Grace Against the Clock

Julie Hyzy

BERKLEY PRIME CRIME, NEW YORK

THE BERKLEY PUBLISHING GROUP
Published by the Penguin Group
Penguin Group (USA) LLC
375 Hudson Street, New York, New York 10014

USA • Canada • UK • Ireland • Australia • New Zealand • India • South Africa • China

penguin.com

A Penguin Random House Company

GRACE AGAINST THE CLOCK

A Berkley Prime Crime Book / published by arrangement with the author

Berkley Prime Crime Books are published by The Berkley Publishing Group.
BERKLEY® PRIME CRIME and the PRIME CRIME logo are trademarks of
Penguin Group (USA) LLC.

For information, address: The Berkley Publishing Group,
a division of Penguin Group (USA) LLC,
375 Hudson Street, New York, New York 10014.

ISBN: 978-0-425-25967-2

PUBLISHING HISTORY
Berkley Prime Crime mass-market edition / July 2014

PRINTED IN THE UNITED STATES OF AMERICA

10 9 8 7 6 5 4 3 2 1

Cover illustration by Kimberly Schamber.
Cover design by Rita Frangie.
Interior text design by Laura K. Corless.

continued . . .

GRACE UNDER PRESSURE

"Well researched and believable . . . Well-drawn characters . . . are supported by lively subplots."
—*Publishers Weekly* (starred review)

"A strong, intelligent, and sensitive sleuth . . . A must-read for this summer!" —*The Romance Readers Connection*

"Julie Hyzy's fans have grown to love Ollie Paras, the White House chef. They're going to be equally impressed with Grace Wheaton . . . Hyzy is skilled at creating unique series characters." —*Chicago Sun-Times*

Praise for the *New York Times* bestselling White House Chef Mysteries

FONDUING FATHERS

"[A] clever plot and fascinating behind-the-scenes glimpses of life in the White House. But it's Ollie who carries the series, and never more so than in this moving page-turner."
—*Richmond Times-Dispatch*

"A mystery delight . . . This is a fantastic installment in the series . . . The White House staff is still quirky and interesting . . . and yes, there is fondue." —*King's River Life Magazine*

AFFAIRS OF STEAK

"Hyzy shines . . . This series burns as bright as the sun during a sweltering D.C. summer." —*Seattle Post-Intelligencer*

"These are wonderful books, enjoyable to read, hard to put down." —*AnnArbor.com*

BUFFALO WEST WING

"[A] top-notch mystery writer. Adventure, intrigue, and a dash of romance combine for a delicious cozy that is a delight to read."
—*Fresh Fiction*

"A captivating story from the very first page until the end . . . Another all-around great read!"
—*The Romance Readers Connection*

EGGSECUTIVE ORDERS

"The ever-burgeoning culinary mystery subgenre has a new chef-sleuth . . . The backstage look at the White House proves fascinating."
—*Booklist*

"A quickly paced plot with a headstrong heroine . . . A dependable mystery."
—*The Mystery Reader*

HAIL TO THE CHEF

"A gourmand's delight . . . An engaging chef's cozy."
—*Midwest Book Review*

"Well plotted . . . A must-read series to add to the ranks of culinary mysteries."
—*The Mystery Reader*

STATE OF THE ONION

"Pulse-pounding action, an appealing heroine, and the inner workings of the White House kitchen combine for a stellar adventure in Julie Hyzy's delightful *State of the Onion*."
—Carolyn Hart, author of *Dead, White, and Blue*

"Topical, timely, intriguing. Julie Hyzy simmers a unique setting, strong characters, sharp conflict, and snappy plotting into a peppery blend that packs an unusual wallop."
—Susan Wittig Albert, national bestselling author of *Death Come Quickly*

To Curt, with love. Always.

Acknowledgments

First and foremost: Thank YOU!

Grace's adventures are extraordinarily fun to write and it is readers like you who allow me to continue writing them. I can never thank you enough for giving me the chance to bring Grace and her friends to life. This is true bliss.

I owe a debt of gratitude to my wonderful editor, Michelle Vega, at Berkley Prime Crime. She's not only fabulous to work with; she's one of the nicest people in the world. I am truly fortunate to have her in my life. Many thanks, too, to my wonderful production editor, Stacy Edwards, and sharp-eyed copyeditor, Erica Rose. Sincere thanks to Paige Wheeler, as well.

As always, much love to my friends and family: especially Curt, Robyn, Sara, and Biz. Special thanks to Sara on this one for suggesting a plot idea. Additional thanks to Curt, Sara, and Biz for their critical input on all my books. After that (oops!) mysterious cell phone incident (different series), I rely on them to help me keep it real. Love you all.

Chapter I

JOYCE SWEDBURG TUCKED HER FINGERS INTO the crook of Bennett's right arm. "Dear man, it's been too long. How have you been?" Without waiting for a reply, the statuesque woman draped her free hand over the other and pressed close, hugging the way a toddler might cling to a parent's leg. "You're as handsome as ever, you devil you." Her lips spread into a serviceable smile as she turned to address her companion. "Don't you agree, Leland?"

Frances nudged me—like there was any chance I might miss Ms. Swedburg's over-the-top performance.

Dr. Leland Keay extended his hand to Bennett. "Good to see you again."

Almost as tall as my boss, Keay's dark features contrasted with Bennett's fair skin and white hair. Keay was younger, by about twenty years, and beginning to sprout gray at his temples. This, along with his Barry White voice, made him quite the attractive package.

He was dressed in a tweed hunting jacket that sported suede elbows and a matching patch at one shoulder. His white shirt was starched, his slacks expertly creased. Handsome and successful, Dr. Leland Keay was widely considered to be Emberstowne's most eligible bachelor.

I'd encountered Keay several times as we prepared for the fund-raiser scheduled for tomorrow night and had come to the opinion that, eligible or not, the rest of Emberstowne's single ladies could keep him. Even though he was a world-renowned cardiothoracic surgeon with a reputation for being witty and charming, I found that Keay carried himself with a faint disregard for others and a perpetual absentminded air.

Keay and Bennett shook hands vigorously—the way men do when they're happy to see one another but not comfortable enough to hug. The action should have dislodged Joyce Swedburg from her perch at Bennett's side, but the woman held on for dear life. Both to Bennett's arm and to her achingly artificial cheer.

The five of us were gathered in a wide, empty section of Marshfield Manor's basement. Accessible via a single stairway, it offered a fun, unusual spot to throw a giant party. And that's precisely what we planned to do.

Two connecting rooms had been reserved for our festive fund-raiser. This, the main section of the party area, would be set up for glittering socialites to enjoy appetizers and drinks. A perfect spot for mingling until the show began. The expansive space was airy and inviting, thanks to creative lighting and creamy-yellow brick walls. The ceiling was brick, too, crafted into neat, arched rows. At our feet was the kind of creaky wooden flooring you might find in an old department store or VFW dance hall. It gave the place charm.

Because we were belowground and centrally located beneath the mansion, no natural light streamed in. In a burst of brilliance, Joyce had arranged to rent six giant flat-screen televisions to serve as faux windows. These had been installed the day before, positioned vertically on two facing walls, and had been programmed to display live views from the highest vista of the closest mountaintop. If you looked closely, you could even see tiny Emberstowne bustling below.

With the dynamic "windows" in place, this main mingling area could have been mistaken for a refurbished warehouse loft in a gentrified urban setting. Banquet-sized and gorgeous, this section had never been included in any public tours. If we ever decided to utilize this area in the future, I'd consider making the flat-screen installation permanent.

"I can't tell you how delightful it is to be working with you again, Bennett." Joyce wagged a finger near his chin. "Your insights at the Chamber of Commerce have been missed."

Bennett acknowledged her compliment. "And I am sorry to have relinquished my seat there. Unfortunately, I've been occupied with many other endeavors. I hope you understand that I couldn't occupy a spot if I was incapable of delivering my best efforts."

She tugged his arm closer and rested her head against his shoulder. "You've more than made up for it with your generous endowments."

Sliding sideways, Bennett extricated himself from her double-handed clutch. "Grace and Frances have been keeping me updated with your plans. We are honored that you've chosen to host the benefit here at Marshfield."

Joyce floated away from Bennett as though it had been her idea to break their physical connection. "There is no more perfect setting in all of Emberstowne. Except perhaps beneath the Promise Clock itself. But can you imagine having this affair in the streets? Then *anyone* would be able to join the party." She gave a dramatic shudder. "We can't allow that."

The Chamber of Commerce, with Joyce as volunteer event planner, intended to raise money to refurbish the area surrounding the giant town clock, which had served as an unofficial entrance to Emberstowne for more than a hundred years. Named the Promise Clock because the citizens at the time believed that Emberstowne held great promise for success and prosperity, it lightly resembled *Le Gros Horloge* in Rouen, France.

The Promise Clock, which had lived up to its titular reputation until recently, was colossally sized. Set in the center of a massive archway that connected two now-abandoned buildings, the Renaissance-inspired glory differed from *Le Gros Horloge* in a couple of key ways: Our town's clock, though somewhat less ornate, sported both hour and minute hands; and the edifice's span was almost double that of its French predecessor.

That the arch's width allowed for two-way traffic to pass beneath it was not the problem—the lack of traffic was. Very few residents traveled through that part of town anymore.

Over the past several years, in one of the ripple effects of the Great Recession, the touristy section of Emberstowne had begun to condense. Businesses at the edge of town had either moved to a more central location or shuttered completely. The establishments already on Main Street, like Hugo's and other mainstays, had weathered the rough patch and were now enjoying a resurgence of business, but the area surrounding the Promise Clock had become a ghost town.

With weeds sprouting in the middle of the pavement, unrepaired sidewalks, and lonely buildings with broken windows, the only promise it held now was that this was an area best avoided. Though rich in history, the stretch was sorely lacking in commerce, making it Emberstowne's biggest embarrassment. If it weren't for the presence of the clock, the entire section of town might have been razed.

Tomorrow night's fund-raiser had been conceived when costs to improve the roads and landscaping and to help smarten up the buildings far overran original estimates.

Despite the deterioration of the surrounding area, the clock's inner workings ran on time and Emberstowne had expended the effort necessary to keep the clock's face unmarred. In the past year, however, experts had noted structural problems. At the recent switch to daylight savings time, a worker who had crawled inside the arch to adjust the hands had nearly fallen through when the crumbling construction disintegrated beneath him.

All maintenance updates on the clock had been halted until a full overhaul and repair of the arch could be done. That took time. And money.

Tomorrow night's benefit sought to solicit contributions from wealthy benefactors willing to donate a thousand dollars per person for the privilege of attending the Marshfield party. Bennett had generously offered to supply the space as well as the food. He'd also purchased tickets for a few of us on staff, to attend as his guests.

Although I'd been in contact with Joyce over the past few months, she'd been working most closely with our catering staff and with Terrence, our chief of security. Today was the first time she and Leland had shown up together. Until now I'd believed she was simply the head of the clock benefit committee and he the president of the Chamber of Commerce. I hadn't been aware that the two had been married to each other once upon a time. Frances had provided that little tidbit moments ago.

Bennett waved his hand as though to encompass the space around us. "I must confess, however, to being surprised when Grace told me that you'd chosen this particular room for the party."

I whispered to Frances, "How long have they been divorced?"

My assistant got that eager-to-gossip gleam in her eye. Drawing a hand up in front of her mouth while ogling the two in question—a conspicuous gesture that practically screamed that we were talking about them—she murmured, "Five years." Her tadpole brows leaping high with glee, she added, "There's quite a story there."

"Not now," I said.

Joyce was nearly as tall as her ex-husband. She sauntered

over to him, ran a hand down the length of his tailored jacket sleeve—I could only imagine how soft that luxurious fabric was—and addressed Bennett over her shoulder. "Leland first suggested we hold the event upstairs in your foyer and adjoining rooms, but he has no imagination, do you, Leland?"

He didn't answer. Arm-rub or no, he didn't appear to be paying attention.

Joyce reached the far end of the space and turned around with an expression that was half bored, half amused. I got the impression that this woman had been born to perform. She extended both arms, hands upraised, looking a great deal like the Imperia statue in Konstanz, Germany, though offering far less cleavage, thank goodness.

Raising her voice, she adopted a beleaguered tone. "*Everyone* who visits Marshfield has seen the foyer," she said. "Hundreds—no—*thousands* of people pass through your front doors each day, clutching their precious tickets. And what do they see first? The foyer. Forgive me, Bennett, but it's not *special*."

Leland wandered to the far end of the first room, stopping at the juncture where it ended and a small hallway leading to the auditorium began.

The doctor raised his voice to be heard over Joyce's. "Where are the bathrooms?"

Joyce rolled her eyes. "Why on earth are you worried about that now?"

"Why do you think?"

She held a hand to her forehead and briefly closed her eyes. "You see what I have to deal with?"

Leland turned to me. "Quite a few of my patients are attending. Several are elderly and may be experiencing incontinence issues."

I answered him. "They're down the alcove to your left."

He pointed. "What's to the right?"

We'd been over this before. "That's where David Cherk

will be presenting 'A History of the Promise Clock' for the guests," I said. David Cherk was a lauded, eccentric photographer who was regularly called upon to chronicle historic moments, and whose work adorned the interiors of most of Emberstowne's municipal buildings. "That's the auditorium."

We used the term *auditorium* loosely. There were no seats, no lights, no sound system, no stage. Like an auditorium, however, the room was fan-shaped, wide at the entrance and narrow at the deep end, which was where the presentation would be held.

Keay disappeared to inspect the accommodations. I exchanged a glance with Frances. Among my concerns with holding the event down here were fire exits, capacity, and washroom facilities. There was only one official entrance to the space, down a narrow stairway that led from an EMPLOY-EES ONLY door on the main level. We would have security officers stationed there tomorrow night to assist guests in finding their way to the party. But if anything should happen that might cause people to stampede out, the restricted egress had the potential to become a dangerous bottleneck.

Weeks ago, at my urging, Joyce had agreed to meet with a representative from the fire department to ensure that the event wouldn't violate code. We'd gotten the all-clear, but I still would have preferred to hold the benefit on Marsh-field's main level. I was certain that we could have found a location that was *special* enough for this gala event.

Although there was only one official door to the party space, an emergency exit had been added some years back, probably when the mansion first opened to visitors. It evac-uated into the employee underground garage, and accessing the exit involved hitting a crash bar, which set off ear-splitting alarms.

I wandered that way now, as Bennett, Joyce, and Frances chatted among themselves. Ahead of me, the auditorium was dark. I tried to envision how David Cherk's entertain-ment would play out. He was due here soon. We'd set up this last-minute meeting between all parties for late in the day, when the mansion was closed to visitors. I wandered back into the main room and glanced at my cell phone to check the time. Almost as if I'd been clairvoyant, the device signaled a text.

Joyce, Frances, and Bennett looked up. "David Cherk is here," I announced as I pulled up my walkie-talkie to alert Terrence to show the man in. Right on time.

"Oh dear." Joyce held a palm up to her powdered cheek. "That man gives me the creeps. He has odd opinions about the strangest things. So precise and peculiar." She shook her head and *tsk*ed loudly.

I understood where Joyce was coming from, though we could do without the theatrics. David Cherk wasn't the sort of person I'd choose to hang out with in my free time, but Joyce's comment still rankled.

With three skinny, black-clad assistants in tow, Cherk descended into our midst. The first time I'd met him, I'd been convinced that he purposely sucked in his cheeks. After a few minutes of conversation, however, I'd come to understand that his skeletal look wasn't an affectation. Right now, as he smiled in greeting, I marveled at how mirth could appear so cold.

"Good afternoon, everyone," he said to us in his sharp, starchy voice. "Are we all ready for the breathtaking presentation I have planned for tomorrow night?" He gave an exultant sigh as he clasped his long-fingered hands together in front of his chest. "So few of our citizens make time to visit the historical office to learn about our town and experience my artistry. I intend to give them a hint as to what they're missing."

Joyce inhaled deeply through her nose, making her nostrils clamp shut with effort. "David, darling." Grasping his shoulders, she air-kissed him next to both cheeks. "So delightful to be working with you on this project. I can't wait to see what you have in store. I would love to stay now and hear all about your little plans, but I'm needed elsewhere."

Cherk blinked, clearly as surprised as I was.

"My understanding was that we were supposed to finalize everything during this meeting," I said to her.

"And things are finalized. Everything is lovely, dear. See you tomorrow."

"But the whole reason we set this up—"

"Other commitments. You understand." She raised her hands helplessly. "You're so capable, Grace. I'm not the least bit worried." She ignored Frances, walking past her to rest both hands on Bennett's arm. "Save me a dance tomorrow evening, my precious man. Will you?"

Bennett shot me the briefest glance. Ever the gentleman, he clapped a hand over one of hers. "Of course."

Dr. Keay returned from the bathrooms, looking confused by the recent arrivals.

"Time to go, Leland," Joyce said.

"Did I miss something?"

Joyce shot him an icy glare. "Don't you always?"

Chapter 2

THE MOMENT JOYCE SWEDBURG AND LELAND
Keay departed, Cherk strode over and nodded toward the
door. "That woman. She'd like nothing better than to see
me fall on my face."

"Then why would she have engaged your talents for the
benefit?" I asked.

Cherk's dark, sunken eyes, his ever-present five-o'clock
shadow, and the curling twist of shellacked, dark hair over
a deep widow's peak made him look like an evil minion
from a 1950s horror film.

"Joyce Swedburg has no choice. She's a moth—a social,
parasitic moth who lives a delusional life, believing herself
a butterfly—and she's stuck with me for this event because
I'm the best this town has to offer. She gets her show, I get
exposure. But we are trapped dealing with each other for
the duration. Let me assure you: Neither one of us is turning cartwheels with joy."

Surprised by his venom, I went momentarily speechless.

David, however, had more to say. "Joyce Swedburg is

convinced I possess the soul of an automaton, rather than that of an artist." He grimaced in her wake. "The woman is an ignorant fool."

Bennett stepped forward. "I'm certain your exhibit will be well received," he said, "and then Ms. Swedburg will be more than happy to brag that she had faith in you from the start." To me, he added, "If you don't require my presence any longer, I'd like to get back upstairs to attend to a few phone calls."

"Thanks for coming down, Bennett," I said. "We may not have accomplished anything, but I suspect it meant a lot to Joyce to have you here."

Bennett gave a good-natured snort. "Who knows what that woman truly thinks? She says what she believes everyone wants to hear. If it weren't for her talent as a fund-raiser, I'd be happy not to have to deal with her ever again."

Cherk wiggled his fingers in the air. "Count me in on that."

"Then we have a quorum," Frances said.

Bennett's mouth twisted downward. He looked away, shaking his head. "I shouldn't have said anything. She's a decent human being, deep down."

"Deep down?" Frances asked. "Where are you looking? There isn't enough depth in that woman for a respectable search."

Visibly pained by having spoken unkindly about Joyce, Bennett turned to me. "I will see you tomorrow night at the benefit. I'm looking forward to meeting your young man again."

"And he's looking forward to seeing you."

The "young man" Bennett referred to was Adam, lead singer of the well-known but not quite superstar-level band SlickBlade. Adam and I had met under difficult circumstances and, after a rocky beginning, had taken gentle steps toward forging a relationship. He lived in New York City, and that, coupled with the fact that he was often on tour with his band, meant that he and I didn't get to see each other too often. I was okay with that. At least for now.

"Are you bringing a date, Frances?" Bennett asked. "You haven't mentioned anything."

My assistant's cheeks colored. "It's enough that I'm attending this soiree on a weekend, isn't it?" Then, as though remembering who she was talking to, she amended, "Not that I don't appreciate you buying my ticket. I didn't mean that. But no, I'm not bringing anyone."

"A shame," Bennett said, which I thought was an odd response. He didn't elaborate. "Good enough. I'll see you all later."

"We plan on blocking off a portion of this room for food storage," I said to David when Bennett had left. We'd arranged to have antique ornamental screens brought in to hide necessary refrigeration and heating units. "I hope that won't hamper your plans to set up."

"Joyce, for all of her aggravations, is an effective organizer. I know precisely how much space I need to leave for you. She was very clear on that detail. Don't worry."

Cherk's assistants hadn't stopped working while we were talking. They kept busy unloading the props and decorations, barely speaking to one another.

I led Cherk to the auditorium, where he shouted, "Hello," up toward the ceiling three times. When he smiled, he showed large yellow teeth. "The acoustics are tolerable."

One of the assistants interrupted. "Where does the stage go, Mr. Cherk?"

"Stage?" I asked.

He tut-tutted. "A platform, really. It will raise me up about eight inches off the ground, but even that small amount will allow better viewing for those stuck in the back of the room. From what I understand, we're expecting a hundred donors."

"Ninety-four at last count." I took another long look around. Our catering team would bring in folding chairs once the rest of the space was arranged.

Two of the assistants walked by, carrying very long, and

apparently very heavy, rolls of purple velvet. I pointed. "What's that?"

"Curtains, of course. If we're to have a presentation here, we're going to do it properly. I rented these from a theatrical supply house. By the time we're set up, this will look like Carnegie Hall."

"Can't wait to see it."

Next to me, Frances gave what sounded like a grunt.

Two more young people arrived to join Cherk's team. "You have this many assistants?" I asked.

Bringing his hands up to face, he tapped the sides of his nose with his index fingers. "Are you always so full of questions?"

I didn't answer.

With affected patience, he continued, "For your information, these are college students I hired to give me a hand. Theater majors, all. They'll assist today and with the disassembling as well. I get the benefit of their expertise. They get extra credit in their courses." Cherk rubbed his nose and started tapping it again. This was either one strange habit or the man had a tic. "Their professor is a friend of mine."

"Convenient," I said.

Two young men carried metal piping and heavy boards, which would eventually be connected together to form the stage. They worked hard, but clearly knew what they were doing. When they needed to ask Cherk a question or request clarification, they were respectful and quick. The stage came together at the far end of the room, right before our eyes.

"See how we've set up wings on either side?" he asked, pointing as the platform was assembled. Two of the assistants unrolled the purple velvet, ran a metal pole through a pocket at the top, and eased the entire length up into place. "This gives me the ability to hide the workings that will make the show come alive."

"Like the man behind the curtain in *The Wizard of Oz*?"

Ignoring me, he blurted a sharp exclamation at the assistants and ran off.

Frances had been quiet for a while. The moment Cherk was out of earshot, she said, "Ninety-five."

"Excuse me?"

"Ninety-five people are coming to this fund-raiser as of the most recent count."

"That's great."

"Jack will be here."

"He will?" I knew I couldn't hide my surprise, so I didn't bother trying. "Isn't that a lot of money to spend on a benefit? Especially for someone who's back in school?"

"The Mister paid," she said. "You know how he is; he likes to keep everybody together, like a family. Even though Jack isn't working at Marshfield anymore, the Mister thought that he ought to be here, so . . ." She let the thought hang.

"Bennett didn't tell me."

"He only arranged it today."

I pulled in a deep breath.

"Good thing you're bringing that Adam fellow as your date," she said.

Not for the first time did it feel as though Frances had read my mind. This news made me especially glad that Adam was coming to town.

Although Jack had professed a willingness to rekindle whatever it was we'd started, recent changes in his life made me doubt his sincerity. His long-ago fiancée, Becke, had returned to Emberstowne, newly divorced with two little kids in tow. Jack had offered his father's deserted home as a rent-free place to stay. There was still unsettled business between the two of them and I refused to be caught in the middle.

Frances added, "Plus the fact that Jack is an Embers . . ."

She let that thought hang, too, but I understood. Jack's family had been among the first to settle in the town. The place was named for them, for heaven's sake. With the historical theme, it made sense for Jack to be here. A long line of Embers men and women had, no doubt, trekked beneath the Promise Clock.

"Davey's coming, too, I assume?" I asked, referring to Jack's younger brother, who now worked for Bennett and lived in a cottage on Marshfield Manor's property.

"He has a ticket. No idea if he plans to use it."

The youngest Embers brother wasn't a fan of parties and didn't socialize much. "I suppose we'll see." I motioned toward Cherk, who was gesticulating wildly and shouting at his assistants. "Having a Davey and a David here at once could get confusing."

"Are you kidding? One's an athletic young man and the other is a walking corpse."

I know she expected me to laugh, but I wasn't feeling particularly amused at the moment. "With all of us Marshfield folks here as Bennett's guests, it'll be a miracle if they raise the kind of money they need. I hope people are generous when it comes to bidding at the silent auction."

"*Pheh*," Frances said. "Wait and see. The folks attending will be only too eager to prove how rich they are. Joyce Swedburg will get all she's expecting and more. Mark my words."

In almost no time at all, Cherk's team finished and had packed up to leave. As they departed, our event planners from the Marshfield Hotel arrived to help finesse the scene. They were experienced in organizing weddings, showers, graduations, and other milestone celebrations often held at the hotel. Today they were charged with transforming this ruggedly beautiful basement into a place of elegance.

Frances and I stood back as tables were rolled in. Men and women, clad in black and white, snapped linen tablecloths into the air, allowing them to settle gently on one round table after another. A woman on a ladder reached high overhead to drape long stretches of tulle along the walls and to suspend more from the ceilings. Candles were placed here and there. They'd be lit the following day, shortly before the first guests arrived. I could already see how gorgeous this space, illuminated by the tall TV monitor-windows and flickering candlelight, would be.

"By the way, Frances," I said as we moved deeper into the auditorium, "I appreciate you staying in town for the weekend. With as large a crowd as we're expecting here tomorrow night, I feel better having both of us in charge."

She pursed her lips and didn't make eye contact. No one seemed to know what Frances did on weekends. All we knew was that she left town every Friday and didn't return until Sunday evening. Beyond that, her life was a mystery. I didn't push her and she never offered a clue.

The thought had occurred to me to have our sometime private investigator Ronny Tooney follow her to discover her secrets, but Frances's life outside of Marshfield was none of my business and spying on her like that, simply to satisfy my curiosity, would be overstepping boundaries. Had our situations been reversed, I believed Frances would have had no such qualms.

"I'd better be getting time-and-a-half for this," she said.

"Of course." I tiptoed onto the makeshift stage, afraid of it wobbling beneath my feet. Within seconds, though, I realized that it was sturdier than I'd expected. "Nice," I said.

Cherk's student assistants had set up eight-foot-tall curtains on either side of the platform, and a wider curtain behind it. There was a sizeable space between the back of the center curtain and the rear wall. Plenty of room for Cherk to hide any equipment before and during the show. I was amazed at how quickly this end of the room had taken on the look of a serviceable, though miniature, stage.

"We ought to keep these students in mind if we ever want to hold a theatrical type of event down here," I said. "They set this up so well and so quickly. It's great."

Even Frances seemed impressed. She perched her fists on her orchid-clad hips and gave the room a long look. "Not bad."

Chapter 3

BACK AT OUR OFFICES, FRANCES TURNED TO me. "By the way," she said as she sat behind her desk, "how are things going between you and Hillary?"

Hillary. Bennett's forty-something, rudderless step-daughter was at my home this very moment, and had been for some time. A few months ago, Bennett had told me that he'd engaged Hillary's fledgling decorator service. I'd told him I thought that was a wonderful idea. That is, until I learned that he'd hired her to work on *my* house.

"It's going as well as can be expected," I said carefully.

Frances regarded me with a shrewd expression. "Cut the polite blather. I want details."

I found myself admitting my surprise. "The good news is that Hillary is a talented taskmaster," I said. "I'd expected her to be difficult to work with, and because she has absolutely zero experience with exterior renovation—"

"She doesn't have much practice in interior renovation either," Frances said.

"Nevertheless, it's been going well. She clearly knows

her limitations and so she subcontracts whatever is beyond her capabilities. For instance, we have a project manager on-site who has been an invaluable resource."

"She can afford to hire talent because she's spending the Mister's money."

"True enough," I agreed. "Maybe that's exactly what Bennett intended. Think about it: She's learning on the job from the project manager. That can only help her succeed in future endeavors. And I have to admit; even though there is still work to be done, the outside of the house looks so much better already."

"Your neighbors must be happy."

"I'll say." I could barely make it to my front steps these days without one of them stopping by to talk about the changes. A few of them congratulated me on the updates, the rest felt the need to weigh in with their opinions. The most recent suggestion I'd gotten was to install a koi pond in the front yard. Lovely idea. Not my style.

"What's the bad news?" Frances asked. "There's always a flip side."

"I shouldn't complain," I said. "Hillary hasn't been unbearable to work with. Believe it or not, she actually listens to my ideas. And when she offers advice, it's usually spot-on."

"But?"

"Not only that, she's incredibly fond of my cat. They've become best buddies, in fact. Hillary is extremely protective of Bootsie and is very careful about not letting her get out."

"I'm still waiting for the 'but.'"

"But." I heaved a sincere sigh. "I'm about ready to scream from the constant activity. There are workers every-where, every day. Every minute, it seems. I can't look out my window without fear of one of them staring back in. I would start counting the days until they're gone, but I have no idea when that might be."

"I wouldn't put up with any of that," she said. "Even if the Mister was paying for it."

"Now that the exterior is progressing, Hillary wants to move indoors."

"I wouldn't like anyone telling me how to decorate my home."

"She's assessing my house even as we speak." I glanced up at the clock. "A little while ago she texted me about an unexpected situation but was weirdly vague about it. I'm sure she'll bring me up to speed tonight." It was true that my house wasn't designer perfect, but it was comfortable. My roommates and I had made it our own. Tackling the interior would be the worst part of the project. I dreaded the next steps.

Frances shot me a withering look. "A conversation with Hillary? That's all the excitement you have planned for a Friday night?"

"Sounds pathetic, but I truly don't mind. Adam won't be in until the morning, and Scott and Bruce will be tied up at their wine shop until late. I might as well get this over with."

"The Mister is a smart man," she said.

That confused me. "I agree, but what makes you say that right now?"

"Hillary is his stepdaughter and you might very well be his niece. He's doing all he can to get you two to work together. I think he wants you to be best friends."

I choked out a laugh. "Not a chance."

"Oh, really? A year ago you wouldn't have had one good word to say about Hillary. And, trust me, she wouldn't have had anything good to say about you." Her carefully penciled brows rose up as though her point were obvious, but she continued anyway. "Seems to me his plan is working."

"I don't think he has any ulterior motive beyond helping Hillary get a foothold in business and helping me improve the appearance of my painted lady." Even as the automatic response streamed out of my mouth, I realized that her observation had struck home. Bennett was fully capable of such a plan. Frances was right. And as much as it irked me, I had to admit that she usually was.

* * *

WITH THE CONSTRUCTION CREW'S TRUCKS and equipment taking up space in my driveway, I parked across the street from my home, marveling at the change in its appearance already. The face-lift, though only half-complete, was remarkable.

Over the years, my painted lady had become more of a flaky lady, with her cracking paint and rotting windows. Old and tired, she'd begun falling apart piece by little piece.

Standing in the sunlight, I shielded my eyes, watching the window crew at work. They'd completed about three-quarters of the job, installing double-hung vinyl replacements, and it looked as though they'd have the remainder done in a day or so. The new windows' bright white frames made me happy. They contrasted with the weathered exterior, but they offered a hint of the beauty to come.

Hillary and I were still in the process of discussing color choices for the siding. I'd seen a sage-green home with redwood- and butter-colored accents that I'd liked, but Hillary was pushing me to take another look at the blue-and-yellow combination she'd picked out. I wasn't completely sold on the green, so I'd promised to give her suggestion consideration but only after the clock fund-raiser event was over. Right now I had its success, rather than color combinations, foremost on my mind.

Workers, mostly men, were in and out of my house constantly these days, whether to shore up a gable, repair a wall, or measure for gutters and downspouts. Although the project manager did his best to keep me updated as to what was going on when, I'd begun to lose track. I made a mental note to get caught up. Even though I'd approved the plans and it was now up to the experts to see those plans through, I preferred to stay closely tuned in.

I'd made it halfway across the street, when I heard someone call my name. I turned to see my next-door neighbor,

Todd Pedota, making his way over, holding up a hand in greeting. Todd was in his late forties, divorced, living alone in a house that was a mirror image of mine. I'd encountered him now and again, and while he wasn't the most unpleasant man I'd ever met, our interactions made my teeth hurt. He'd been the last of my neighbors to come over and chat. That had been by design. I'd worked hard to avoid him.

"Grace," he said, "haven't seen you around much since all the work began. You win the lottery or something?" He was one of those people who laughed at his own comments, funny or not.

"Nothing like that," I said.

At about five-foot-ten, Todd kept himself hard-body fit. I suspected that he purposely flexed his biceps whenever women were around, in the hopes that they'd swoon. Today he wore a solid gray T-shirt that fit him like a second skin, and his rippling muscles looked like they were trying to wave hello. I ignored them.

I couldn't say that Todd wasn't good-looking. The cleft chin, chiseled jaw, and full head of highlighted hair combined for the kind of look that graced department store sale flyers. Handsome, yes, but the fact that I couldn't read any emotion from his sunken eyes always made me wary. When he took a step closer, I took one back.

"A beautiful young woman like you suddenly decides to update her home for no reason?" His tone was teasing. Taunting, even. "What's the occasion? Is there a new man in your life?"

"What could one possibly have to do with the other?"

"So you're still single?"

Here we go again. "I never said there was no reason for the renovation," I answered sweetly. "But I see no purpose in sharing that reason with you."

Unfazed, he arranged his mouth into a smile showing his even, over-whitened teeth. His perfect choppers were the faintest shade of blue. "Maybe you're dating one of these guys?" He gestured toward the half-dozen workers who were starting to pack up for the night. One of them waved to me. Oh, perfect timing.

"Aha," Todd said. "Bingo."

"Thanks for chatting, but I have a friend waiting for me inside."

Todd raised his eyebrows, still smiling hard enough to blind me. "A friend, huh? Tell you what. If your friend ever lets you down, you know where I am." He tilted his head toward his property.

"See you later," I said, eager to get away.

"Hope so." He lifted a finger and waved it at my house. "Nice changes, Grace. I like what you're doing with the place. Keep it up."

My jaw was tight. "So glad you approve."

Chapter 4

INSIDE, I DROPPED MY PURSE ON THE KITCHEN
table and called out to Hillary. She'd texted me before I'd
left Marshfield to let me know that she would be waiting
with blueprints I needed to see. I wandered through the first
floor but my designer was nowhere to be found.

About to start up the stairs, I tried again. "Hillary? Are
you here?"

I heard the basement door open. "Grace," she called
from the kitchen. I wasn't used to hearing women coo at me
the way Hillary did. I supposed she'd grown so used to
doing it with all the men she flirted with, she'd forgotten
how to shut that little trait off. "You're home."

I retraced my steps through the dining room to greet her.
How in the world she managed to look so cool and put-together
even after a full day on a construction job was beyond my
comprehension. Granted, she wasn't doing the hammering
and refinishing herself, but still. There was dust flying every-
where, yet apparently none of it dared land on her.

Hillary had been here this morning before I'd left for work, as she had most mornings since the renovation began. Although I knew she left the premises periodically throughout the day, she always looked as though she'd stepped out from a go-getter women's magazine. Even now, having emerged from my dingy basement, there wasn't a speck of dirt on her pink cropped pants, white wedges, and white silk twinset. I'd been in the house for less than a minute and I could already feel the construction dust settling into my skin and hair.

She'd come upstairs with Bootsie. The little rascal, who had been—at best—tolerant of the leash with me, now apparently delighted in her time in the harness with Hillary. Bootsie scampered between Hillary's chic summer wedges, pouncing on the woman's toes and making her laugh.

Bennett's vacuous, self-centered stepdaughter had morphed into a smart businesswoman with good instincts. It didn't hurt that she had a partner in this venture, Frederick, a man I had yet to meet. The elusive fellow had apparently provided financial backing for Hillary's business, but I suspected he provided life-coaching advice as well. There was no way she could have made this dramatic of a turnaround in such a short period of time without help.

"Look," Hillary said to my little tuxedo kitten as she lifted her up and held her close, "Mommy's here."

She handed her over. I accepted the bundle of fur and took hold of the leash, relaxing as Bootsie purred against my chest. It was good to be home.

"I got your message," I said to Hillary. "When you say 'unexpected,' I take it to mean 'trouble.' What's wrong?"

"I didn't get into details in my message only because it's so difficult to explain in a text. Come downstairs, I'll show you."

Her wedges clunked the bare wood steps that led to the basement, making it sound as though a giant was marching down the stairs. "We ought to get these carpeted at some point," she said over her shoulder.

Bootsie appeared to have no opinion on the matter. She

was content to be carried for now but would probably get antsy soon.

"Are the indoor workers almost finished for the day?" I asked as we reached the bottom. "I'd like to take Bootsie off her leash."

"As a matter of fact, I was doing a final walk-through to make sure the coast was clear, when you got home." She gave the cat an indulgent smile and scratched her under the chin. "You've been such a good girl today, haven't you?" To me, she said, "The basement was my last stop. We're all locked up. You can let her down if you like."

I put Bootsie on the floor and unclasped the leash. Whether it was the freedom, the fact that things in the basement had been moved, offering a rearranged playground, or simply pure kitten joy, I wasn't sure, but she immediately leaped away and out of sight.

Hillary laughed as we watched her go. "She's such a character, that one." Turning to me, she said, "But back to matters at hand," and gestured for me to follow. I'd been in my basement a hundred times, but had to admit that I didn't know it intimately.

Measured end to end, this belowground level stretched approximately seventy feet long by fifty feet wide. We sat at a high enough elevation to avoid flooding problems, which rendered the basement dry, yet the area remained musty. Smelling much like an antique shop, it was broken into smaller spaces by the furnace in the center, a storage room along one wall, and our laundry area near the base of the steps. A handful of above-grade windows dotted the walls, delivering scant light through dusty panes thick with cobwebs.

As basements go, it was no beauty. Bare plywood planks had been affixed haphazardly to its uneven walls. These sagging, stained shelves held cans of leftover paint, extra cleaning supplies for upstairs, and junk we didn't know where else to store. A handful of pull-chain lightbulbs provided meager illumination.

Hillary pointed at a pile of boxes that had been relocated from the front of the basement to a spot closer to the washer and dryer. "I know you can't fit any more in your garage at this juncture." She gave me a pointed stare that I took to mean she expected me to clean that out soon. "But I thought that perhaps some of these things would be easier for you to get through if I left them out."

"How thoughtful," I said. She missed my sarcasm. Truth was, I did need to get through everything and do a massive purge, both here and in the garage. I simply hadn't had the opportunity. When I finally got to the project, I wanted to do it right. That meant devoting lots of free time to going through all the "stuff" that my mom had relocated when she'd returned to live here after my dad died. I was looking forward to spending time with my mother's belongings. I'd stumbled on one secret she'd taken to the grave. I wondered if there were more.

I followed Hillary past the storage room, around the furnace, to a spot near the front of the house along the west wall. Hillary stopped and pointed.

"That's a workbench," I said, stating the obvious. It was loaded with coffee cans full of nails, a toolbox, and at least a dozen cardboard boxes all labeled HARDWARE. I shrugged. "I'm guessing that my grandfather built it originally. It's been here for as long as I can remember."

Even though the bare wood structure was built into a space between two stone abutments, it squeaked and moved when Hillary gripped one side and wiggled it. "I don't know for sure, but I'd bet this workbench has been around since long before your grandfather was." She blinked. "Or should I say, your grandmother's husband?"

We both knew what she was talking about, but I chose to focus on the implied question instead. "You think it has to go?"

Hillary scrunched up her pert little nose. "Definitely,"

she said, not bothering to couch the answer in polite explanation. "It's a hazard. Worse, it's ugly."

I tucked my hands into my hips and looked at the workbench, really looked at it, something I hadn't done before. "You're right," I said. "It is an eyesore. And I wouldn't want it to fall over on Bootsie."

She pointed to the very top of the structure. "The only thing I'm concerned about is whether we'll need to be prepared to shore up that area above it. See?"

I looked. She pointed to what looked like a railroad tie, except it was four times wider and at least three times the length. It sat above the workbench, holding up—

I couldn't tell what it was holding up. "What an odd place for a beam that doesn't seem to be attached to anything," I said.

"When I pointed it out to the project manager, he thought it was possible that this was a load-bearing wall and warned me to be very careful about removing the workbench. He promised to take a closer look tomorrow." She took a few tiptoe-y steps around the dusty monstrosity and pointed again. "Here's the part that puzzled him most. The shelves are only about twelve inches deep, but the beam above looks to be more than two feet wide. Do you have any idea what's behind here?"

"Not a clue." I dragged an old chair over and stood on top to see if I could determine anything. Not that I would recognize a load-bearing wall versus one that wasn't. Nor could I figure out why the beam was so much wider than the workbench itself. I'd never looked at it closely before— it had simply always been there and I'd accepted it as a given. "Hey, this is odd," I said. "The beam looks as though it's attached to the top of the workbench."

"Exactly. Which means we can't simply tear the thing out without first making sure the floor above won't crash down on top of us."

I got down from the chair. "Let me know what the project manager says."

"Frederick had a marvelous thought about this," she said. "I wanted to show you when you came in, but you needed to see the bench first." She curled her finger and started back toward the laundry area.

"Frederick was here today?" I followed her. "I thought he was your silent partner."

She giggled as though I'd said something truly witty. "Frederick is here every day."

"How strange that we haven't run into each other yet."

"I keep forgetting that you haven't met him. You will."

When we returned to the area near the stairs, she made a beeline for a long, shallow plastic bin with a hinged white top, like the kind I kept under my bed to store sweaters. "I can't take credit for this," she said, "it was all Frederick. He's the one who ran over to the Emberstowne historical society this afternoon. And good thing he did."

"What did he need at the historical society?"

"Blueprints for your house." She pulled up three packets of rolled drawings and stretched one out. "Isn't this a find? We can study these and know precisely how to restore the interiors." Catching herself, she added, "I mean, if you think that's a good idea."

"I think it's a great idea," I said. It was true. I spread my hands along the edges of the blue-tinted paper in order to get a better look at the drawings. This was like finding gold. I couldn't keep the excitement out of my voice.

Hillary's face lit up with what may have been the first genuine smile I'd ever seen on her. She was clearly taken aback by my reaction and it occurred to me, belatedly, that she'd probably been as leery about working with me as I was with her. Worse for her, in this situation, she was the one with something to prove. The pressure on her to succeed must be sky-high.

Up until now I'd been the one under the microscope. Even though Bennett had accepted me—had practically taken me in as family—Hillary had remained aloof. Recently, however, after she'd learned about my possible blood relation to Bennett, she'd begun to warm up a little.

Here, in my home, I wielded the power. She needed to work to make me happy with her changes and suggestions. Although I'd understood our new dynamic on a logical level from the very start, it wasn't until this moment, after her spontaneous reaction to my happiness, that it had hit home.

"Frederick says that they're probably not as old as the house," she said. "But they're the closest thing to an original plan that we have. Frederick borrowed them from the historical society and promised we'd return them no later than Monday morning."

"I didn't know that the historical society kept records of every house."

"Not every," she said with a little shrug. "Most, though. I think some were lost or misplaced through the years. Frederick was delighted to find out that yours were there."

Each of the three rolls she'd pulled up was actually a set of multiple sheets. I flipped through them slowly, seeing the floor plans to my first level, the bedroom level, even the attic, before returning to the drawings of the basement.

"I can't really read these," I said. "I mean, I can figure out where the walls are." I traced a finger along the line that represented the wall in front of us. "But when I look over here to where the workbench is, I don't see it."

"Which is why Frederick and I think it wasn't considered permanent. The foreman will get a chance to study these tomorrow, but I think it's good news for us. If it isn't part of the original structure, that means that we can tear it out. Won't that be fun?"

Chapter 5

BOOTSIE RAN IN AND OUT, OCCASIONALLY KEEP-
ing me company while I dined alone at the kitchen table. As
it was Friday night, I knew that Scott and Bruce wouldn't be
home from Amethyst Cellars until very late. Tourist season
was always good, but business at their wine shop had really
taken off this year.

After cleaning up, I pulled out the blueprints and took to
studying them again, one room at a time. Although my
house hadn't undergone major changes since it had been
built, there were a few notable updates, mainly having to do
with bathrooms. From the looks of it, the original structure
had had one bathroom, up on the bedroom level.

A powder room had been installed much later, on the
main floor near the back of the house. Two additional full
baths had been added through the years, making three total
on the bedroom level. These added conveniences had
allowed me to open my home to boarders in the first place.
My roommates had their own private bath, I had mine, and
there was a spare. We used it for guests, but it provided the

option of opening the house to another boarder, if we ever decided to expand our little family.

My cell phone rang.

"Hey, Grace," Adam said when I answered. "It's good to hear your voice."

"Yours, too," I said.

I'd gotten to know him enough to expect cheerful banter. Today he skipped that and asked, "How are plans for your benefit coming?"

"Really well. We had our final walk-through today. I'll have to get there early tomorrow to oversee things, but I think we're all set."

He made a noise I couldn't decipher. "That's great." His voice was off.

"What's wrong?"

"Something has come up." He pulled in a deep breath. "I'm sorry, Grace, but I'm not going to be able to make it to the fund-raiser tomorrow night."

"What happened?"

"I have an aunt who's sick. More than sick; she's probably not going to make it through the weekend."

"I'm so sorry, Adam," I said. "You need to be with her."

"I do," he said. "I hate to disappoint you, but I knew you'd understand."

"Of course. Which aunt is this?"

"One of my dad's sisters. She's about fifteen years his senior and the oldest in the family. My dad is quiet, reserved, and staid. Aunt Tessie is a pistol and always has been. Married four times, buried all but the most recent husband. I think he's in shock that he's going to outlive her."

"I'm sorry. This has to be tough for you."

"We saw it coming, but yeah. It is. I'm sorry to miss your party, Grace. I really wanted to be there."

"It's all right. I'm probably going to be busy most of the night anyway."

"When all this—" He stopped himself. "When things

have settled down again," he amended, "I'd like to come out there and see you."

"I'd like that, too."

"Would you?"

"Yeah." I almost told him that I missed him, but at the last second, I kept the words tight inside. I'd been too open, too transparent, too eager to be hurt in the past. Fear held me silent.

"I miss you, Grace."

My breath caught.

I heard the back door swing open. "The boys are home," I said. "I have to go. I know you're facing a difficult time ahead. You take care of yourself, okay?"

I wasn't sure if the sound he made was one of disappointment or resignation. Or both. "Talk soon," he said, and hung up.

I brought Bruce and Scott up to speed about the workbench in the basement, showed them the blueprints, and updated them about Adam's change in plans. Neither of my roommates planned to attend the benefit tomorrow, mostly because Saturdays at the wine shop were even busier than Fridays, but they had been looking forward to seeing Adam again.

"Speaking of the fund-raiser, your friend came in again this evening," Bruce said. He turned to Scott. "I thought we'd gotten lucky and he'd found a new place to hang out."

"Apparently not." Scott rolled his eyes. "What did we ever do to you, Grace?"

"Who are you talking about?" I asked.

"David Cherk."

"I'd hardly call him my friend," I said.

"That's not how he sees it," Bruce said. Imitating Cherk's pontificating tone, he went on, "'Grace and I are working together, you know. She's depending on me to bring brilliance to her fund-raiser.'"

"*My* fund-raiser?"

"Oh yeah," Bruce said. "And because you're his dear

colleague, he insisted that Scott or I take care of him. Had to be one of us. He wanted to make extra sure we knew that he was working with you and that the entire event is dependent on him."

"The guy barely tolerates me."

"He had motive. We get these types from time to time, don't we?" Scott asked Bruce. "Cherk is a user and a complainer and an all-around pest. Our favorite kind of customer. Not."

Bruce shot me a weary look. "He made it sound as though you told him to come into the shop and mention your name if he wanted to score deep discounts."

"I did no such thing."

Bruce and Scott both managed smiles at that. "We know," Bruce said. "Don't worry about it."

"For heaven's sakes, why would he do such a thing?"

Scott waved as though shooing a fly. "Don't take it personally, Grace. He's one of those people who wants a better deal than anyone else, and thought that if he dropped your name into conversation, we'd throw freebies his way."

"Did you?"

They answered together. "No."

Bruce picked up the story. "He put on quite a show, broadly suggesting that after having to deal with Joyce Swedburg he deserved special treatment."

Using the fingers of his hands like pincers, Scott gripped the front of his shirt and waved it in and out. "Sweat. He told us about how he worked up a sweat. Poor baby."

"And he thinks that entitles him to a free bottle of wine," Bruce said. "Or two."

"How does he figure that?"

"I don't know." Bruce shrugged in a way that let me know he'd gotten over the annoyance. "All I can tell you is that people like Cherk—you can't change them. He's got this bloated sense of entitlement and believes he's above us all. I think that's what drives him—he truly believes he deserves to be treated better than the rest of the world."

"That's it exactly," Scott added. "If he isn't lobbying for free stuff, he's complaining about prices, selection, or service. And he never hesitates to share his nasty mood with our employees. They cringe—literally cringe—when he walks in. I've seen it happen."

"I'm sorry you had to deal with him today. Especially if he made it sound as though I'd sent him there."

"We know you better than that, Grace."

"Seriously, don't worry about him," Scott said. "We only told you so that you'd know who you're dealing with."

When my roommates retired for the evening, I went upstairs and stood in the doorway of the spare bedroom I'd prepared for Adam's arrival. I flicked on the overhead light and sighed.

Bootsie, who had been missing for some time, circled my ankles until I picked her up. I nuzzled her face, craving the kitten's comfort, even though I knew I'd pay the price later. My allergies had gotten more manageable over the time we'd had her, but her saliva still caused hives when it came in contact with my skin and I hadn't completely conquered the sneezing bouts yet.

"It's worth it," I said into her neck as I took a long look around. I'd stocked the spare room and bathroom with new towels and toiletries, freshened the sheets, and tidied up in anticipation of Adam's arrival. I'd been looking forward to having him here—to getting to know him better. I was far more disappointed about this change of plans than I cared to admit.

FRANCES AND I WERE OVERSEEING THE LAST-minute setup in the basement of Marshfield the next afternoon, when David Cherk arrived. "You're here early," I said. "The benefit doesn't begin for another four hours."

He gave an insouciant shrug. "There are always details that need to be attended to, unexpected problems before a big event. I want to do another full walk-through before I return home to change into proper attire."

"We'll join you on the walk-through," I said. "I'd like to go over everything one more time as well."

His smile didn't reach his eyes. "I prefer to make this final round on my own." He tapped both temples with his index fingers. "Helps me to see things more clearly."

I exchanged a look with Frances. "By all means. Don't let us stop you."

He winked and pointed a finger at me, gun-like. "Try not to interrupt."

"My," Frances said when he had retreated to the stage room, "someone ought to inform Mr. Cherk that he doesn't own this place."

"True enough. But neither do we, so let's chalk his attitude up to eccentricity and get back to work."

"You might, though."

"I might what?" I asked. "Get to work?"

She gestured, arms wide. "You might own this entire estate someday."

I held up a finger. "Don't go there."

"I speak the truth as I see it."

"Clearly, you need new glasses." Before she could retort, I walked away. Workers were occupied with final tasks, and the last thing I wanted to do was get in their way.

David Cherk had disappeared behind the stage. I could hear him humming a fragmented tune, but we were too far away to make it out. Frances followed as I moved closer to listen. Behind the humming, we heard the quiet but unmistakable notes of a Johann Strauss waltz, probably coming from an iPod.

She nudged me. "Look," she whispered.

The back curtain moved. Twice, three times. We kept watching, noticing that the fabric's movement synced with Cherk's music. It looked like he was hitting the back of the curtain with a pointed elbow, every third beat or so.

"Is he dancing?" I asked quietly.

Frances held a hand up to her mouth. "You think that's why he didn't want us following him?" she asked from between her fingers. "What is wrong with that guy?"

I took her arm and led her away. She balked at my touch but didn't fight me. When we got far enough away, I said, "Maybe the music moved him and he got caught up in it. Let's let him be."

Frances clearly wanted to break in on Cherk, to see what he was up to, but I had better things to do.

"Let it go," I said. "Focus on the party tonight. Are we missing anything?"

She frowned but admitted, "I think we're in good shape."

I gave the space a long, admiring look. The tables were covered in linen, the chairs in the auditorium set up in precise rows. Lighting was gentle, décor was soft. I was proud of how we'd pulled it all together.

"Everything is wonderful," I said. "Glittery and bright. I'm hoping the benefit is as successful as our preparation for it has been."

Frances checked her watch. "Shouldn't you be leaving for the airport? Isn't that band leader boyfriend of yours due to land soon?"

"He had to cancel."

"Oh?" Her tone was high-pitched and inquisitive. "He's got something better to do?"

It was none of Frances's business, but I didn't care for the implication that Adam had chosen to stand me up. "His aunt is dying."

She looked away, but didn't respond immediately. "Sorry to hear." A second later, she added, "Assuming it's true, that is."

AT QUARTER TO SEVEN, WE WERE READY FOR the party to start. Everything was in place, the room glowed, and Frances and I made ready to greet the first guests.

Frances wore a nun-worthy eggplant pleated skirt with matching jacket over a mauve blouse. Having forgotten Frances's penchant for purple when I was out shopping, I'd splurged and bought myself a tea-length violet-blue dress for the occasion. I was now second-guessing my color choice. Heaven forbid that anyone assume that my assistant and I had coordinated.

Frances pulled up the antique watch she wore on a chain around her neck. "They should be showing up soon." She clucked as she looked around the room. "I wonder how much it's killing Joyce Swedburg not to be here."

An hour earlier, our illustrious organizer had phoned to tell us that she'd fallen ill with a nasty bout of food poisoning and wouldn't be able to attend. Frances had taken the call.

"I can only imagine," I said. "I feel bad for her."

Frances gave me a "You've got to be joking" look. "And you wonder why you get into trouble so often. You feel sorry for everybody."

"The woman grates on my nerves, but she worked hard to make tonight's benefit a success. Unpleasant personality aside, she deserves to be here."

Frances didn't say a word, but for once she didn't disagree. I took that as a positive.

Because the closest working kitchen was up one floor and across the main hall of the first level, and because that kitchen was extremely small, our catering staff had had to get creative about supplying food for our guests. Fortunately, we weren't serving a full dinner. Tonight's menu consisted of appetizers, desserts, and drinks. It had taken some precise organization, but we'd arranged to have hot hors d'oeuvres delivered from the kitchens at the Marshfield Hotel, where they had plenty of space and many hands to help.

Food continued to arrive as we waited. We'd set up several decorative screens in the main room and kept both hot and cold storage units behind them.

Two men carrying a large hotbox edged too close to one of the tables, snagging a corner of its linen tablecloth. I was making my way over to straighten it when Frances sidled up. "Look who's here," she said under her breath. "Twinkletoes."

Chapter 6

DAVID CHERK SWOOPED INTO THE ROOM looking more like Count Dracula than anyone should when it wasn't Halloween. He wore a trim-cut black tux with white silk vest and white bow tie. What sealed the deal, however, was the red silk–lined black cape. Its high collar turned up against Cherk's veiny neck.

"Good evening," he said.

When he smiled, I was surprised not to see fangs.

Frances kept her mouth tight, but her shiny cheeks turned as purple as her dress.

"Good evening," I said, working to keep my own reaction at bay. "You look ready for our big night."

His face creased into an even creepier smile. "I most certainly am."

Bennett strolled in behind Cherk, and the two men greeted each other cordially. I could detect absolutely no surprise on Bennett's face when he encountered our vampire in charge.

I told both men about Joyce's illness. Bennett expressed genuine regret.

Cherk said, "All that work and she doesn't get to enjoy the fruit of her efforts." He make a *tsk*ing noise that was more sarcastic than sincere.

A few moments after Cherk and Bennett left us to mingle, Dr. Leland Keay walked in, smiling. And with good reason, it seemed.

"Ooh," Frances whispered. "What have we here?"

The fifty-something doctor was accompanied by a golden-haired woman who had to be a least ten years younger than me. She had lovely, mild features and held tight to Doc Keay's arm. They made their way toward us. Unsteady on five-inch, icepick-thin heels, she reminded me of Bambi taking his first steps.

I worried, not because she might topple and hurt herself— this girl was young enough to bounce—but because there was very little left to the imagination with the tiny red bandage dress she wore. One wrong move, one unexpected sneeze, and Marshfield could be cited for promoting public indecency. The stretchy, scarlet garment fit her so snugly that she probably had to baby powder herself to get into it.

Keay introduced us. "This is Serena," he said, with a protective hand around her waist. "When Joyce informed me that she wasn't going to make it tonight, I knew her ticket would be going to waste. Serena didn't mind joining us at the last minute." He turned to the younger woman. "Did you?"

She blinked sweetly up at Dr. Keay. "I didn't mind at all."

I supposed I shouldn't have been surprised by her high, soft voice, but I was. Not only did she look barely legal, she sounded like an eight-year-old.

Serena smiled hard enough to hurt, and I caught a glimpse of what might be her only aesthetic flaw. Her teeth were a mess. Crowded together, sideways and twisted, they were jammed uncomfortably in her tiny mouth. "I'm so excited to be able to attend this benefit," she said, squeezing the doctor's arm. "Leland has told me about how a lot of the people from his hospital will be here. I'm super excited to meet all his friends."

"I'm betting the good doctor is super excited as well," Frances said.

I shot her a look.

"It's very nice to meet you, Serena," I said. "I take it you live in Emberstowne?"

She shook her head, making her shiny hair swing into her face. How old *was* this girl? "Westville," she said, practically wrapping herself around the doc's arm. "It's so exciting to be in the actual town where Leland works. I'm so excited."

I wanted to hand this girl a thesaurus. "You may be interested in learning about Emberstowne's clock, then. I'm sure Dr. Keay will be happy to show you around the fund-raiser and tell you more about it."

She gave a little giggle before he spirited her away.

"What the heck?" Frances whispered when they were out of earshot. "Where did he find the bimbo?"

"She's young," I said. "Cut her some slack."

With a glance back over her shoulder, Frances grunted. "Old enough and clever enough to snag a rich old codger like Keay."

I nearly laughed out loud at that. "Codger? Really, Frances. He's probably all of fifty-five."

"Coot, then," she said, refusing to cede the point. "Curmudgeon."

"How are things going?" Bennett asked as he rejoined us. Frances and I hadn't moved from our position at the entrance. As it was the only way in, we'd decided it was our best bet for allowing us to greet guests as they arrived and direct them to food, drink, and entertainment, right from the start.

"So far so good," I said. "It's not even twenty minutes after seven and most of our guests are here." I gestured. Men and women in their festive finery chatted in groups. "Seems as though everyone is having a good time. I admit I didn't expect the party to take off this quickly. It's a great sign."

Bennett's expression softened. "Joyce is very good at organizing such things. It's clearly her influence at work. Such a shame that she's ill." He smiled at me indulgently. "I'm sorry your young man couldn't make it, either."

"Thank you," I said.

"There must be plenty of eligible bachelors among tonight's crowd," he went on. "And you should dance. A beautiful young woman like you would have her choice of partners."

I knew he was doing his best to be kind and complimentary, but I was eager to halt this particular line of thought. "Thanks, Bennett, but I'm fine on my own. Adam will be back to visit again soon, I'm sure," I said, ignoring Frances's pointed smirk.

A friend of Bennett's pulled him away from our group to join a jovial crowd across the room. The moment he was gone, Frances said, "How much do you want to bet that the Mister is expecting you and Jack to hook up at this event?"

"I don't plan to 'hook up' with anyone. Do you even know what that means?"

"*Pheh.* Of course I do. Why not give Jack another chance?" she asked. "Tonight's benefit is for the Promise Clock. Seems like an omen to me."

"None of that," I said. "I don't even want to hear Jack's—"

The words died on my lips as he walked in. This was the first time I'd seen him in a suit and I needed to suck in a quiet breath to stop myself from exclaiming how handsome he looked. Not only would it have been awkward to stare; it would have been mortifying as well.

Jack wasn't alone.

"Becke," I said, making myself smile over the hard pit of disappointment that was doing belly flops in my stomach. "What a lovely outfit."

The woman cleaned up well, I had to give her that. Her

dark-rooted white-blond hair had begun to grow out from its spiky punk style and she'd shellacked it smartly into finger waves. Coupled with her drop-waist sleeveless dress, she looked as though she'd stepped out of a 1920s fashion magazine. I hated to admit it, but she looked darling.

One thing about Becke hadn't changed, though. Her eyes were hard as ever. "This belonged to Jack's grand-mother," she said, performing a pirouette. "Fits like it was made for me."

"Your grandmother's?" I said to Jack, nearly choking on the words. "How nice that you were able to find it."

Barely two months ago, Jack had sworn he wasn't inter-ested in Becke. Swore that he was allowing the woman and her two young children to live in his dad's vacant home only because he wanted to be a good guy. He wanted to help them out until Becke got back on her feet.

Seems as though she'd done so. Quickly, too.

To be fair, I'd told Jack that I wouldn't wait, not again. He'd taken me at my word, and why shouldn't he? These days I was seeing Adam, so there was no reason why Jack shouldn't be out there dating as well. Still, his being here with Becke, after his earnest assertions that there was noth-ing between them, caused me a sharp pain I could never have anticipated.

Frances stepped in, dragging Becke by the arm. "Over there is the bar. We have waiters and waitresses offering appetizers, but if you want to help yourself."—she tugged her to turn—"there's a buffet on that side of the room. Beyond, in the back to your right is the entertainment. You may want to stake out your seat early. Good spots will go fast."

Becke pushed Frances's hand away. "Thanks, but Jack and I are happy to go exploring together." She started to reach for his arm—what was with women hanging onto men lately?—but Jack turned, effectively slipping out of her grasp.

He took a step closer to me. "I'm looking forward to meeting your beau," he said, giving the partygoers a cursory glance as though hoping to pick Adam out of the crowd. "Is he here yet?"

Frances made a noise I couldn't decipher.

"Adam's not coming," I said. About to lapse into an explanation as to why, I bit my tongue and kept silent.

"Oh?" Jack said. "Anything wrong?"

Frances answered with a dramatic shrug. "Things happen."

Becke urged Jack to get a drink as another couple entered, requiring me to get back to my hostess duties. But Jack wasn't ready to leave yet. "I'm interested in all the work that's being done on your house, Grace," he said. "You and I will have to talk later."

Becke's expression darkened. "Oh, I'm sure you'll be too busy to chat, Jack. You're in for a very special night tonight. I guarantee it."

As if her words weren't blatant enough, she reached up to finger his hair.

"Becke," he said sharply as he stepped away, his J-shaped scar whitening ever so briefly. He turned to me with an apologetic look on his face.

I pretended not to notice as I spun around to greet the new arrivals.

AN HOUR LATER, I WAS TALKING WITH A group of financial advisers who regularly golfed with one of Emberstowne's gastroenterologists. The four women had been regaling me with tales of their shenanigans on the links. I'd found them to be charming and fun, but when they started sharing stories about their caddies, cars, and vacations, I began to realize how much I didn't belong in their circle.

I excused myself when I saw Frances wandering about with a puzzled, determined look on her face.

"What's up?" I asked her.

"Dr. Keay is supposed to get the program started with

the opening speech." She tapped the watch hanging around her neck. "He's due to be onstage in five minutes."

I knew that. "What's the problem?"

"I can't find him. David Cherk can't find him."

"Maybe he's off in a quiet corner with Serena," I said, but even as I spoke the words, I knew there was nowhere private down here. Not tonight. And I could vouch for the fact that Dr. Keay hadn't left. Even though I'd mingled, I'd stayed close enough to the entrance to greet any stragglers who came late. I knew with certainty that no one had left the space since the party began.

"Serena is sitting in a chair in the auditorium"—Frances gestured toward the entertainment quarters—"all by herself."

"Has anyone checked the men's room?" I asked.

Frances gave a brief nod. "I had the Mister take a look."

"You asked *Bennett* to search the men's room?"

She blew off my reaction. "He didn't mind."

"The only other place I can think of—"

"Is the food storage area, behind the screens," she finished for me. "Already checked."

As I started for the auditorium, David Cherk joined us. "Where is he?" the agitated Dracula asked. "I've looked all over."

"Did you check behind the stage?" I answered his question with one of my own. "Do you think he went back there to collect his thoughts before taking the spotlight?"

Cherk's skeletal face appeared even more gaunt than usual. "Of course I checked." His dark, wiry brows arched in emphasis. "That was the first place I looked. In fact, I thought for sure that's where he'd be because I was certain I'd heard the sound of scuffling back there earlier." Slicing the air with both hands, he said, "Nobody."

"Why haven't you taken that off?" I asked, pointing to the cape, which caught the breeze behind him as the three of us hurried toward the stage. "Aren't you uncomfortably warm?"

"I am exceptionally relaxed in my garb," he said, clearly confused by my question. "We are so seldom called upon to dress up. Today, at least, I'd hoped to impress our audience with my unexpected elegance. Historical presentations can be a bore, which is why I always add my own personal flair." He tapped the sides of his nose with his fingers. "Assuming I'm able to perform tonight at all. If we can't find our guest of honor and keynote speaker, then everything will be ruined."

"I'm sure he's around," I said, but doubt was beginning to creep in.

Bennett joined us. "No luck finding him?"

"Not yet," I said.

We entered the auditorium, where, as Frances predicted, Serena sat, drink clutched in two hands, perched on a chair in the back row, alone. Because the presentation wouldn't begin until we announced it and invited everyone in here, the place was otherwise empty.

Wide-eyed, and so skinny that her bare, knobby knees and too-tall shoes made her look like a toddler who'd borrowed Mom's dress-up clothes, she turned as we entered, looking hopeful. I could read expectation on her smooth face, then despondency when she noticed that Leland Keay wasn't with us.

"What happened?" I asked her. "Where's Dr. Keay?"

I'd thought her eyes couldn't get wider. I was wrong. "He left me at the bar and told me he'd be right back. I saw him come in here. He was gone so long that I came to look for him."

He *had* to be behind the curtains. There was no other possibility. I glanced up at the low platform, wings, and backdrop. Even though Cherk had claimed no one was back there, I asked her, "Did you check behind the stage?"

She shook her head. "I didn't know if I had permission to go back there."

Permission? I found myself hoping that the caramel-colored liquid in her glass was a soft drink.

Cherk tapped the bridge of his nose with two fingers again, only this time he used enough force to leave white marks on his skin. "The longer we wait to start the program, the more this crowd will have been drinking. You know they all intend to get their donations' worth." He began to pace in small circles. "I don't care to perform before a drunken throng or to deal with hecklers. It's not pretty."

"A drunken *thong*?" Serena asked, swiveling her head between Cherk and me. "I've never heard of one of those."

"Throng," I corrected her absentmindedly. "Another word for 'crowd.'"

Frances seemed to be waiting for me to do something. If she and Bennett maintained that Dr. Keay wasn't in either the men's room or the food preparation area, then I knew it to be true. I couldn't say the same for David Cherk here, or depend on uncertain Serena. Time to check for myself.

Heading for the stage, I said, "I'll have a look back there, just in case."

Cherk started to protest, but stopped mid-sentence as Dr. Keay stumbled onto the stage from the wing on my left.

"There you are," I said, but my words died as he fell onto his hands and knees, slurring curses at whatever had tripped him up. To me it looked as though he'd fallen over his own feet.

Drunkenly, he attempted to stand up again.

By the time he waved a hand in the air, we were at his side. "Dr. Keay," I said, as I held his arm, attempting to ease him into a sitting position. His skin was cold and clammy. The sickly sweet smell of liquor poured off of him. "What happened?"

He stared at me, unable to focus. His lips moved, but his words were almost indistinguishable. It sounded as though he said, "Injection."

"Are you diabetic?" I asked.

He blinked and moved his lips, but nothing intelligible came out.

"Is Dr. Keay a diabetic?" I asked those around me.

Getting no response, I ordered Cherk back to the other room. "We've got at least a dozen doctors in there," I told him. "One of them will know what to do. Get them."

Cherk took off.

Keay tried to speak again, but he couldn't get the words out. Clutching at his chest, he fell to his side, eyeballs rolling up high into his head. His body went limp and all struggling ceased.

"Dr. Keay," I said, my voice rising. "Dr. Keay." I shook him and shouted, "Leland."

He didn't move. I brought my face down close to his mouth and nose, my hand on his chest, then my fingers against his neck. I hoped to feel breath, a pulse, something.

I was about to begin chest compressions, when one of the doctors summoned from the other room pulled me away. He took over, beginning CPR and ordering those around him to help loosen Leland's clothing.

Scrambling to my feet, I looked at Frances. "I think he's dead."

Chapter 7

DESPITE THE FACT THAT THE ROOM WAS filled with many medical professionals, all of whom performed heroically, no one was able to save Leland Keay.

Paramedics who had been called to the scene attempted to revive the deceased doctor as well. It was obvious the surgeon was dead, but also apparent that no one wanted to be accused of not trying hard enough to bring him back. Efforts to resuscitate Dr. Keay went on for a long time. Finally, however, we all had to admit it: He was gone.

The paramedics began packing up their equipment as partygoers slowly made their way to the door. There would be no entertainment tonight.

In the aftermath, I'd asked one of Keay's friends if the man was diabetic and found out that he was not.

"Then why would he have said, 'injection,' I wonder," I murmured to Frances.

"It's a mystery. And look," she said with a sour lemon grimace, "here come Mutt and Jeff. Maybe they'll help you solve it."

I glanced up. Our local homicide detectives, Rodriguez and Flynn, were making their way over to us. I'd worked with the pair before and had always found portly Rodriguez to be affable and kind, though slow to react. His younger partner, Flynn, was jumpy, wiry, and prone to quick accusations and reluctant backpedaling.

"What are you doing here?" I asked. "It looks like Dr. Keay died of a heart attack. Natural causes. For once, thank goodness, your services aren't needed."

"Nice to see you, too, Miz Wheaton," Rodriguez said. He took out a plaid handkerchief and wiped sweat from the side of his face. "How about after that warm welcome, you tell us what happened here tonight."

"I'm sorry," I said. "You're right. That was no way to greet you. Maybe I'm still in shock."

"No worries, *amiga*," he said.

I gave him a quick rundown about how Dr. Keay had gone missing and how we'd come upon him here in the auditorium moments before he collapsed. "That's really it," I said.

"How long was he missing?" Flynn asked. The tenor of Flynn's question set me on edge. It shouldn't have, but it did.

"I don't know precisely," I said. "We needed him to make a speech and when the time came, he was nowhere to be found." I pointed. "Unfortunately, when he showed up, it was too late for anyone to help."

Rodriguez labored across the room to take a closer look at the scene surrounding Dr. Keay's body. Speaking over his shoulder, he added, "The station was alerted when the 9-1-1 call came in. We're here simply as a precaution. With all that happens at the estate, you never know." Gesturing to the wing on his left, he asked, "He came out from here?"

I nodded.

"Anybody back here with him?" Rodriguez asked.

"No," I said. "While one of the doctors tried to revive Dr. Keay, Frances went to check. She wanted to see what

Dr. Keay might have been doing back there. She said it was completely vacant."

"No way out?" Rodriguez disappeared behind the wing.

I raised my voice. "Solid brick walls." I turned to Flynn. "Is this really necessary? It's bad enough that a man died in front of us all. Having you here makes everyone queasy."

"Can you blame us for being careful?" he asked. "Never a dull moment at Marshfield."

"Your high opinion of us leaves me breathless," I said.

Flynn was as cocky as ever, but this time, at least, he didn't sneer. "As well it should."

While we waited for the stout detective to reemerge, I lowered my voice. "Is Rodriguez okay?"

My question must have surprised Flynn. "Why do you ask?"

"I don't know," I said. "I haven't seen him in a while. He looks pale. He's gained weight, hasn't he?"

"What are you, his mother now?" Before I could snap back a reply, Flynn gestured with his chin. "Who's that?"

Behind me, Serena sat in the same folding chair she'd been in since we'd arrived, both hands clutching her face. She moaned quietly, rocking back and forth in her seat.

"The deceased doctor's date for the evening," I said. "After we"—I faltered—"after we knew that Keay wasn't coming back, I got her a drink of water and asked if there was anyone she wanted me to call to pick her up."

"And?"

"A friend is coming. From Westville. She's stuck here for a while."

Rodriguez came around from the right and took a knee next to the corpse.

Flynn shot a glance at him. "I'll talk with her."

Had I not known Flynn, I would have assumed that the younger detective was eager to swoop in and play knight on white steed to Serena's damsel in distress. But this guy was all business all the time, and from the glint in his eye, I could tell he intended to interrogate the distraught girl.

Serena wouldn't stand a chance under the detective's harsh tactics.

I made it to her side two steps before he did. "Serena," I said, "this is Detective Flynn of the Emberstowne Police Department." When she looked up at me through tear-filled eyes, I asked, "Are you doing okay?"

"I knew he was older," she said, "but I didn't think he was old enough to *die*."

Flynn whipped out a small notebook and pen. "What was your relationship with the deceased?"

Serena turned to me, mouth open in surprise, bottom lip quivering.

"Detective Flynn wants to ask you a few questions," I said, doing my best to keep her tears from starting up again.

"You're a detective?" she said to Flynn. To me, she asked, "Did Leland do something illegal?"

"No," I said. "Not that I know of. The police are simply here to make sure everything goes smoothly."

She blinked and nodded. Turning to Flynn, she said, "Leland is my boyfriend." She held a hand up as though to shield herself from seeing Keay's motionless form on the stage floor across the room. "I mean, he was."

Serena didn't see the judgmental smirk on Flynn's face, and for that I was grateful.

"How long were you two a couple?" he asked. Could the man ever pose a question without sounding so snarly? "How long had you been seeing each other?"

"We had our three-month anniversary last week. I was really excited because he took me to a special dinner and then dancing."

I tried to envision that. Couldn't.

"Where did you first meet Dr. Keay?" Flynn asked, still taking notes.

"At a club in Westville."

Flynn stopped writing. He looked up. "Dr. Keay went clubbing?"

She gave a tiny shrug. "I guess. I'd seen him there a few times before we met. He came over and introduced himself one night. We've been together ever since."

I decided to join the conversation. "Do you know if Dr. Keay needed to take any injections? Do you know if he had any illnesses he was fighting?"

She shook her head.

Flynn looked like he was about to cast me away, but remembering the smell I'd noticed when trying to rouse the doctor, I pressed on. "Was he a big drinker?"

"Oh, no," she said, eyes wide. "That was the weird part about meeting him at a club. He never touched alcohol. He'd buy drinks for me if I wanted them, but he stuck to soda and stuff."

"Really?" I said. I looked over at Flynn.

He'd fisted one hip and now gestured with the hand holding the notebook. "Oh, please. Proceed with your line of questioning, Detective Wheaton."

Ignoring his sarcasm, I continued, "Serena, you saw how he stumbled onstage right before he collapsed. It looked to me as though he'd been drinking. Heavily."

"I was with him all night," she said. "He ordered club soda with a twist of lime from the bartender. That's all he had."

"What about when he left you alone? He could have been drinking then."

She gave me a skeptical look, which I deserved. There was no way she could know what he'd done when he'd been on his own. Plus, she pointed out the obvious: "That would have to be a lot of drinking in a super-short period of time. I've never seen anybody get that drunk that fast. And some of my friends can really pound down a lot of liquor super quick."

"Did Dr. Keay say or do anything before he left you alone that could explain where he was going?"

"He said he needed to talk with someone privately, and that it was better if I stayed back."

Flynn went back to note-taking and took a step forward, effectively, though gently, elbowing me out of the way. "Who was he meeting?"

"I don't know."

"A friend?" Flynn asked. "Coworker?"

"I don't know," she said again.

Flynn's voice hardened. "He must have told you why he was leaving you alone for so long."

She shook her head. "He kissed me on the cheek and told me to wait for him at the bar while he talked with someone. He said he'd be right back."

"How long was he gone?" I asked, ignoring Flynn's glare at my interruption.

"I'm not sure. It seemed like a long time. I didn't know anyone else at the party so I wandered around for a while, then came in here to wait."

"Why would you sit here if the rest of the party was in there?" Flynn asked, gesturing.

"When I came in here to look for him, I saw all the empty chairs." She pointed. "My feet hurt."

Flynn rolled his eyes.

"Partner," Rodriguez called. Whether or not Flynn expected me to stay with Serena, I didn't care. I accompanied him as he made his way to the stage. Rodriguez grimaced, struggling to get up from his position on the floor. When he was upright, I noticed how much the man was perspiring. His breathing was fast and shallow.

"Are you all right?" I asked him. Some maternal instinct caused me to place the back of my hand against his forehead. Cold and clammy, a lot like Keay had been seconds before he died. "You don't look so great."

He massaged his chest and quirked up one side of his mouth. "Indigestion," he said. "Too many hot peppers with dinner tonight."

"You had a turkey sandwich," Flynn said. He moved closer, assessing his partner. "Maybe we need to take you in."

Rodriguez waved a pudgy hand. "No worries, amigo. Catching my breath is all." He showed teeth, but I couldn't tell whether he was smiling or experiencing pain. "I wasn't prepared for more excitement at Marshfield tonight. I'm fine."

I could tell Flynn didn't believe it. I didn't, either.

At that moment, someone touched my arm. I turned to face Jack. "You need any help?"

I looked past him to see Becke waiting far back, in the doorway. "I think we've got it handled. Thanks."

"You and I need to talk," he said.

"I don't think we do."

"I invited Becke only because you were bringing a date," he said quietly. "Davey wasn't using his ticket so I asked him for it. If I would have known—"

"Jack, this is not the time or the place."

His expression tightened. "You're right. I'm sorry. Let me know if I can do anything. I mean it."

"I will," I said. We both knew I was lying.

When he was gone, I left Flynn and Rodriguez to go find Frances. She and Bennett had formed a sort of anti-receiving line, thanking guests for attending the benefit, expressing their sorrow at the loss of Dr. Keay, and promising to keep everyone updated about the man's sudden demise, as details became available.

The music had been silenced, the waitstaff had begun to clean up, and there were only a few stragglers left, waiting to say good night.

"I'm sorry for Dr. Keay's family," I started to say to Frances, then blurted out, "Joyce! His ex-wife. Someone ought to let her know."

Frances sniffed. Bennett, overhearing, leaned closer. "I'll call her as soon as we're wrapped up here. Better coming from a friend than hearing it secondhand, I'll wager."

Serena's friend, a young man about her age with unruly hair and silver chains hanging from his low-slung jeans, came in, escorted by one of Terrence's staff.

Frances said, "I'll get her."

There was a lot of activity at once: The paramedics carried the unused gurney past me out the door and up the stairs as my assistant made her way toward the auditorium. Serena's young friend remained silent except for a quick chin-lift and a muttered, "Hey, how's it going?"

"Serena will be here in a moment," I said. "She's upset."

"Yeah."

"Did she tell you why she needed you to pick her up?"

"No."

I took a deep breath. "The gentleman she was with tonight"—I had a tough time using the word *boyfriend* where Dr. Keay was concerned—"collapsed and died." I gestured. "In the other room. In front of her."

His eyebrows almost rose. "No kidding?"

"Be nice to Serena, okay? I think she probably needs to go straight home."

He made a face. "Whatever."

Bennett shook hands with the gastroenterologist I'd been talking with earlier. "I'll be in touch," he said, to at least the twentieth person in the past fifteen minutes. "It's a shame. A terrible loss for us all."

"Grace!" From behind me, Frances shouted, an edge to her voice I'd never heard before. I turned to see my assistant gesturing violently from the auditorium doorway. "Come quick."

Chapter 8

SHE GRABBED MY ARM. "IT'S RODRIGUEZ. HE needs help. Have the paramedics left?"

"They're on their way out now," I said, moving past her.

"I'll get them. You know CPR. Get in there and do what you can."

With that, Frances was gone, moving faster than I thought she was capable of. I raced past Serena, who had stood up on wobbly legs. She said something as I hurried across the room, but I couldn't make out what it was. "Go." I pointed back the way I'd come. "Your friend is here."

Up at far end, there were now two men lying on the stage. The one on my left, Keay, was dead. The one on my right, Rodriguez, clutched a bicep, his eyes squeezed shut.

Flynn crouched by his side. "They're going for help," he said, "hang in there."

I knelt on Rodriguez's other side. "What happened?" I asked as I loosened his tie and pulled it away. "You're okay," I said softly, pressing my hand against Rodriguez's damp cheek.

He was still breathing, still conscious. "The paramedics haven't left yet. They'll be here in a second. You got lucky."

Through gritted teeth, he fought to get words out. "Don't feel lucky right now."

I glanced up at the doorway as the paramedics raced back in. One of them was shaking his head as he took up a position next to Rodriguez and Flynn. I backed off, giving them room to work.

"Thought maybe the dead guy had come back to life or something," one said to the other.

His partner made a face. "The first guy is way past help."

"I'm not," Rodriguez said. "Quit talking and get the pain to stop."

They'd begun working even as they conversed, taking Rodriguez's pulse, stripping the detective's shirt to bare his furry chest, and setting nodes all over the man's body to send telemetry to the nearest hospital.

"Good thing they were still close by," I said to Flynn.

His attention trained on Rodriguez, the younger detective ran a hand up through his hair. He worked his jaw, but didn't respond.

Frances and Bennett had followed the paramedics into the auditorium. I met them halfway across the room. "Is everyone gone?" I asked.

Bennett stepped sideways to be able to watch the goings-on. "I hope he'll be all right."

"He's talking. I'm no medical professional, but I assume that's a good sign."

We chatted idly the way people do when they're forced to stand by, helpless, during a crisis such as this. I was sure none of us would remember later what we talked about. All we could do was watch the paramedics in action, doing what they did best. It could have been ten minutes, it could have been a half hour—I lost track of time—but soon they had him sitting up, and I was relieved to see that the detective's color had improved.

Behind us, one of Terrence's team cleared his throat. "The coroner is here," he said. "What do I do?"

The paramedics had begun preparing Rodriguez for transport. I knew that the narrow corridor and steps between the front door and the party room wouldn't accommodate two stretchers at once, so I said, "Bring them in and have them wait off to the side, okay? Dr. Keay isn't going anywhere."

Flynn still hadn't said much. He stood apart from us, constantly rocking onto the balls of his feet as though preparing to sprint. He rubbed his chin and stretched his neck, watching the medics attempt to lift his half-naked partner onto the gurney. Rodriguez was a big man, and they were working hard to move him without disturbing Keay's body, not four feet away.

"Let me help," Flynn said. Though wiry and slim, the guy had muscle. Within seconds the heavyset detective was safely in place. The paramedics began strapping him in.

The coroner and his assistants hurried by, apparently unaware of Rodriguez's health crisis. "Coroner coming through," they said, then asked, "Where's the body?" loud enough for everyone in the room to hear.

The awkward silence that followed was broken by Rodriguez's labored though wry exclamation: "Whatever you do, don't get us mixed up!"

ONCE RODRIGUEZ HAD BEEN RUSHED OFF TO the hospital with Flynn by his side, and Keay's body had been removed to the morgue, Bennett, Frances, and I pulled folding chairs from the auditorium and set them up near the buffet while the waitstaff worked to clear the detritus and pack up the remaining food.

Frances fixed herself a plate of appetizers and sat down. "Shame to let all this go to waste." She lifted a mini beef Wellington and took a bite. "Still hot," she said around the mouthful.

"Any suggestions for what to do with it all?" Bennett asked.

One of the waiters had been listening in. "There's still quite a bit that we haven't even unpacked from the hotboxes," he said. "I know of a homeless shelter on the outskirts of town. I've volunteered there a few times. I'm sure they'd be willing to accept a last-minute donation."

Bennett clapped his hands. "Wonderful. Will you see to it?"

The waiter said that he'd be happy to.

Before he could pack any more of the displayed food away, Frances got up and refilled her plate. When she resumed her seat, her gaze flicked between us, defensively. "Didn't get a chance to eat."

"What I want to know," I began, "is who Dr. Keay needed to talk to. Clearly, it had to be someone in attendance because Keay said he'd be right back. There was no way in or out beside the entrance—"

Holding another appetizer aloft, Frances sucked at a tooth, making her cheek bulge. "Except for the emergency exit, remember."

"That sets off an alarm," I said. "But what if it isn't working?" I stood. "Hang on, I'll be right back." I hurried to the door in question, pressed the crash bar, and winced when the shrill siren pierced the air with its shriek. I made my way back to Bennett and Frances with my hands over my ears.

All the waiters and waitresses had stopped in their tracks, putting down whatever they'd been carrying to cover their ears as well. Bennett and Frances had done the same. I waited, counting aloud, though no one could hear me, "Twenty-eight, twenty-nine, thirty . . ."

Silence, sudden and deep, slammed like an invisible hammer.

"You had to do that, didn't you?" Frances said. Her plate was balanced precariously on her lap. She gripped it again with both hands.

"There's no way anyone could have come in or out through the emergency door," I said. "We wouldn't have missed that."

"Gracie," Bennett's voice was a warning, "there is nothing suspicious about the way Dr. Keay died. You've got that look in your eye again. Leave this alone."

"I don't know," I said. "Even though both Keay and Rodriguez got the cold and clammies, there were differences in the way they went down."

France wagged a finger. "Not all heart attacks are by the book, you know."

I sighed, restless. "Who was Keay meeting? Why couldn't anyone find him?" I held up my hands as though grasping the air around me for answers. "Cherk claims Keay wasn't behind the stage, and yet, that's where he turned up. He said 'injection.' Of all the last words he had to choose from, why 'injection'? He was a preeminent cardiothoracic surgeon. If he was having an attack why wouldn't he say 'heart' instead? And why did he smell like liquor when Serena insists the man never drank a drop? Nope," I said. "There are too many unanswered questions."

The two stared at me in silence for a long moment.

"You really do have a hard time letting things go, don't you?" Bennett asked.

"Only when they don't make sense," I said. "I can't help it. I prefer it when loose ends are tied up." I took a look around as the cleanup continued. "I hope Rodriguez is okay."

Chapter 9

EVEN THOUGH SUNDAY WAS USUALLY A DAY off for me, I returned to Marshfield to oversee Cherk's student team as they took down the stage and repacked all the photographs the man had brought for the presentation but never got a chance to show. Frances joined me.

When they were almost finished, Frances and I took a very Jane Austen–like turn about the room, examining the area closely to see if there was anything amiss.

Cherk had been a brisk taskmaster, but now that his students had completed their jobs and were on their way back to unload the truck at the theater, he became very chatty.

"You here at Marshfield certainly know how to throw the kind of party that gets the whole town talking," he said. "I was initially disappointed not to be able to make my presentation, but who can compete with a dead body followed by a cop suffering a heart attack, all in the same room?"

"You're too kind," I said, returning his sarcasm.

"That detective went down so quickly after Keay died—I started to worry who might be next." When Cherk's face creased into a grin, I suppressed a shudder. One minute he was fish-faced, the next, Dracula. Now a scary clown, complete with fake smile. The deep lines set in his pale skin made him look like an aged person wearing white greasepaint. Except he wasn't all that old. And that was his natural skin tone.

"I called Flynn this morning," I said. "Rodriguez is stable, but may be looking at valve-replacement surgery."

Frances had already heard this update. She made a *tsk*ing noise. "And to think that he could have had Dr. Keay perform the surgery, if only he'd had his heart attack a week sooner."

Cherk said, "Poor planning on his part."

Frances apparently missed the mockery. "Dr. Keay was the best heart surgeon these parts have ever seen." She got a familiar look in her eye and adopted an enticing tone. "He certainly turned his life around."

"Oh?" Cherk asked. "Do I detect the delicious waft of gossip?"

"Don't you know?" Frances asked sweetly, warming to the opportunity to share what she'd hinted at. "I know Grace wasn't living here at the time, but I'm not sure when you moved here."

Cherk didn't answer the unspoken question. "Spill, darling. Please. You have me on tenterhooks."

She perked up. "I thought you'd never ask."

Frances had warned me shortly before the benefit that there was a story behind Joyce Swedburg and Leland Keay's divorce. Now, as she settled in, I got the feeling we were about to hear the whole sordid tale, whether we wanted to or not.

This time, I opted to let her continue. With all the unexplained happenings from last night, I thought it might behoove me to know a little more about the late Dr. Keay and people in his life.

Tugging at the hem of her three-quarter-sleeve peasant blouse, she set her feet apart, like a fighter staking her ground. Vinyl sandals strapped her wide feet about as well as the gurney had strapped Rodriguez's girth in the night before.

Savoring the moment, she pushed up one sleeve and then the other.

"It was a dry autumn. I remember," she began in a tone that belonged around a nighttime campfire, "almost a drought. That's important because it wasn't like Keay could blame what happened on the weather."

I had no idea what Keay might want to blame on anything, but Frances was on a roll, so I didn't ask.

"Dr. Keay and Joyce Swedburg had been married for about fifteen, maybe twenty years at that point. No kids. She was, and still is, a high-powered attorney, and he had already achieved status as a world-renowned heart surgeon. They were living the good life, the two of them."

"Rich, accomplished, people. No dependents. Got it," Cherk said.

"The thing is"—Frances's eyes sparkled; we were clearly getting to the good stuff—"Keay was a lush. A functioning alcoholic the likes of which I'd never seen before. Joyce pretended not to notice, and mostly everyone in town looked the other way."

"He operated on people? Drunk?" I asked.

Frances shook her head. "Never touched a drop when he was on duty, but the minute he was off, or come the weekend, he partied hard."

"What about emergencies?" I asked. "Was he so irresponsible that he didn't consider middle-of-the-night calls for help?"

"He only performed scheduled surgeries. He'd made such a name for himself that he saw patients two days a week for consultation and two days a week in the O.R. He kept a strict, limited schedule." She held up her hands at the unasked question. "He got away with that because he could. People flew from all over the country to see him. There was always a year-long waiting list because Keay almost never lost a patient. Desperate folks lined up and people treated him like a god." One corner of Frances's mouth turned up. "So what if he let loose on his own time? Everybody rationalized that the guy was under such stress while he was working that he ought to be allowed his vices. As long as it wasn't hurting anyone."

Cherk and I exchanged a look. "Vices?" I asked. "Plural?"

"Mm-hmm." Frances allowed her buildup to sink in before continuing, "Keay and Joyce kept up appearances and lived their life of luxury, looking like the happiest, most successful couple Emberstowne had ever seen."

I felt an "until" hovering in the air.

Frances obliged. "Until the accident."

"I thought I'd find you down here."

We all jumped. I spun.

Bennett had come into the room so silently we'd missed him. Either that or we'd been so drawn into Frances's story that we'd tuned out everything else.

"Good morning, Gracie, Frances, David," he said. Then, perhaps reading the scene—the three of us huddled close together, with Frances holding court—Bennett asked, "What have I missed?"

"Background on Joyce and Leland's relationship," I said. "Frances was about to tell us about an accident of some sort."

Bennett cocked an eyebrow at her. "Speaking ill of the dead, are we? So soon?"

She held up both hands. "Facts are facts."

Bennett sent Cherk an almost apologetic look. "I'm sure I don't need to warn you to be careful what you say around our dear Frances here," he said. Resting a hand on my shoulder, he added, "Gracie knows what I'm talking about."

Unfazed, Cherk said, "Back to the accident."

Bennett held a hand out toward Frances in a silent "Go ahead" move.

As though she hadn't been interrupted, Frances jumped right back in. "One night, the good doctor was out carousing again. Joyce kept busy the way she usually did, working on briefs, alone. She got a call at about nine in the evening letting her know that her husband had wrapped his car around a tree in Westville. Totaled the car. Blood alcohol was way over the legal limit."

Bennett, not usually one for gossip, chimed in. "It was bad enough that he'd been driving drunk, but—"

I could tell that this was the reveal Frances had been leading up to, and she wasn't about to let Bennett steal her thunder. Her voice rose and bulldozed over his words. "But he wasn't *alone*." She wagged her brows at me and Cherk. "He had a *woman* in the car with him. A *married* woman."

"Were they hurt?" I asked, adding a faint question, "Was she killed?"

"Lucky for him, no. She was banged up pretty badly, but eventually recovered. The doctor was fine. Maybe being all liquored up kept him loose, who knows? He barely had a scratch."

I had a feeling there was more.

Frances continued, "Can't say that Keay stayed in one piece after Joyce got ahold of him, though. He'd been having affairs with women in town for years. Lots of women," she added with a knowing look. "He probably could have kept it going, too, if it weren't for the bad luck smashing up his car like that."

"So that's why Joyce divorced him?" I asked.

"Yes and no," Frances said. "Whether she'd known about the other women before the accident didn't matter. What mattered was that her husband was a public spectacle and—you know Joyce—that is *not* the kind of attention she craves. Keay called her from jail but she refused to bail him out. Made sure no one else bailed him out, either. Couple of my friends in the police department were there when she finally showed up. She screamed at Keay, told him he could sit and stew for a couple of days and think about where his drinking had gotten him."

Frances looked around as though she needed a drink of water to continue. There was nothing, so she went on, "Joyce defended him in court against the DUI charges. Got him off with a warning if he promised to go into rehab. Keay's passenger sued him and Joyce got that settled out of court. She came off looking like the devoted wife who had forgiven her husband this one transgression. The minute Joyce got him safely free, however, she kicked him out of their house and filed for divorce."

"All that's true," Bennett added. "And if there was any good that came out of it, it was that Dr. Keay has been sober ever since."

"Until last night," I reminded him. "You saw how he stumbled. He was clearly under the influence of something." I waved a hand near my nose. "If that wasn't enough, I could smell it on him."

"Who knows what pushed him over the edge?" Cherk said. "We all have darkness lurking in depths we presume others will never see."

Frances blinked at him.

Clearly unaware of the sinister undertone in his pronouncement, Cherk continued, "Whether he was concerned about disappointing his adolescent date later, or he was worried about having to make a speech, clearly the man found the pressures too much to bear and succumbed to the lure of the drink. There is a devil within us all."

"That's what's bothering me," Bennett said. "Leland has made many speeches in his career. This was nothing new. Why would he have been nervous? There was nothing at stake. These were all people he knew and worked with."

"And if Serena is to be believed, he wasn't out of her sight long enough to drink the volume necessary to impair him to such a degree," I said.

"Things aren't making sense." As Bennett spoke the words, he made eye contact with me. "Not that we need to do anything about it. I'm sure the autopsy will reveal that he died of natural causes, and that what looked like drunkenness may have simply been signs of a stroke."

I opened my mouth to argue that Bennett's theory didn't account for the unmistakable scent of alcohol, but decided to let it go.

Chapter 10

I'D LET FRANCES KNOW THAT I'D BE A LITTLE late arriving at work Monday morning. Hillary had impressed on me—multiple times—that the blueprints Frederick had borrowed from the historical society needed to be returned as soon as possible. I decided to drop them off on my way to work.

I set out for my quick stop at the society's offices in town, thinking about everything that had transpired over the weekend. Last night at home with my roommates, we'd opened a chilled bottle of rosé and simply talked the night away. That quiet respite, being able to relax with two of my closest friends, had turned out to be the relief I'd needed from the stress of managing the Marshfield party and the double heart attacks that had claimed one victim and threatened another.

Scott, Bruce, and I had gone over the blueprint plans closely, trying our best to glean whatever information we could about the house we lived in. We'd found it fun to think about what life had been like more than a hundred years earlier. I didn't have paperwork to tell me when the first shovelful of dirt had been turned over when the house was built, but there was no doubt the home had survived a great deal of history. Oh, the stories it could tell.

The three of us had also decided to take another look at the workbench in the basement and had agreed that the wobbly built-in should go. Better to take it out on our timeline than to wait for it to collapse on its own.

I arrived at the historical society's office moments after it opened for the day. Opening the front door wide, I could smell history the moment I stepped in: musty, and familiar. I took a deep breath and savored it. Although I'd returned to Emberstowne to live more than a year ago, I hadn't spent any time here yet. I knew the society existed, but I had so much of historical significance to sort through at Marshfield before I even began to explore the rest of the town, that I hadn't paid this place proper attention.

The room's ceilings were high. Bookshelves, crammed tight with leather-bound volumes in shades of navy, black, and the occasional faded red, beckoned to be perused. The narrow storefront doorway gave the illusion of the space being tiny and cramped, but walls within had been knocked down between the original store and the adjacent buildings that flanked it, making for a wide, spacious area. There were glass display cases showcasing artifacts that had been collected over the years.

A shiny oak counter stretched along the length of the wall to my left. "Good morning," I said to the man behind it. The dark wooden floor creaked as I made my way in, and the man behind the counter came around to greet me.

A head taller than I was, he was probably a couple of years older than Adam and good-looking, but with a noticeable paunch. He wore 1970s-style glasses, a plaid flannel shirt open over a solid gray tee, and stonewashed blue jeans. With his trim beard and full head of hair—both of which sported a slight touch of gray—he looked like Central Casting's ideal choice for "handsome nerd."

He leaned to look out the front windows, peering up at the sky before answering. "It is," he said, then returned his attention to me. "Let me guess. You must be Grace Wheaton."

"I am," I said. "And you are?"

"Wes McIntyre. I'm the historian in residence." He extended his hand, causing me to shift the rolls to my other arm so we could shake.

"In residence?" I asked. "You don't really live here, do you?"

"Not in the office, although it sure feels like it sometimes. I live in the apartment above. One of the perks of the job." As we stepped back into our own spaces, he added, "Very pleased to meet the woman who everyone in town is talking about."

"Me?" I asked with a self-conscious laugh. "Why on earth would anyone be talking about me?"

"You've earned quite a reputation for yourself," he said.

I waved my free hand dismissively.

"I'm not kidding," he said with an infectious grin. "Did you really take down a thief with an antique sword? Singlehandedly?"

I couldn't resist. "No way," I said. "That sword was heavy. I used two hands."

His eyes sparkled. "I'd love to hear more about that someday."

"I'm sure the tale has grown with the telling and the truth would be a disappointment," I said, eager to change the subject. It always surprised me to find out when my exploits were the topic of conversation among people I'd never even met.

He must have sensed my discomposure because he pointed. "A big hint as to who you are is the fact that you're carrying those blueprints. I signed out three sets last week." He counted aloud as he tapped the tops of the rolls I carried. "One, two, three. The gentleman—Frederick—who picked them up, explained all about your renovation plans." He pointed again. "Let me take those from you."

Happy to be unburdened, I handed the blueprints over. "We really enjoyed going over those drawings. I didn't even realize you kept those sorts of records here."

His eyes crinkled up and he cast a loving gaze around the room. "There is so much here to discover. I wish more of our citizens would take better advantage of all we have to offer."

"I'm one of those guilty of not visiting before now," I said. "If it weren't for Hillary and Frederick, I probably wouldn't even be here today." A framed picture on the wall caught my attention. "This is a great shot of the Promise Clock," I said. Peering closer, I noticed the photographer's name. "David Cherk's work?"

"Most of the modern shots on display are his," Wes said. "We hire him from time to time for specific projects, but he also donates whatever doesn't sell."

"That's nice of him."

One corner of Wes's mouth twisted up. "I get the feeling he's more interested in tax deductions than philanthropy." He carried the blueprints around to the other side of the counter. "He told me about what happened at the benefit. That had to be horrible."

"Already? When was he here?"

Wes scratched the side of his head. "Stopped by yesterday afternoon to drop off a whole stack of donations. The one of the clock seemed to fit that space so I hung it up last night. I haven't had time to put any of the others up yet."

Behind the long oak counter was a wall of wide, short drawers. Wes opened one of them and gestured for me to come around. "Here's where we keep your house's plans," he said as I joined him.

The drawer was filled with other sets of plans, which I asked about.

He lifted one corner of the pile and riffled through. "Your neighbors. We don't have floor plans or original blueprints for every home in Emberstowne, but we have quite a few. They're filed here according to address."

"Can anyone take them out? Like at a library?"

He made a so-so expression. "We discourage people removing items from the premises, because not everyone is diligent about returning them." Closing the drawer again, he smiled. "But as you can tell, we do make exceptions."

"I appreciate that. And because we were so prompt at returning them, will that help in the event we ever need to look at them again?"

"Anytime."

I turned to make my way out along the back area, passing a desk that had been tucked into a nook behind the counter. A jar of clear liquid sat next to a framed photo of a thirty-something woman with dark hair and a winning smile. The glass container wasn't labeled—it looked to me like a pickle or canning jar that had been repurposed—and it seemed out of place.

"What's that?" I asked.

He peered around to see what I was pointing at. "That's David's. He left it here by accident yesterday when he dropped off the photographs."

"What is it?"

Wes tapped the metal cap. "I have no idea, but I assume it's chemicals. You know, he still prefers print over digital photography."

"He mentioned that," I said. "Several times."

"He called to ask me if he'd left stuff here. He forgot this, too." Wes picked up a taped-shut cardboard box and shook it. The top of the box read: PERSONAL AND CONFIDENTIAL. Whatever was inside rattled, sounding like hollow plastic balls bouncing against one another.

"That's curious."

Wes shrugged. "He didn't mention what was inside, and with a sign like that scrawled across the top, I wasn't about to look. Doesn't matter; David said he'd be back today to pick it all up."

I pointed to the framed photograph at the desk's edge. "Is that your wife?"

Wes picked up the picture. "Lynn."

"She's lovely."

"Thank you." His mouth tightened briefly before he continued. "We would have been married fifteen years this December."

"Would have?"

"She died."

"I'm sorry," I said. "I didn't—"

"Don't apologize. You couldn't have known. Lynn passed away well before I moved here."

I was at a loss for words. "I'm sorry," I said again. "Was it an accident?"

"Aneurysm." He put the photo back on the desk. "Never saw it coming. She'd been sick for a while, but we'd gotten through the worst of it. Thought we had all the time in the world. But fate had other plans."

I struggled to find solid conversational footing. "Where did you live before moving here?"

"Seattle," he said. "Lynn loved it there, but once she was gone, I couldn't bear to stay. I looked around for whatever job would take me as far from Seattle as I could get." He held out both hands. "That's how I ended up here."

Searching for something positive to add, I said, "We're glad to have you."

"Emberstowne has been good for my soul." He took a long look around the room. "I'll never stop missing Lynn, but here at least I'm starting to find peace."

I took a look at the black-rimmed schoolhouse clock on the wall. "I ought to get going," I said. "Thank you again for all your help."

"My pleasure," he said. "Keep in mind that our files are open and if there's ever anything you need, all you have to do is ask."

* * *

WHEN I GOT BACK TO MY OFFICE, I RAN INTO Flynn, looking surly as usual.

"I told him you'd be here shortly," Frances said with a frown of disapproval. She checked her watch. "But he was about to leave."

Not looking at my assistant, Flynn said, "I don't have all day. I'm not about to sit on my hands and wait for you when I have a potential homicide to solve."

"Homicide," I repeated. "Do you believe Dr. Keay was murdered?"

He looked like he was about to say, "Yes," but thought better of it. "Now that you're here, I can spare a couple more minutes." He pointed. "Your office."

"Please," I said, allowing him to go first. Behind his back I sent Frances a wide-eyed "I wonder what this is about" look.

I didn't shut the door between my office and Frances's. Flynn didn't complain.

"How's Rodriguez?" I asked as I took a seat behind my desk. Flynn lowered himself into a chair across from me. The man fidgeted constantly and his gaze never seemed to rest on any location for more than a beat or two.

"He's better. Specialists are taking a look at him today. Looks like he *will* need a new valve."

I grimaced. "That's a tough surgery," I said. "Is he a good candidate?"

"Because he's so overweight, you mean?" Flynn asked, dropping any pretense of being polite. "Doctors are worried about that. When I find out more I'll let you know."

I was about to ask about that "potential homicide" comment, but he didn't wait for the opening. "I'm here to take another look at the scene," he said. "You don't need to accompany me or anything. After all the incidents you guys have had here, I can find my way around pretty well."

Feeling prickly after his comment about past troubles at Marshfield, I said, "Thank you for making it clear that you aren't asking permission or for company. But then why come talk to me at all? Is this a social visit?"

His gaze stopped bouncing and he shot a withering, arrow-straight look at me. "If that's what you want to call it, be my guest. I came to let you in on some information. Information I am not *required* to share. Given the circumstances, I thought it best to keep you posted."

"I'm sorry for being flip, then." And I was. "Go ahead."

He resettled himself in his chair, perching on its edge, and leaned forward. "You may or may not know that taking blood alcohol level readings on a dead body can be tricky."

I'd heard as much, but let him continue without interrupting.

"Part of the decomposition process involves putrefaction," he said as casually as if he were discussing what he intended to have for lunch. "Putrefaction can cause higher blood alcohol readings than are wholly correct. I mean, it depends on other considerations, like what the victim ate. That can factor into it. Readings might not always give you an accurate idea of how much liquor the victim consumed."

"Putrefaction?" I said. "That takes a while, doesn't it?"

He gave an emphatic nod. "Depends, again, on the circumstances. What's important here is that the accuracy of a blood alcohol test diminishes the longer a person has been dead. Which is why I asked the coroner to take a reading Saturday night."

"You did?"

"Everybody there claimed that Dr. Keay didn't drink. They swore he never touched the sauce anymore. But you told me you smelled alcohol on him."

"I did."

"Based on that, and knowing that our window of accuracy would be closing soon, I made the call to take a reading."

"And?" I prompted.

"Levels are off the charts," he said. "The coroner couldn't believe that Keay managed to stand upright, even for that brief moment you saw him, with that quantity of liquor in his body. He took a second reading to confirm. The coroner says it was like nothing he'd ever seen before. They'll be doing a full autopsy today."

I'd seen Leland Keay when he'd first arrived. I'd bumped into him a few times before David Cherk had alerted me that the doctor had gone missing. The man hadn't been drunk—not even tipsy—when I'd seen him. How could he have consumed that much alcohol in such a short period of time? It didn't make sense. And if he had given up liquor completely the way everyone believed, then why had he done such a dramatic flip-flop? And why at a high-profile fund-raiser?

"There are too many questions surrounding this death," Flynn said, echoing my thoughts. "I'm not letting it go until I have answers."

"That's a commendable attitude," I said. "I'm glad."

One eye narrowed.

"I mean it," I said. "Whatever you need from me, from Marshfield, let me know. You have our full cooperation."

"That so?" he said. "Then I'll ask you to stay out of my way and not get involved in the investigation."

"I never intend to."

He got to his feet. "That's the part that scares me."

I stood up to walk him out. "Will you have a new partner assigned until Rodriguez returns to the force?"

He shrugged. "Right now my chief isn't convinced this is a homicide. He wants to wait and see until the autopsy results are in. Which means I'm on my own."

"I hope, for both our sakes, that it turns out that Dr. Keay died of natural causes."

"So do I," he said. At the doorway, he turned and added, "But we both know better, don't we?"

Chapter 11

WHEN THE DOOR CLOSED BEHIND FLYNN, Frances folded her arms across her chest and said, "So it is a murder, after all."

"We don't know that," I said.

The look on her face told me that she, Flynn, and I were in agreement, maybe for the first time in our lives.

"The guy was one of the most respected cardiothoracic surgeons in the country," I said. "From the little bit I talked with partygoers, everybody loved him. Who would want him dead bad enough to kill him?"

"Joyce Swedburg, maybe?"

That made no sense to me. "You told me they've been divorced for years. Why now, all of a sudden?"

"Because he was pressuring her to sell their house. I told you she kicked him out, right? When they settled their divorce, she got to stay in the house for a specified amount of time. From what I've been hearing, that time was up and he wanted the place sold. She refused to go." Frances lifted one shoulder.

"Why didn't she simply buy him out?" I asked.

"Can't," Frances said. "You look at her, you see a successful attorney. She's got to be rich, right? Not so much. A couple years ago she invested in a friend's company that went belly-up. Her retirement accounts took a huge hit. She's not destitute, but there's no way she could afford to buy out half that mansion she lives in. Not with her current state of affairs."

"How do you know this?"

Frances got a sly look on her face. "Friends."

"Friends who share confidential information?" I said, aghast yet not entirely surprised.

Another shrug. "What else are we going to talk about around here? We thought that once you started dating that rock star guy we might have a chance for juicy gossip. Keeping an eye on you two has been as boring as watching concrete harden."

I ignored that. "I don't know," I said. "That seems like a pretty lame motive for murder. Dr. Keay was very well off. I can't imagine why he'd try to push Joyce out if he didn't really need the cash."

"It's not always about money," Frances said.

She was right about that. "I suppose if Keay felt somehow emasculated by having his wife defend him, then subsequently dump him, this could be his way to reassert power."

She flapped her hands up. "Ooh, you're a psychologist now."

I glared.

"All I'm saying is that the two of them weren't getting along so well lately," she said.

I thought about their interactions when they'd been together in the basement before the party. "You are missing one important point."

"I know." Frances's mouth twisted. "Joyce Swedburg wasn't at the party."

"Exactly."

"She could have met him earlier and fed him some poison that only *presents* like alcohol when it takes effect."

"Oh?" I knew my expression conveyed my skepticism. "What kind of poison does that?"

"How should I know? You're the one who finds answers when people get themselves killed around here." She pointed to the computer monitor. "You should look that up. Figure it out. Whatever she fed him would have to have been a time-release kind of drug."

"I don't think such a thing exists."

"What, you're a pharmacological expert now?" She rolled her eyes. "However do you find the time?"

I pulled in a deep breath. "What about the mistress, the woman who was in the accident with Keay?" I asked. "I understand that was five years ago, but could she have harbored a grudge all this time? Maybe she was one of the attendees Saturday night."

Frances shook her head. "That ship has sailed. Once the story was out, her husband filed for divorce. She left Emberstowne as soon as it was final. Haven't seen or heard from her since."

"One night of carousing resulted in two divorces," I said. "Sad."

"One night?" Frances repeated with a snort. "It was that woman's bad luck that she's the one who got caught. The way he ran around town womanizing, it could have been almost anybody."

The way she said it made me think, for one second, that Frances might be speaking from experience. I tried to imagine what she'd been like five years earlier. I doubted the woman would have ever kept company with a married man, but I couldn't resist the urge to needle her a little bit. "Anybody?" I asked. "Don't tell me you fell under the handsome doctor's spell?"

"Certainly not," she said with a haughty glare. "I've got

good sense enough to know better than to go for those smarmy types. How could you even suggest such a thing?" Without waiting for me to answer, she shifted gears. "You may find this interesting: The woman from the accident used to live in the house next to yours. Her husband still lives there, though why he keeps such a big place for only one person is beyond me."

"Next door?" I had neighbors on both sides, but only one was a divorced man living alone.

Frances and I said the name together: "Todd Pedota."

THAT NIGHT, IN MY BASEMENT AT HOME, Scott, Bruce, and I unloaded all the dust-covered supplies that had accumulated on the workbench through the decades. When that task was complete, we toasted the structure a fond farewell.

"So it's coming down tomorrow." With a glass of Malbec held aloft, Bruce used his other hand to push sideways against one of the now empty inner shelves, making the whole contraption wobble and squeak. "I think there's mold growing in there." He regarded his fingers then wiped his hand on his jeans. "This demolition project's coming not a moment too soon."

I sipped my wine and then took a few steps back, tilting my head to look at the warped monstrosity from another angle. Turning my back to it, I looked at the rest of the basement and wrinkled my nose. "Doesn't this seem like an odd place to put a workbench?" I asked.

I turned back to face them. Bruce and Scott looked confused.

Bootsie took that moment to join us, coming around the far corner with an air about her that seemed to ask what the three of us were up to.

"If it were me," I said, reasoning aloud, "I'd position the workbench closer to the rear of the house, nearer to the steps and back door. I mean, if you're going to make the effort to create a work space, wouldn't you situate it more conveniently?"

My roommates appeared either unconvinced of my logic or unsure of where I was going with this. I continued, my thoughts flowing full force as I put them into words. "I can't imagine why a person would put a workbench all the way at the home's front, when there was plenty of space in the area at the bottom of the stairs."

Scott ran a hand across his chin. "You know, now that you mention it, I always accepted that this was just here." He waved a hand toward the rotting wood construction. "I never questioned its existence."

He handed his glass of wine to Bruce and moved to examine the bench more closely. "What?" I asked after a few silent moments.

"What if it *wasn't* a workbench?" he asked. "Originally, I mean."

"What else could it be?" I asked.

He walked back and forth again. "Maybe I'm second-guessing it because of what you said about its placement here, but when I was a kid, I spent a lot of time with my dad around his workbench and I'm starting to wonder about this one."

He reached into one of the shelf spaces and pressed his fingers against the back of the unit.

"Why?" he asked.

"Why, what?" Bruce and I asked in unison.

"This is old, I get it," Scott said. "But look around. The basement walls are sturdy. Put up a couple of studs and they do a fine job of supporting shelves." Bruce and I scanned the perimeter, where random shelves had been installed over the years. "Here, though, everything is anchored to a wooden backing. Why do extra work to build a back when it wasn't necessary? In fact, I'd go as far as to say that it's a detriment."

Not having an answer, I crouched to the ground and peered underneath. "It looks like the backing goes all the way to the floor."

"Odd," Scott said, reclaiming his glass.

Bruce asked, "What now?"

Scott leaned in again, this time tapping the wall behind the bench. "Does that sound hollow to you?" he asked. We shrugged. Turning to face us both, he added, "My imagination may be running wild here, but what if whoever built this bench used it to cover up something?"

"Like what?"

"I don't know. An old painting?"

Bruce laughed. "What, like an Italian fresco?"

"You never know," Scott said. "We may discover that a famous artist lived here once and behind that workbench is that artist's greatest creation of all time."

"I like the way you think, Scott." I lifted my wine, clinking it against my roommates' glasses.

"To tomorrow's unveiling."

Chapter 12

BENNETT PACED THE AUDITORIUM, HANDS clasped behind his back. "What now, Gracie?" he asked. "How do we stop the madness?"

I didn't have an answer for him. I'd brought him up to speed on the fact that Flynn believed that Dr. Keay's death was a homicide. "Remember, nothing has been confirmed yet. Maybe . . . " Words dissolved in my throat. Was I really about to say that perhaps we'd be lucky this time? That felt wrong, no matter how it came out.

"I appreciate the optimism," Bennett said, "but you believe Flynn is right, don't you?"

I couldn't lie. "I suspect he is, yes."

The auditorium room was empty now. All the chairs had been carted away, the stage disassembled, and the temporary back and sides long gone. The room was a bare, bricked-in space.

I ran my hand along the wall that had been hidden by the stage and curtains. "David Cherk said he looked for Dr. Keay, but there was no one back here at the time."

"And we both know that Dr. Keay didn't leave the party. There are only the two exits, the main staircase to the room—"

"And the emergency exit," I finished. "Which would have sounded an alarm."

Bennett scanned the area exactly as I had a moment earlier. "It's a conundrum."

Thinking about Scott's intriguing comment regarding hidden treasures last night, I asked, "There aren't any secret passages to this part of the basement, are there?"

Bennett squinted, as though working to remember. "None that I'm aware of."

I watched as he continued to think, and I could tell he was ticking off locations on a mental checklist.

"How many are there? You've only shown me one or two."

"A little mystery never hurt anyone," he said. "You'll know them all. In time."

The man, and this house, never failed to surprise me. "I look forward to that. In the interim, however, we have to figure out what happened to Dr. Keay in that space of time he went missing."

"The question, as I see it," Bennett said, picking up my train of thought, "is whether David lied about not seeing him here, or he lied about checking."

"Exactly. To what end, though? I know the man is eccentric, but he certainly doesn't strike me as the murderous type."

Bennett sighed. "They never do, do they?"

"You'd think we'd have gotten better at sniffing them out by now."

He smiled. "You're doing fine. Better than anyone else on the job, I might add." Looking up, he whispered, "Speak of the devil."

I turned. "Flynn," I said, tamping down a smile as Bennett's comment registered, "I'm surprised to see you back so soon. Any news about Rodriguez?"

The detective crossed the long room in a few quick strides. "He's scheduled for an aortic valve replacement tomorrow.

His wife is convinced that he's not a good candidate for surgery, even though the cardiologist assures her otherwise. The woman is a wreck."

"Of course she is," I said. "This has to be frightening for her."

"Everything is frightening if you let it be," he said.

I didn't know how to respond to that.

Bennett stepped in. "Grace told me that you ordered an autopsy—"

"Of Leland Keay, you mean?" Flynn asked.

"Certainly not of Detective Rodriguez," Bennett said with a touch of exasperation before continuing, "Have you gotten any word from the coroner? I must confess that I'm eager to hear that Dr. Keay, rest his soul, died on his own and not at the hands of another."

"Well, then," Flynn said, drawing out the words, "I'm afraid you're about to be disappointed. As of today, this is officially a homicide investigation." His eyes clenched and he worked his jaw. "Why couldn't the guy have gotten stabbed, or shot, or something?"

"Why on earth would you say something like that?" I asked. "Would that make investigating it easier for you?"

"As a matter of fact it would, Miss Priss. Remember that everybody—including my chief—believed that Keay suffered a heart attack in the middle of a party. Because it looked like he died of natural causes, nobody bothered to protect the crime scene." He paced away from us then turned back. "Look at this place. Cleaned like nothing happened. You guys probably had maids rush in to spiffy it all up, didn't you?"

We had, but I decided not to answer.

He continued to rant. "You think we're going to be able to find a single clue here anymore?"

"My apologies," Bennett began.

Flynn waved a hand. "Not your fault. Mine. I should have taken steps to secure the scene, no matter how ridiculous it seemed at the time. With Rodriguez's real heart attack and the fact that no one suspected foul play, everything went crazy. You guys have been good about those kinds of things in the past. No, this one was our screwup."

Flynn not blaming us at Marshfield for a misstep? I couldn't believe it.

"What did the coroner say?" I was probably pushing my luck, but I had to know. "How does he know this was a homicide?"

Whether it was because he was on his own and no longer following in the more seasoned Rodriguez's shadow, or whether we'd simply caught him at a weak moment due to his irritation with his own department, I didn't know. Either way, he answered me without his usual antagonism.

"First thing: defensive wounds. Keay struggled with whoever killed him. There's enough bruising on his face, neck, and hands to make it unmistakable that he fought back."

I remembered the last thing I'd heard Keay utter. "He said the word *injection*," I said. "Was he poisoned?"

"In a way," Flynn said. "The guy who killed Keay—and we are operating under the assumption that the killer was male—did more than overpower the man. He definitely injected him. Twice. One of them here." Flynn pointed to a spot inside his own thigh. "The other here." He pointed again, this time to his neck.

"He was able to subdue Dr. Keay long enough to get two injections in?"

Flynn was on a roll. I almost got the impression he was enjoying his chance to hold court. "Keay wasn't a young man, remember. Even though he was a famous surgeon, that didn't mean he lived a perfect, healthy lifestyle. You guys heard that he was a recovering alcoholic?"

We both said that we had.

"Keay came close to dying back in those days. More than once. A body can't take that much punishment without there being long-term consequences. We figure that in a fight, he didn't stand a chance against a younger man, or even an older gentleman if, say, he was in the kind of shape you're in."

This last part was directed to Bennett, who nodded acknowledgment, then asked, "Do you know what Dr. Keay was injected with?"

"That's the most interesting part," Flynn said.

We waited.

"Keay was shot up with liquor. That's why you smelled it on him. Tests are still running, but the coroner suspects pure grain alcohol, the kind you can't find in a store. Moonshine."

"Moonshine?" I repeated. "Isn't distilling illegal in the United States?"

"Unless you're licensed—and that license is not easy to get—yes, it most certainly is."

"Does the coroner know how long it was between the time Keay was injected and when he died?" I asked, hoping against hope that this had all transpired well before the party began. Of course, if it had, why wouldn't Dr. Keay have alerted anyone?

"Best guess, twenty minutes. Maybe less, maybe as much as a half hour. He can't be exact. Injected alcohol takes effect much faster than when it's consumed. Our digestive systems have the capacity to work off some of the poison, but when you inject the stuff, it can be deadly. And this time it was."

Clearly perplexed, Bennett asked, "How could anyone have smuggled moonshine into our party? And how did no one notice a scuffle between two men?"

"I'm hoping you two can help with that. I'll need the guest list and I'll ask you both to write up as much as you can remember about the evening." To me, he said, "Get that Frances woman to write something up, too, okay?"

"Sure," I said, still trying to understand how any of this could have happened without anyone noticing.

Flynn rocked back and forth on the balls of his feet. "You know what this means, don't you?" he asked.

I had a sense of what the detective was about to say, but kept quiet. Bennett did, too.

"Two things." Flynn held up fingers. "One, this was premeditated. And two: This was personal."

Chapter 13

❧

"THAT WAS PROBABLY THE LONGEST CONVER-
sation Flynn and I have ever had," I said to Bennett when
the detective left. "He's not as abrasive when he's on his
own, have you noticed?"

"I have." Bennett adopted a thoughtful expression. "Perhaps we've overlooked this young man's potential."

I wasn't about to go that far. "He hasn't helped his own
cause in the past," I reminded him. "But I'll try to keep a
better attitude where he's concerned. He seems determined.
I sincerely hope he comes through."

"And I sincerely hope you don't get pulled into this
mess. Let's leave it to our man Flynn this time, shall we?"

My cell phone rang at that moment, preventing me from
answering. The truth was that as soon as Flynn had confirmed
that Dr. Keay had been murdered, I knew I had to be involved.
Not enough to annoy Flynn or worry Bennett, but enough to
satisfy my curiosity. There were far too many "impossibles"
surrounding Keay's death for me to let it go. This murder had
happened on my watch and I felt responsible.

"It's Adam," I said to Bennett. "Do you mind if I take this?"

"No, please. Go ahead." With a wink, he headed for the door. "I'll catch up with you later."

I could hear the smile in Adam's voice when I answered the phone. "Hey, Grace," he said. "How are things going?"

"I'd rather know how you are." Not finding the right words, I hesitated. "And how's your aunt?"

"She—" I heard a hitch in his voice. He took a long three seconds before continuing. "She had a good life, a long life, and died peacefully surrounded by people who loved her."

"You can't ask for more than that," I said. "But I'm sorry, Adam. Truly."

"I wish you could have known her."

"I wish I could have, too."

We were silent for another uncomfortable few seconds until Adam said, "Her wake is tomorrow, funeral Thursday. It's been a rough time here so I thought maybe I'd take a few days before returning to rehearsal. What would you think if I came out there on Friday? You could show me more of the area or we can take a drive? I did homework and there's a national park with a whole lot of great historical sites only a few hours away from you."

The hope in his voice was palpable and I felt bad about that. He'd pursued me and, despite untold obstacles, had hung in there. After other recent troubles had been resolved and the guilty parties identified, I'd begun to see Adam for who he was, rather than who I thought he might be. I liked him. Very much.

The problem between us—if there was one—was all mine. I'd had my heart broken in the past. I'd been played for a fool in the past as well. I fought the attraction I had for Adam because I couldn't let myself be pulled in too soon. And, after all I'd been through during the past year and a half, it was most definitely too soon.

"Friday?" I could hear the anticipation in my own voice as the possibility danced in my brain. "That would be great—" I stopped mid-sentence. "Oh wait, maybe not."

"Why?" he asked.

"It's not that I don't want to see you," I assured him quickly. "Or that I don't think your idea to spend a few days together is a good one."

I heard him release a breath of air that could only be disappointment. I knew he thought I was blowing him off. "Okay," he said. "Some other time."

"No, you need to understand. It's not that. It's—I've got a little problem here."

Alert again, he asked, "What's up?"

How to explain? "You remember the fund-raiser Saturday night?"

"Jack was there." Adam's voice was flat, disheartened.

I took a deep breath. "Yes, he was." Before Adam could respond, I added, "But you need to know that he brought Becke as his date and that's not the problem I'm talking about."

"Then tell me. What's going on, and is there anything I can do to help?"

"Remember I told you about the people in charge of organizing the fund-raiser? How one of them was a well-known surgeon?"

"Yeah?"

"Well, he collapsed in the middle of the event Saturday night."

"Oh, no. That's terrible. Is he all right?"

"He's dead." I heard Adam's sharp intake of breath. "What's worse," I continued, finding it tough to put all that had happened into words, "is that Flynn believes he was murdered."

"Not possible," Adam said with vehemence. "Absolutely not. You can't be involved in another murder. What's going on there? Why didn't you tell me sooner?"

I waited for him to calm a bit before continuing. "It looked like a heart attack at first," I said, "but the coroner believes otherwise. As of today, it's officially a homicide. In fact, Flynn delivered that news moments ago."

"I don't know what to say."

"Complicating the situation," I went on, "the older detective, Rodriguez, really *did* have a heart attack. Right
there, right then. At the scene of the crime." I thought to
add, "Even though no one realized it was a crime scene at
the time."

"Grace," Adam said, "I'm going to ask this again. What
in the world is going on there? Are you safe?"

"Of course I'm safe. Flynn thinks that Dr. Keay's murder was premeditated and personal. I have to believe that
none of us here at Marshfield are in any danger."

"I don't know—"

An incoming text interrupted. "Hang on a minute,
Adam," I said, then clicked to check. Hillary had sent an
imperative: *Can you get away? Come home ASAP.*

I clicked back to my conversation with Adam. "Looks
like I have to run. Hillary needs me back at the house."

"No problems there, I hope."

"I'm sure it's nothing," I said, but fought a quiet sense of
unease. Hillary hadn't ever asked me to come home during
my working hours. I wondered what was up.

"Keep me updated?" Adam asked.

"I will."

I told Bennett and Frances that I was running home for
a bit, explaining that Hillary needed me. Neither of them
commented, but Frances clucked her disapproval. I wasn't
sure what she found more distasteful: my leaving the office
during the day or Hillary summoning me home. Not that it
mattered right now.

I pulled up and parked across the street from my house,
trying to imagine what the emergency was. Workers were
there, as always, some on scaffolding, others busy on the
lawn, sawing, drilling, and hammering pieces of house.
None of them appeared troubled or overly concerned.

I hurried up the driveway, walking around to the back
door, saying hello to some of the workers, feeling less appre-
hensive as I made my way in. When I'd responded to Hillary's

text, letting her know I was on my way, she'd replied simply: *Okay.*

Even though that message didn't offer a clue as to what she needed me for, I suspected that it had to do with the removal of the workbench in the basement. I hoped no one had been hurt.

I made it down there, my heels clunking on the bare steps, announcing my arrival. In the far end of the basement I could hear people chatting. Quite a few people, from the sound of it. The hum of conversation quieted enough for me to realize that they were aware of my approach.

Hillary came around from the front of the basement, hurrying on her own near-stiletto heels, to meet me in the laundry area.

"I'm so glad you're here," she said, taking me aback with her eagerness. Never in my life would I have expected Hillary to say those words to me.

She must have felt it, too, because she stopped, gave a peculiar twitch, and began again. "We have something to show you."

"Where's Bootsie?" I asked.

She pointed. "I locked her upstairs in your bedroom. I hope you don't mind. I had her on the leash for a while but things have gotten crazy here and I didn't want her to get hurt."

I opened my mouth, but she interrupted.

"She has food, water, and a litter box. I made sure."

"I appreciate that."

Before I could ask what had caused the craziness and, presumably, the text that had rushed me home, she waved a manicured hand. "Come on. You've got to see this."

Intrigued, and a little uneasy, I followed her and the sound of conversation, to the front of my house.

The "crowd" consisted of three men in dusty jeans and T-shirts: the construction foreman, who I'd met a few times; Wes from the historical society; and Larry the Locksmith. There was a name I never forgot. He was on speed dial at Marshfield because we had so many antique locks that required regular maintenance, and he'd helped me here at home with an antique lock issue I'd encountered several months ago.

As I followed Hillary deeper into their midst, I started to ask "What's up?"

The question died on my lips. The workbench had been reduced to a haphazard pile of stained, moldy wood on the basement floor, the smell of which caused me to bring my hand to my nose. But it was what had been revealed on the wall behind it that left me speechless.

Curiosity drew me closer. Notwithstanding Scott's wishful imagings from the evening before, I'd expected the aged structure to have been hiding nothing more exciting than plumbing pipes. Nothing like this.

"It's a door," I said, unnecessarily. The group of onlookers waited with patient smiles. Clearly, they'd come to that obvious conclusion well before I'd returned home. "Wow," I said, and reached to skim my fingers over the cool, black-painted metal. Iron, I guessed. Set about a foot up from the ground, the door was about two and a half feet wide by three feet tall, looking a lot like the sort of closure one might see between sections of a submarine. Except, instead of jutting into the room the way a vault door might, this was flush with the wall. "Amazing."

"You see why I called you," Hillary said.

"Yeah." The door's handle was a thick pull-ring, countersunk in a hole. I lifted the rusty metal, which responded with grating disapproval. I tugged; the door didn't budge. I ran my fingers over the lock positioned immediately above the handle.

"That's why you're here, I take it?" I said to Larry.

"Unless you happen to have an old key about yea big." He held his index fingers about four inches apart. "It looks like I have a challenge on my hands."

"No key that I know of," I said. "This is all news to me."

Hillary fairly gushed. "You see what wonderful surprises my home renovations can bring?"

Chapter 14

BECAUSE I COULDN'T PRODUCE A KEY, THERE was little to be done at the moment, and because Larry needed different tools than he'd brought along on this trip, we all agreed to wait until tomorrow for the momentous door opening. I practically bounced with excitement. A secret door. In my own home. The thought made me giddy.

I remembered being enthralled, back when I was a young girl, with a special on television featuring a reporter opening up Al Capone's vault. The event had been spotlighted in the news for weeks and the country was antsy with anticipation. My mom, in particular, had been breathless awaiting the great unveiling. She'd insisted that the whole family gather together to watch.

Even though Geraldo Rivera must have been shocked when he opened the vault and found nothing, I don't believe his disappointment was nearly as acute as my mother's. My mother's father—or the man who, up until recently, I'd believed was her father—had had a dubious connection to the late mobster. Even though my mom didn't much care for her father-of-record personally, she'd always been interested in histories of the shady characters he'd purportedly hung out with.

My dad teased her about the empty vault for a long time following the broadcast. In that case, at least, I think she may have gotten off easier than Geraldo Rivera did.

"We'll have more answers tomorrow," Hillary said as she shooed some of the workers out.

While nothing had come of the Geraldo Rivera extravaganza or my mother's unlikely connection to whatever she thought may have been secreted in the vault, the experience—the crushing disappointment—had left an indelible impression on me.

An optimist by nature, I'd come to realize that I never truly counted on something now until it was a done deal.

This time, the promise in question—of what? adventure? exhilaration? treasure?—sat behind a locked door in my basement. Where some homeowners might envision stacks of cash secreted behind it, I expected to find little more than an outdated coal bin. But even that was a little thrilling.

As Larry finished packing up his tools, he promised to get back to my house the next day as soon as he was free. "I have a couple of other appointments," he said. "You understand."

Hillary looked as though she was about to tell him to ignore those other appointments and make this his priority, but I stepped in. "Whatever is back there has been waiting to be discovered for a very long time. I don't think another day or so is going to hurt anyone."

Hillary wrinkled her nose.

When Larry left, Wes pointed to the blueprints lying on a nearby table. "Frederick called and asked me to bring these by again, just in case." He pointed. "I stuck around when things got exciting. None of us can find anything on file that describes that door, or hints at what could be behind it. Do you want me to take these back with me, or do you want to hold on to them here for tonight, in case there's something I missed?"

I was about to tell him that he could take the blueprints back, but Hillary jumped in before I could get a word out. "Leave them here, Wes. If you don't mind. Knowing Grace, she'll probably want to study them herself, to make sure we haven't missed anything."

"No problem," he said. "You guys have been good about keeping them safe. Let me know when you want me to pick them up."

"Thank you, Wes," Hillary said, placing a hand on the man's arm. "You are such a sweetie."

I saw them out, and when the house was finally empty again, I scooped Bootsie up and returned to the basement to give the door a longer look. "What do you think is back there?" I asked as I scratched behind her ears. As though answering me, she delivered a long, vocal *meow* with such conviction that if I could have understood cat-speak, I think I would have had my answer.

Later that night, when Bruce and Scott returned home, I didn't tell them why, but suggested they both follow me downstairs again.

"Seems as though we're spending a lot of time in the basement lately," Bruce said. "Except for doing laundry, I don't believe I've ever made this many trips down since we've lived here."

"After tomorrow," I said, adopting my most mysterious tone, "we may have a whole new reason to visit the basement."

"What's happening tomorrow?" Scott asked.

Holding Bootsie again, I led them to the front of the house, into the nook where the workbench had once stood. "See for yourselves."

"Whoa," Bruce said. He gave me an inquisitive look before reaching for the handle. "May I?"

Scott had taken an involuntary step back. "What's in there?"

"It's locked," I said unnecessarily because, by that point,

Bruce had given the counter-set ring a hearty tug. "Larry the Locksmith said he should be able to get it open tomorrow."

"You are full of surprises, Grace," Bruce said. "You and this house."

"First you find out that you're Bennett Marshfield's niece," Scott began.

I held up a finger, which Bootsie tried to swat. "That hasn't been proved yet."

My roommates shot me such immediate and similar "give me a break" looks that I would have bet they'd practiced in a mirror.

"Well, it hasn't," I said, but my words sounded lame, even to me. Changing the subject back to the matter at hand, I said, "Do you want me to call you when Larry gets here?"

"Yes," they said in unison, the way people often say "Duh!"

"Wes left the blueprints again," I said, nodding toward the large sheets lying nearby. "He couldn't find anything on the plans that indicated a door here." As I pointed, Bootsie squirmed out of my arms to land silently on the floor. "He did mention that if we can determine when the door was installed, we may be able to do research on the home's owner at that time. He said he'd help me with that."

Scott's eyebrows rose. "Interesting. Does Adam have anything to worry about?"

I hadn't even thought of Wes's offer in those terms. "No," I said. "He's simply being nice. There's nothing there."

"That's what you said about Adam at first, too," Scott reminded me. When I reacted, he went on, "I'm not telling you this to make you uncomfortable," he said, "but you're a catch, Grace, and without Adam around here regularly, no one really knows about him." He held both hands up and shrugged. "I'm only saying it because you tend to be blind-sided when you find out a man is interested in you. I want you to be ready this time, in case I'm right."

"Do you even know Wes?" I asked.

Bruce scratched his chin, clearly taking up Scott's train

of thought. "Let's see, he's close enough to your age to be a prospect. A smidge older, maybe. Interested in history and artifacts the way you are. Pretty sure he's single."

"He's a widower," I said.

They both cringed. "Oh," Bruce said. "I'm sorry to hear that. Recent?"

"Not really. He moved here from out West a few years ago."

"Years ago? Then he's fair game, Grace. And I've never seen him with anyone else," Scott added. "Romantically, I mean."

"Do you two make it your business to know who in town is attached and who isn't?"

Bruce seemed surprised by the question. "Not on purpose. Remember, though, Amethyst Cellars is right on Main Street. We're always talking with people: tourists, neighbors, people who don't even drink wine. You get to know a little bit about everybody."

I'd been fairly clueless in the past where it came to matters of the heart. Maybe my roommates were right. I decided right then to be sure to drop Adam's name into my next conversation with Wes. "Got it, thanks," I said. "I am officially forewarned."

"Not that there's anything wrong with Wes, you understand," Scott said. "But we know you're not the type to lead a man on if you're not interested in him."

"Thanks," I said again. "I'm lucky you guys have my back."

THE NEXT MORNING, ON MY WAY TO WORK I stopped by the historical society to drop off the blueprints. Hillary hadn't been mistaken about my wanting to study these further, but I hadn't done much more than scan them last night. I'd originally wished she'd taken Wes up on his offer to grab them, thereby sparing me the trip, but Scott's and Bruce's warnings—unlikely as their suppositions were—made me see it as an opportunity to let Wes know that I was seeing someone.

"Good morning," he said as I entered the musty storefront. Smiling broadly, he came around the counter to take the blueprints from my arms. "Twice in one week. How did I get so lucky?"

It could have been politeness on his part, and I was betting that's all it was. Still, the thought that he may have meant it flirtatiously rendered me tongue-tied. I couldn't find a proper segue into the topic of my love life without making it feel forced. Instead, I asked if he'd seen David Cherk recently. Knowing that Flynn was treating Dr. Keay's death as a homicide made me want to question our resident Dracula a bit more.

"Oddest thing," Wes said as he returned the house plans to their drawer. "He came in yesterday and hurried out, barely speaking a word."

"Is that unusual for him?"

"Yes and no," Wes said. "Because we employ him from time to time, he's generally pretty chatty. This time, though, he seemed to be in a hurry."

Instinctively, my gaze shot to the nearby desk. "And he took that jar with him? The one you thought might be photo developer?"

"And the rattling box, too." Wes shrugged.

"Maybe he is out taking pictures then," I said. "I'm disappointed. I wanted to talk with him a little more about the events of Saturday night."

Wes's expression tightened. "That detective Flynn was here looking for him, too."

"Oh?" I said. I wasn't sure how much Flynn had shared with Wes so I let him lead the conversation.

"Word was Dr. Keay died of a heart attack. Now Detective Flynn is saying that it was murder."

"Yeah," I said. "They're treating as a homicide."

Wes lowered his voice, even though there was no one there to hear us. "I got the impression that the detective thinks David might have had something to do with Dr. Keay's death."

"Flynn has that effect on people. I don't mean to downplay his investigation, because it's possible that Flynn has more evidence than he's choosing to share with me, but he does come on strong with everyone he questions." I thought about my past interactions with the man. "David Cherk doesn't strike me as a murderer."

"Me neither," Wes said. "He's eccentric, but hardly dangerous."

"The thing I want to know," I said, "is that if Dr. Keay was murdered—and the coroner says he was—how could it possibly have happened? We were in the middle of a bustling, crowded event. Dr. Keay never left the premises and no one saw him being attacked."

Wes shrugged. He looked as helpless as I felt.

"David said he checked behind the stage and Dr. Keay wasn't there," I continued. "And yet, a short while later, that's where he appeared from. It makes no sense."

"You were there when it happened?"

"I was," I said, replaying the scene in my mind. The story had been spreading like wildfire around Emberstowne and I welcomed the chance to share what I considered the most accurate version. "Keay had been alone behind the stage. My assistant, Frances, had the good sense to take a look back there while we were trying to help revive him. According to Flynn, Keay had defensive wounds and bruises. Yet how can that be? No one saw an altercation between the doctor and anyone else. It's impossible." I stopped for a moment to take a breath. "The only clue we have is that when Dr. Keay collapsed he said one word: *injection*."

"Injection?" Wes asked. "Was he a diabetic?"

"That was my first question. He wasn't. Apparently he was trying to tell us that he'd been injected with booze."

"Was Dr. Keay an alcoholic?"

"So I've been told," I said.

"Could he have injected himself?"

"Why would he do that? And how to explain the defensive wounds?"

"Good point." Wes looked thoughtful. "I'm no detective, but shouldn't they be looking for whoever had a motive for killing Dr. Keay? Mind you, from what I've heard of the man, everybody loved him."

I was wondering the same thing, thinking about Frances's disclosure that Keay had been trying to force Joyce Swedburg out of their marital home, when Wes very nearly echoed my thoughts.

"The only person I can think of is his ex-wife. She's been in here a lot lately"—he gestured to encompass the area—"and made no secret of the fact that she wished he would drop dead."

"Seriously? Why was she here, if I may ask?"

"She wanted to go through blueprints and house plans. She said that if she had to move, she wanted to build new. She needed inspiration. Still, real estate isn't much of a reason to actually kill a person, is it?"

"You'd be surprised at motives," I said, enjoying the banter with Wes more than I'd anticipated. "But there's one thing we're forgetting."

"What's that?"

"Joyce wasn't there that night. She'd gotten food poisoning and had to cancel. After all that work."

"Joyce wasn't there?" Wes repeated. "I thought she was in charge of the event. When she talked about it, you'd think it was the only thing of importance in her life this year. Besides being forced to move, that is."

"Nope. She was taken ill," I said. "In fact, I have no idea if she's recovered. Nor any idea how she took the news of Keay's death." I made a mental note to ask Bennett how that conversation had gone. I made a second mental note to ask

Flynn if he'd spoken with the woman. There was no possible way she could have killed her ex-husband, not unless she possessed magical powers that allowed her to walk through walls or move about in a crowd unseen. Still, she could have hired someone to do it for her. I wanted to talk with her if I could manage it; she might shed light on who else may have held a grudge against the illustrious Dr. Keay.

"Then I have no clue," Wes said. "Good thing that's not our job." His smile grew wider. "Although it's your job sometimes, isn't it?"

His playful tone wasn't exactly flirtatious, but it reminded me. "Funny you should say that," I said. "The man I'm seeing—Adam—said almost the very same thing to me when I told him about the murder."

It was subtle, but I caught a change in his eyes, making me wonder if Scott and Bruce had been on target. I sensed that Wes didn't know what to say next. The slight tension in the air kept me talking. "Believe me, I'm happy to let the police take care of this one."

Teasing again now, but in a more relaxed way, he said, "From what I hear, they should put you on the payroll."

I laughed, the awkwardness gone. "No, thanks. I've had more than my fair share of adventure." Taking a look around, I said, "I should be getting back to work. Thanks for letting us borrow the plans."

"Anytime," he said. "Happy to help."

I waved a hand in the direction of the drawer where he'd replaced the blueprints. "With this newly discovered door, it looks like I've got a mystery of my own to solve at home. I'll leave murder to the professionals."

"Speaking of your secret door, I'd love to know what you find down there when it's finally unlocked."

"Hillary promised to call me home when that time comes. I'll let you know and if you want, you can come by and see for yourself. I have a feeling we're going to have quite an audience."

He smiled again and this time I read it as friendliness, nothing more. Part of me was glad I'd mentioned Adam. Part of me wondered if I should have waited.

"I'd like that a lot," he said.

Chapter 15

"STROLLING IN LATE AGAIN, ARE WE?" FRAN-
ces said when I walked in.

"Dropping off blueprints at the historical society. I
thought I told you that."

"The Mister was looking for you," she said with a sharp
glance at the clock. "You might want to let him know you
finally showed up for work."

"Gee, thanks, Frances."

I was about to cross the threshold between her office and
mine when I stopped. "David Cherk," I said.

Her neck wobbled when she turned to make eye contact.
"What about him?"

I folded my arms, resting my hip against the door frame.
"This morning when I talked with Wes down at the historical society, he told me that Flynn had been asking to talk
to Cherk in connection with Keay's death."

That got her to raise an eyebrow. "Oh?" she said as calmly
as anything, yet I could see possibilities racing behind her

placid expression. "What does Flynn want to talk with him about?"

"That's what I'd like to know," I said. "Think about it. We didn't know that Keay was missing until Cherk told you. We have only his word that he checked behind the stage and that no one was there when he looked."

Frances's whole body straightened. "So what you're saying is that he might be lying. And why would he lie unless he's the one who murdered Dr. Keay?"

"I'm not suggesting that—"

"Oh yes, you are." Her hands tapped her desk blotter absentmindedly as though she was working out a particularly complex problem. "And you say Flynn is looking for him?"

"Wes assumes that Cherk is out on a photo shoot."

"Hmph," she said. "Pretty convenient, don't you think?"

"Let's ask Ronny Tooney to see if he can find him."

Frances held her tongue, and for that I was grateful. My assistant's opinion of the would-be private detective was far from complimentary, but she'd grudgingly come to accept that he had helped us, more than once. To Frances's deep disappointment, the hapless man was slowly worming his way into our Marshfield Manor family.

"I'll call him soon," I said. "You said Bennett wanted to see me?"

Frances had already lifted the handset of her phone. "I'll talk to Tooney, get him started on the search for Cherk," she said. "You go on upstairs. The Mister is waiting."

BENNETT INVITED ME INTO HIS OFFICE AND sat behind his massive desk. This room was dimly lit and intimidating, smelling of old leather, faded books, and stale cigars. The walls were rich mahogany and the draperies dark and heavy, blocking out most of the day's sunlight. Bookshelves lined three walls, but fiction was relegated to the study. In here all the titles dealt with contracts, law, economics, and investments.

"Have a seat," he said.

We made small talk as I lowered myself into a bloodred chair that was at least twice as old as I was.

Had I not known Bennett as well as I did, a first glance at this space would have led me to believe the room belonged to a stuffy, elderly lawyer, rather than this energetic septuagenarian. Because Bennett used this room for conducting business, he showcased no personal items whatsoever. There were a number of beautiful and important antiques decorating his shelves, including a celadon jar from the Jin Dynasty and a Picasso skull sculpture that was fake but held sentimental value known only to a few of us. Nothing on display gave insight into the man, himself.

Bennett was, and had always been, a force to be reckoned with in the business world. Colleagues invited to this room would find no clue as to what made Bennett tick. There were no photographs of his late wives, none of his family. He had no awards on the walls or the shelves that spoke of his prowess—years ago—in polo, target shooting, or swimming. Bennett preferred it that way. He didn't like the idea of giving others an edge or providing insight by sharing personal details. Bennett believed that knowledge was power and he preferred absolute control.

Still, I thought the room was too empty.

Bennett owned more antiquities and priceless objects of art than most museums did. Hundreds of his treasures were on display in the public rooms of the mansion, for guests to *ooh* and *ahh* over as they wandered past during their tours. The bulk of Bennett's belongings, however, were stored out of sight, some here in his private apartment, others elsewhere in the house or on the grounds, away from tourist traffic.

Now he caught me looking around. Reading my mind, he said, "You can't wait to get your hands on this room, can you?"

"You're taunting me again," I said. "Maybe someday we'll get started on that inventory you keep promising."

I longed to catalog everything he owned, both for potential display purposes and for insurance concerns. Mostly I wanted to touch these treasures, smell them, and immerse myself in their history.

"And I'm willing to deliver, Gracie. I'm simply waiting for a quiet time when we're not up to our ears in murder."

"Is that what you wanted to talk with me about?"

"That," he said, "and . . ." He ran the tips of his fingers along his neck and I noticed he was avoiding eye contact. "I would like to know how things are going with Hillary." I'd never known Bennett to be sheepish, but at this moment he came close. "Working on your house, I mean."

I waited until he met my gaze. "You really want to know?" I asked with a stern expression. I could tell he didn't know I was teasing.

"That bad?"

I smiled. "Believe it or not, Hillary is doing a wonderful job."

Relief whooshed out of him. "Really?" he asked, leaning forward now. "You're not just saying that to make a foolish old man feel better?"

"You are neither old nor foolish," I said, "but no, I'm not just saying that. I have to admit that she surprised me. Hillary is on top of things, constantly. She runs things efficiently and she takes good care of my home and of Bootsie."

Again, he let out an audible breath. "You don't know how happy I am to hear that."

"Maybe I do know," I said with a smile. "Want to hear what's even more astonishing?"

"What?"

"She's been in a good mood throughout. I'd even go so far as to say she's been pleasant to be around."

"Hillary?"

"You had a gut feeling that this would be good experience for her, didn't you?"

He nodded.

"So far, I'd have to say that things are going far better than I'd expected. In fact, she's supposed to call me later." I told him about the locked door we'd discovered in the basement, and how we were waiting for Larry to figure out the best way to open it without breaking the mechanism. "It seems as though my house has its share of secrets, too."

His lips pulled to one side. "Let me know what you find there."

"I will." I scooched forward. "Now, let me bring you up to date on the investigation."

FRANCES WASN'T AT HER DESK WHEN I RE-turned. A bit later, hearing the unmistakable sounds of her arrival coupled with furious huffs of indignation, I got up to talk with her. She must have had the same idea, because we nearly bumped into one another in the doorway. I held out my hand toward my desk. "Have a seat. Were you able to get in touch with Tooney?"

"That man," she said.

"Problem?"

"About a year ago he was down on his luck, trying to shoehorn his way in to Marshfield Manor."

"I remember," I said.

"You gave him a chance to make something of himself. He should be grateful."

"I believe he is. Very."

Frances gave a pursed-lip frown. "Sure he is. Do you know what he said when I called?" Without waiting for my response—not that I had one—she continued, "He said that he'd fit us in. Told me that business has picked up and that he has a few new clients."

"That's great news."

She sniffed unpleasantly. "The man doesn't know which side of his toast is buttered."

"We don't pay him a retainer," I reminded her. "And even if we did, I'd want him to know that he's free to take other jobs."

"Jobs he should drop like a hot charcoal when *we* need him," she said with a proprietary huff. "Who does he think he is?"

"Frances," I said, in a calming voice, "I don't even know if this job is worth Tooney's time. This could be a wild-goose chase. I only suggested asking him for help because I want to talk with David Cherk. Maybe ask the photographer a few questions. It isn't critical."

"But it could turn out to be. When you say, 'Jump,' Tooney ought to ask, 'How high?' "

I laughed, then sobered. "How's Rodriguez? Any news?"

She gave a brief nod. "Out of surgery. He's expected to make a full recovery."

"Do you know if he got the flowers we sent?"

"Haven't ordered them yet." She shook her head. "Flowers aren't allowed in ICU and he'll probably spend a few days there. I'm waiting until he gets the all clear." Her lips curled downward. "Of course, he could take a turn for the worse and then we won't need to send anything at all."

"Frances!"

"You never know," she said without malice. "I don't want to waste the Mister's money on a gift if Rodriguez won't ever see it."

Her logic astounded me.

She must have read my mind because she added, "Nothing wrong with being pragmatic."

My phone rang. I reached for it instinctively, then hesitated. "It's Hillary," I said to Frances.

Her always-expressive brows conveyed her surprise.

Taking a look at her watch, she said, "Do you think they've gotten that secret door open so quickly?"

"I suppose I'm about to find out."

A HALF HOUR LATER, I PULLED UP TO MY house and parked the car. Frances had been right as to the reason for Hillary's phone call. Larry the Locksmith had worked his magic.

The secret door had engendered more interest than I'd expected. As I pulled up, workers who had been crawling up scaffolding or hanging from open windows hurried to join me as I made my way to the basement. Every one of them expressed interest in what we might find.

About halfway down the stairs I detected the hum of conversation—much heavier and deeper than Hillary and Larry could possibly conjure together. Hillary must have invited a few extra people to join in the fun.

I worked to keep the look of shock off my face when I finally made it down to the basement landing. Someone took my picture, but I wasn't sure who. Practically half the population of Emberstowne was gathered there. Okay, that was an exaggeration, but it seemed as though there were at least a dozen extra people milling around, a couple of whom I didn't even know. Conversation stopped and they all turned to face me at once.

I raised a hand. "Hi," I said, thinking that I should have invited Frances along. She would have loved this.

Hillary elbowed her way from the back to greet me. "I hope you don't mind. I thought it might be fun to bring in the local newspaper and a videographer." She held her hand out toward two people: a young woman holding a couple of cameras and a young man pushing a small recorder into my face. Like Cherk's assistants, they were both dressed in head-to-toe black. His clothes were too big, hers too small.

"What do you expect to find inside the door?" he asked me.

"Not much, to be perfectly honest." I wasn't quite sure what to make of their presence. The woman hung back behind the guy, looking as though she longed to be anywhere else. "This may turn out to be nothing at all. I can't believe the paper sent you both out here for this."

The young man shrugged. "I'm a freelancer. If you open that up and find a couple of dead bodies in there, then I'll have a story I can sell to the local news." He thumbed backward toward the woman. "That's my girlfriend. She's a film major."

I looked over to the young woman, noticing for the first time the streaks of royal blue in her dark hair.

She lifted her chin, offering a weak smile. "'S'up?"

I couldn't believe Hillary had brought these kids in. Even if they weren't mainstream media, I worried that this would be a huge bust and we'd have wasted everyone's time. Not to mention the fact that there were strangers in my house photographing my cluttered basement. Visions of the Geraldo Rivera debacle danced through my brain. Except I don't remember there being this many spiderwebs in Capone's vault.

"What if there's nothing in there?" I asked, hearing the wildly plaintive tone in my voice. "What if everyone has come out here for nothing?"

"Don't be such a pessimist," Hillary said, flicking her fingertips against my forearm. "What if there's treasure? You might turn out to be as rich as Papa Bennett." She cocked one eyebrow and moved closer, whispering, "Uncle. Niece. Both independently wealthy. Wouldn't that be interesting?"

I wanted to remind her that a familial link hadn't been proved, but this was neither the time nor the place. I wanted to tell her that having toddler reporters here made me uncomfortable, but she'd already begun dragging me toward the far end of the basement, flapping her free hand at the others as we passed them. "You know everyone else, of course."

I did. The project foreman was there, along with a

couple of his assistants. I exclaimed my surprise when I saw Bruce. "I'm so glad you're here."

"After Hillary got in touch with you, she called us. Scott would've liked to come, but one of us had to stay back at the shop. I won the coin toss." He gave a pointed glance over toward Wes from the historical society, who blushed when I said hello.

Larry the Locksmith, on the other hand, stood in front of the big black door beaming like a man who'd won the lottery. "Told you it wouldn't take me long," he said by way of greeting. "There isn't a lock made that I can't open." He held up a finger. "Without destroying it in the process, that is. That's the trick of it."

I provided the requisite adulation he clearly expected, then turned to Hillary. "You haven't opened it, even to peek?"

"Of course not," she said. "As soon as Larry got it unlocked, we tugged on the door to see if it was still stuck." She shook her head. "Even though it's heavy, it moved well enough. We pushed it shut again and called you."

I turned to see everyone in the basement gathering into a semicircle around the door. "Up to me, I guess," I said.

They all laughed politely, but their faces were bright with anticipation and their eyes said, "Get on with it, woman!"

One of the window installation guys said, "This feels like that sword in the stone—Excalibur. Only one person can pull it out."

"Does that makes me king of this castle?" I asked. "I don't know about that."

"Come on, come on," someone else said. "We've been waiting to see what's in there."

"You know as well as I do that it could be nothing," I said, again. In my heart, I was pretty sure that's exactly what we'd find. A small, empty room. Probably a former owner's coal storage. "Here goes."

Grasping the metal ring with both hands, I pulled.

Chapter 16

THE WEIGHTY DOOR OPENED AS SILENTLY and smoothly as Hillary had described. That is, until I got it about six inches wide. At that point, the hinges delivered a shrieking wail that caused everyone in the basement to wince and cover their ears.

"I'm sorry," I said, cringing. Turning to Larry, I asked, "Is there anything we can do for that?"

He'd already moved to the door's far edge to examine it. "These aren't normal hinges. They're an unusual design, set up to be invisible from the outside, which means I can't get to them to lubricate until we get the door open far enough for me to reach in." He patted his substantial gut and grabbed for the metal handle. "Looks like we got a ways to go yet. You need help?"

I wrapped my fingers through the metal ring before he had a chance to beat me to it. "Nope. It isn't hard to open. It's the noise I'm worried about."

I knew he meant well, but I should be the one who

opened the door for the first time. This was my house and my responsibility. Plus, I wanted to do it.

"Stand back," I said to him. I raised my voice and addressed the rest of the group. "Cover your ears, I'm going in."

I wished I could take my own advice. Shriek-y, high, and horrible, the noise was worse than nails on a chalkboard times a thousand. The hinges screamed for mercy as though they were being torn apart by a surprise enemy. Maybe that's what I was.

"I can get some grease on those now," Larry said over the din.

I blinked and ceased pulling. A cool, earthy gust rolled in as the door screeched its last protest. The overpowering smell of wet dirt held an underpinning of rot. I worried how much that dank aroma might permeate the rest of my house and I started to wonder if maybe there *were* dead bodies in there.

"Ugh." I waved a hand in front of my face. "Can we get some windows open?"

Hillary turned to one of the workers and directed him. "See to that, Joe, will you?"

I peered into blackness. The room, or whatever it turned out to be, was definitely deeper than I'd expected, but I couldn't tell precisely how large. The darkness was blinding, although I detected a faint reflection of light on a back wall. Cupping my hand to my mouth, I called, "Hellooo?"

"No answer, thank goodness," Larry said.

"I would have fallen over," I said. Looking around the interior, I asked, "Anybody got a flashlight?"

Larry pressed one into my hand. "Here you go."

I turned and noted the group's rapt expressions. "Anyone game to join me?"

Larry put his hands up and took a step back. "I open doors. I have no need to go through them."

Rather than dissipate, the cold aroma of wet earth grew stronger. Wrinkling her nose, Hillary leaned to peer into the void and shook her head. "Dirt floor." Pointing to her feet, she went on, "My heels will sink."

I raced my flashlight back and forth, seeing nothing. "It doesn't look too promising."

The video person had come up behind me and flicked on her spotlight. I felt crowded with her hanging over my shoulder, but her light illuminated the entire space far better than the little flashlight could.

"There," I said. My tone was triumphant but only to mask my disappointment. "It's exactly as I expected. A tiny room." I pointed to bits of long-forgotten coal. "Nothing."

Larry leaned in, took a long look, and when he straightened again, he agreed with me. "Yep. Old coal bin."

"No treasure?" someone asked.

Larry answered him. "Doesn't look like it."

The camera girl, probably disappointed to have accompanied her boyfriend only to come up empty, gave the room a long, final sweep, the bright beam light hitting every chunk of coal, every pitch-black angle of the rock-walled room.

"Hang on," I said.

When she didn't respond, I touched her arm. "What?" she asked.

"Can you direct the light that way again?"

The back wall of the little room was solid, smooth. But that didn't make sense. Why should it look different from the sides? The rest of the room's walls consisted of jutting, uneven stone, blackened from decades of storing coal. I pointed my flashlight upward, looking for a chute. "Where did the supply come in from?" I asked. "When it was delivered, I mean."

"Probably sealed up the opening a long time ago," Larry said. "To keep intruders from sneaking in."

The cameraperson started to move away, but I asked her to give it one more pass with her spotlight. That smooth back section didn't look right. "I wonder if the coal chute was behind that wall at one point," I said, still trying to figure out what was amiss.

Larry was already packing up his tools. "Could be."

I thought about it. "I'm going in," I said.

Hillary blinked. "You'll get dirty."

"Something isn't right."

"What do you mean?" she asked.

"I don't know. But while we're all here, I may as well check."

The group shuffling ceased. The audience had come for a show and apparently decided to stick around a little longer in the hopes of getting one.

The camerawoman gave the space a dubious glance and asked, halfheartedly, "You're not expecting *me* to go in there?"

With enthusiasm like that, no thank you. "I'm sure there's nothing worth filming," I said.

She backed away, shut off her spotlight, and held the camera at her side.

I lowered my head and eased myself through the small opening, standing up straight once I was fully inside. I traced the flashlight's beam along the left side wall, to the corner, where it met the back.

"Hey," I said. My voice echoed against the metal wall I'd climbed through, making it sound as though I was in a giant cavern rather than a small coal room.

"What?"

I couldn't tell who'd asked that, the camerawoman or Hillary.

Didn't matter. My focus was elsewhere.

The corner wasn't right. Using my flashlight as a guide, I placed my hand against the back wall and skimmed all the way to the left, where I should have hit brick. I didn't.

"This back wall is—" I didn't have the words.

"Is what?" Definitely Hillary this time.

I ran my fingers up and down the back wall's edge—which, if it had been attached to the side wall, shouldn't have been possible. "It's like a freestanding board here," I said. Not only that: It smelled terrible. Of wet and rot. I was afraid of slivers and the long-buried germs that would accompany them. Using my flashlight again, I started to realize that there was a sizeable space between the side and back, running from ground to ceiling. "I think this is a fake wall," I said, then checked the far right. Same thing.

"What do you mean, fake wall?"

I nearly rolled my eyes in exasperation. *What else could I mean?* "I think I can squeeze behind it." I wasn't thrilled with the idea of getting my clothes filthy, but I couldn't stop now. "They're washable," I said under my breath.

"What?"

"I'm going to try," I said. Easing slowly to the far left, I flattened myself as much as possible in order to fit into the space between the walls. I had no idea what I'd find behind the fake wall—probably nothing—but I wanted to get my head around the corner, if only to take a peek.

There was more room than I'd anticipated. My flashlight had distorted the perspective, and squeezing through turned out to be not hard at all.

I eased my left hand, the one holding the flashlight, around the corner, then followed with my torso, moving gingerly, worried about dislodging the giant wooden barrier and having it land on me.

When I managed to get my face around the corner, I pointed my flashlight forward. Nothing. But this time, there was lots of nothing. "Oh my gosh," I said aloud.

"What, what?"

I pulled back into the coal storage room and crouched to face the group gathered at the opening. They stared at me, wide-eyed. "What's back there?"

"A passage," I said. "It's a secret passage."

Chapter 17

I STEPPED OUT OF THE COAL ROOM AND BACK into the basement. "Well," I said to the group as I slapped fine, black dust from my clothes, "there's more back there than I expected." I explained how I'd been able to sneak around the fake wall. "I'm going all the way in. If I'm not back in ten minutes," I said, half joking, half serious, "send a search party."

Bruce had elbowed his way to the front. "You are not exploring an underground tunnel by yourself," he said. "I'm going with you."

Wes rubbed his beard, looking perplexed. "Count me in, too." He pointed. "I have a guess as to what this is. I'd like the chance to take a look and confirm. You don't happen to have another flashlight, do you?"

Bruce knew where we kept extras, and hurried to get a couple more. While he was gone, the reporter offered to join us. I declined. "Thanks, but until we really know there's a story here, I'd rather you stay back." I did think twice because his partner's spotlight would come in handy, but I preferred not to be accompanied by a stranger, and in close quarters, three flashlights ought to serve us just fine.

"You don't really think they buried people in there?" one of the workers asked. "I mean, that smell is pretty bad."

"Can't be dead bodies," another person said. "Look at how old that wood is that was covering the door up. Anything buried here would have disintegrated long ago."

"Burying people at home would have been illegal, anyway. It wouldn't be allowed."

One of his colleagues smirked. "Only if the law found out. I mean, if whoever owned this place murdered people, then no one would be the wiser, right?"

I shivered, both from the idea of walking into a homemade crypt and from the chill of the dank, deep air.

"Do you think we should call the police?" Larry asked.

"No," I said quickly, imagining Flynn's reaction. I didn't want to deal with his snide commentary about how I was always caught in the middle of things. The chances of my basement turning out to be a tomb were slim. Less than that. My best guess was that this had been some sort of root cellar, closed up years ago when the owners no longer used it, or to keep pests at bay. That's what I told myself, and that's what I believed.

"There's nothing here to see," I said firmly. I forced a laugh. "You people have been watching too many TV murder mysteries."

"I don't know," Hillary said. Her pert little nose remained squished up tight. "Things get hairy whenever you're involved, Grace."

"There's nothing to be afraid of," I said with more bravado than I felt. At that moment, Bruce returned with two more flashlights. He kept one and handed the other to Wes. As he did, I continued, "Let's all tamp down our imaginations, shall we?" To the other two men, I said, "You ready?"

They both nodded.

I climbed back in. Bruce followed and hung to my left,

Wes to my right. This was tricky because there wasn't much room for three adults in this small space. We ran the beams of our flashlights up and down the sides, and I immediately headed back to the space between the left and back walls and began to inch my way through. I was aware of the rest of the group crowding the doorway behind us to watch, jockeying for position.

Bruce stayed with me. Wes moved to the far right side, where he managed to make his way around as well. We waited for Wes, who gave an appreciative whistle as he cleared the wall into the tunnel of darkness. "Who'd have ever guessed," he said.

"We should check out how far this passage goes," I said. They murmured assent and we moved forward.

The temperature was cooler in here than in the basement, but the smell had become less intense. "Hang on," I said, tracing a path at our feet. "I think we're on a slope."

We took a few steps forward, downward and deeper into the room. The dirt floor was surprisingly solid.

"Brick walls," I said as my flashlight traced a path along one side and then above my head. "Wood beams above."

"Thick beams," Bruce said. He waved the bright light from side to side. "They look like railroad ties but thicker. Like the one that was installed over the top of the workbench."

"I don't recall coming across wood beams buried underground when we were working on the landscaping," I said, but suddenly I did. "Wait. Remember those chunks of concrete?"

"Yeah," Bruce said. "They were too big to pull out easily, so we left them there for another day."

"We wondered why someone had buried concrete," I said. "Now we know. They wanted to cover this room, or whatever it is."

Wes aimed his flashlight deeper in. "Can't see a thing, yet. It keeps going."

"Going where?" I asked.

"Only one way to find out," he said. "Would you like me to lead?"

The thought of insects, spiders, and other critters roaming around with us in here made me want to say, "Yes, please," but my ego got the best of me. "No, I'll go first," I said. "Makes me feel a little like Nancy Drew."

Wes chuckled.

Bruce said, "I preferred the Hardy Boys."

I nudged him in the side. "You look like a Hardy Boy. You and Scott both."

"I'm sure their fans would love to hear *that*," he said.

"Ready?" I asked.

Hillary raised her voice from the basement. "Of course we're ready! What's down there? Have you found anything yet?"

I rolled my eyes good-naturedly before answering her. "Not yet. You want to come down and see for yourself?"

She mumbled a reply, which I took as a refusal.

"How far down are we?" I asked my companions.

Wes studied the walls and floor, but didn't answer.

Bruce placed a hand atop his head and then reached up, gauging. "The walls here are about six and a half feet tall. When we first came in we were probably standing about ten feet underground, if you figure three and a half feet of dirt between the ceiling and the ground outside. Now, however—" He turned to face the way we'd come and ran his beam up along the descending walkway. "Maybe fifteen feet down?"

Wes scratched his beard, still saying nothing.

I turned to him. "At the outset, you told us that you had a guess as to what this was. Any theories you care to share?"

"Mm-mmm," he said. "I'd like to do some digging, pardon the pun. I've visited many of these, but I've never encountered one quite this large."

"One of what?" Bruce asked.

Wes flashed his light up, sideways, and deep into the

dark again. "The small door was the first giveaway. Easy to camouflage and it's likely we'll find latches that can be worked from the inside. It will be interesting to see what we find on the other end. Depending on when this was created, it could be either a secret passage for bootleggers during Prohibition or a hideout for escaped slaves. A safe haven along the Underground Railroad."

I thought about that. "Or both."

Wes nodded. "Or both."

We continued walking. The passage was dark as a tomb and probably as chilly. Bruce and I kept our beams forward, expecting to encounter an endpoint. Wes swept his light back and forth across the floor.

We'd gone another twenty feet or so when Wes gave a happy exclamation. Bruce and I stopped as Wes reached down to pick something up.

"Look at this!" he said.

Wes beamed his light at a small dark-blue glass bottle, turning it one way, then the other. The skinny flagon, not much bigger than Wes's palm, had raised, vertical ridges and had been closed up with a stopper.

Bruce asked, "Is that significant?"

"It's a poison bottle," he answered with obvious delight.

"Poison?"

"These little bottles are highly collectible," I said, taking the item from Wes and shaking it close to my ear. I hadn't really expected there to be any liquid remaining inside, but was disappointed nonetheless. "Reproductions have been manufactured in mass quantities over the years because collectors like them a lot." I exchanged a glance with Wes. "This one is probably an original."

"That would be my guess," he said.

I continued to explain to Bruce. "Originals, like this one, came into popularity during the nineteenth century, to help prevent accidental deaths. The thought was, if the bottles were easily identified as holding poison, fewer folks would be likely to take a curious swig."

"You know your history," Wes said.

"Part of the job." I rolled the small bottle in my palm then fixed the light on it to do a closer inspection. "This one appears to be in beautiful condition."

"With its stopper intact," Wes said.

"How valuable is it?" Bruce asked.

"Not enough for us to retire on," I said with a laugh. "But if this is as old as I think it is, a collector might be willing to spend a hundred dollars on it. Maybe a little more than that."

Wes took the bottle back and held the blue against his flashlight. "Yeah, maybe a little more," he said.

I thought about it. "I'm not going to be able to do any homework on this find. Not for a while."

Wes's expression lit up. "I'd love to take that on. We don't have any current projects at the historical society," he said. "You don't mind?"

I thought about my responsibilities at Marshfield, the continuing renovation here at home, and, most important, the investigation into Dr. Keay's murder. I'd have no time to look into this myself. If Wes was as eager to dig as he appeared to be, it was a win-win for us both. "Not at all. I'd be thrilled."

We continued walking. Bruce and I directed our lights forward; Wes kept his pointed toward the ground. We were silent for about a minute as we made our way through, which is a long time to be underground in a tunnel with no windows or ventilation. I wasn't prone to claustrophobia, but I wasn't wholly comfortable, either.

"How far does this go?" Bruce asked.

As though in answer, the ground began to rise. To say we walked uphill would be to overstate the situation, but as the floor had gently sloped down before, it now began sloping up.

"Wherever we're going, I think we're here," Wes said.

This time, when we faced a freestanding wall in the

center of the passage, we knew exactly what to do. We scooched around the wall's sides to find ourselves in a coal storage room that was virtually identical to the one in my house.

"Where do you think we are?" Wes asked.

I'd been playing a guessing game with myself as we'd traversed the passage. "I think," I said, "we're in Todd Pedota's basement."

Bruce ran his hands against the metal door, which looked exactly like the submarine hatch on the other end. "The direction we walked supports that theory," he said. When he pushed on the door's handle, I held my breath.

Part of me wanted to stop him. After all, we could be trespassing into someone else's home and I knew I wouldn't appreciate strangers stumbling into mine. The other, more adventurous, part of me wanted to know what was behind that door.

"It's locked," he said.

I let out a breath of relief, coupled with disappointment. "I'll have to let him know. I wonder what his side looks like."

"Oh boy," Bruce said. "Todd Pedota with a secret passage between his house and yours. That's a dream come true for a guy like him."

"I hadn't thought of that," I said. "Thanks a lot, Bruce."

Wes seemed enchanted by it all. "When we get back I'd like to look into prior owners' occupations," he said. "That is, if you don't mind my doing homework on your house."

"Please, be my guest," I said. "What will you be looking for?"

"You noticed the brick walls that lined the passage? They were installed by someone who knew what he was doing."

"What does that tell us?"

"Think about it. What good would it do to have a hidden space such as this one if you have to bring in a professional to help create it? Then the secret is out, isn't it?"

"So you're saying that if you discover that one of the home's owners was a bricklayer, you might have a good idea as to when the passage was constructed."

"It's a place to start," he said.

"The group in my basement is probably getting restless," I said. "Let's head back before they really do send in a search party."

Chapter 18

OWING PERHAPS TO THE FACT THAT WE WERE
more relaxed on our return trip, the three of us found two
buttons, another poison bottle, and several pieces of crockery
that we'd missed on our exploratory journey. By the time we
made it back to my basement, we had our hands full.

The gathered group must have heard us coming because
the camerawoman had her camera rolling. She filmed us
emerging from the coal cellar. "Oh, great," I said when I realized how awkward I would look as I climbed out, all dusty
and having to lift my legs to clamber through. Before exiting
fully, I handed the treasure in my arms to Larry. "Here, take
these. I'll be enough of a klutz climbing out of this submarine
hatch. If I try to do it with all this, I'll fall on my face."

Questions came so quickly and from so many directions
that I couldn't answer them all at once. I couldn't even tell
who was asking what.

"Were there any dead bodies?"

"Where did it lead? What was back there?"

"How far does it go?"

"What's all that stuff you found?"

As Bruce and Wes emerged, I raised my voice to explain. "It's a passage. Wes thinks that it may have been built during Prohibition or even before that—it might have even been a safe hiding spot on the Underground Railroad."

The assembled crowd went silent, waiting for more. "Wes has generously offered to do some research for us on that matter. In the meantime"—I turned my back to them and faced the passage's entrance—"this seems to be facing north by northwest, would you all agree?"

There was murmured assent.

"Let's go outside and see if this leads where we think it does."

The reporter and his camera-wielding girlfriend seemed much more interested in the story than they had earlier. With them and the rest of our ersatz audience in tow, Bruce, Wes, and I trooped up the stairs and out the back door. I would have liked to have stopped long enough to have gotten Bootsie out of my room. We could have brought her along on her leash, but the risk of her getting stepped on was great. Reluctantly, I left her behind.

We all traipsed to the south side of the house, near the front. Although everyone had a slightly different guess as to how far back from the front of the building the passage started, we all agreed that it was between ten and fifteen feet from the corner.

"Too bad you weren't able to measure how far you walked," Hillary said.

"I counted," I said. "On the way back."

Wes grinned at me. "Good going."

There was no doubt in my mind where the passage ended, but we followed through nonetheless. When our 123rd step brought us to the side of Todd Pedota's house next door, the reporter suggested we ring my neighbor's doorbell. Everyone joined in, clamoring for me to get Pedota involved. The group wanted resolution and they wanted it now.

"He's probably at work," I said when he didn't answer. "I'll talk with him when he gets home."

Disappointed, the reporter shoved his recorder in my face. "Do you think he knew about this passage? Why didn't he ever mention it to you?"

I held both hands up and pushed the tiny silver device away from me. All of a sudden the dozen or so people on Pedota's grass made me uncomfortable. "We need to go back," I said. "We're trampling my neighbor's lawn." I pointed to one of the construction crew. "Don't back up, you'll step on his daylilies. Please don't crush them."

To everyone, I said, "Let's all be very careful, shall we? I shouldn't have brought you all along. We're trespassing here."

"But if this"—the reporter read from his notes—"Todd Pedota didn't know about the secret passageway, he's going to want to explore it from his side, isn't he?"

"I can't presume to speak for him," I said. "Let's all get back to my yard, okay?"

"What about ownership?" the reporter asked. "Who owns the tunnel?"

I tried to catch Hillary's eye, to enlist her help in getting away from this guy, but she was on camera with his girlfriend, talking about her design and renovation business, using my house as a backdrop. There was no way to get her attention when she was performing. The earth was soft beneath her spiky heels and I watched them sink slowly into the ground. Hillary seemed far less worried about her shoes out here, where she had the opportunity to talk about her business. I decided not to call her out on that.

I turned to Bruce. "Can you make sure that we didn't mess Pedota's yard up too badly while I get everyone back to our side?"

"You got it, Grace," he said.

Wes sidled up. "I would imagine that ownership would be shared between the two parties. Unless, of course, there

was some agreement the homeowners came to years ago."
He shook his head solemnly. "I went over your blueprints
and house plans a number of times, Grace. I don't think that
was the case. I'm afraid this may have to be settled between
the two of you." He gave me a sheepish look. "But I'm no
lawyer. You'll need to consult someone who specializes in
real estate law to figure this out."

I felt my shoulders slump. With the murder and now this,
my to-do list was growing by leaps, bounds, and underground tunnels.

"Bennett Marshfield can probably recommend someone," Wes added.

"I'm sure he can, and will. I have to admit though, I'm
tempted to tell Todd Pedota that it's all his if he wants it."

Wes grimaced.

"What?" I asked.

"This is none of my business, and I should be grateful
you let me participate this much."

I waited for the "But."

"But," he said, "you've made it clear that you respect
history. You're a curator, for heaven's sake. That's what
drives you. I don't want to add undue pressure, but this tunnel is an incredible find. We came up with a few artifacts,
but I'll bet there are a lot more in there."

I could see where he was going with this.

"Todd Pedota is an unknown," he continued. "Maybe
he'll be open to our exploration of the passage. Maybe he'll
want to keep it sealed shut. If you give up all rights to it,
those become his calls to make. If you fight for half, or
discover that the entire connection belongs to you—"

"That's a big if."

He acknowledged me with a so-so shake of his head. "In
either case, you'll have a say in what happens down there.
I have to believe that you would make good decisions."

The reporter guy had been paying rapt attention and was
writing everything down. "This is all off the record," I said.

He gave me a look. "Are you kidding? You can't be off the record. You're a local celebrity. You're always involved in murders around here. This is big news."

"The murders aren't enough?" I asked before I could stop myself.

"Yeah, well, they give those juicy stories to the older reporters. And their photographers." He sent a glance at his girlfriend, who was still recording Hillary's impromptu info-mercial. "This is the first time I have something to offer that's bigger than a shop opening, or somebody's dog being found."

"Oh, well, then," I said, "I'm happy to oblige."

I'd meant it sarcastically, but the young man didn't notice. That was good because the moment the words left my mouth, I regretted them. We all want to be important in our own worlds, and if delivering a human interest story like this one made his day, who was I to judge?

Wes looked like a man who'd been granted his fondest wish. "I'll go back and collect the items we picked up before I leave, if that's all right?" I nodded, but before I could answer, he continued, "I'm going to get right on this. I have a feeling that some of what we found will help us discover the answer to who built the tunnel."

Bruce had gotten the remainder of the audience to disperse. After asking a few more questions, the reporter left, with his photographer girlfriend in tow. Finished in front of the camera, Hillary hurried over to talk to us as we made our way back up my driveway.

"This whole story started because of my renovations in your home," she said in a rush and with such high-energy elation that I barely recognized it was Hillary talking. "When this story goes live, everyone will want to hire me. This is the best thing that could have happened to my business."

"It's probably too late to keep this quiet," I said, thinking about how that young reporter had salivated over the story. "But I think it's only fair to let Todd Pedota know about the tunnel before the rest of Emberstowne finds out."

"Five minutes!" she shouted, flinging her hands out, arms extended, as though ready to give me a hug.

With no idea what she meant, I hesitated.

"He couldn't have been here five minutes ago?" she asked rhetorically, and in that moment I realized who she really wanted to hug. "Your neighbor is home. Let's go tell him the good news."

Todd Pedota barely had time to get out of his car before Hillary started for him. Wiggling her fingers high above her head, she singsonged, "Oh, Toh-ohdd," as she scurried to his driveway in her mud-caked heels.

He spun at the sound of her voice. Todd Pedota had never been a man who backed off where an attractive woman was concerned, and he didn't now. Despite the fact that he clearly hadn't expected anyone to come running when he pulled up, he was quick to welcome her. Hillary practically squirmed with excitement and Todd, clearly misreading her approach, grasped Hillary's upper arms and rubbed his hands up and down her bare skin. "What a wonderful surprise," he said. "What brings you—"

He cut himself short when he caught sight of me and Bruce coming up from the sidewalk. Letting his hands drop from Hillary's sides, he took a step back, suddenly wary.

Hillary turned, making eye contact with me, as if to say, "Let me handle him."

"What is all this?" he asked. "Are you planning a block party? Looking for donations? Count me out."

Hillary ignored his questions. "We have the most exciting news."

From the look in Todd Pedota's eyes, the only thing exciting that Hillary could tell him right now was that she'd be happy to scamper up his front steps, accompany him inside, and shut the door on the rest of the world.

"What are you doing home so early?" I asked.

Hillary had moved closer to him, close enough that their shoulders touched. She slid a hand around his arm. It took a moment, but he recollected himself. The self-assured lounge lizard was back.

"I've been working from home a lot lately. Even with all the construction noise going on at your house, a bad day at home is always better than the best day at work, right?"

I smiled at the cliché, which he took as encouragement.

"Seems like today was a particularly good day to be home." With a glance around at us all, and a fond assessment of Hillary, he asked, "Tell me, beautiful, what's going on that's so exciting?"

"Well," she began, running a perfect fingernail down the front of his dress shirt. "We have a surprise for you."

The man couldn't have been more confused.

Hillary pulled back slightly. Enough to make eye contact. "We uncovered a secret passage in Grace's basement," she began. "And we think it leads to your house."

"Wait, what?" Pedota took a step back, his expression darkening. "You're crazy," he said. "What are you talking about?"

It took some convincing and a great deal of Hillary's charm, but she finally persuaded the man to allow us to take a look inside his basement.

Pedota was as flustered as I'd ever seen him. He walked us up to his front porch as the realization that we weren't kidding began to seep in. "Wait here a minute," he said at the door. "I have a few things I need to put away."

Bruce, Hillary, and I exchanged a glance, which Pedota caught.

"Get your minds out of the gutter," he said. "I live alone and didn't expect company. I may have left a few personal items lying around."

He disappeared inside.

While we waited, I made a swift appraisal of Pedota's abode with its clean and freshly painted façade. The home's pristine appearance made me doubly glad I'd allowed Hillary to begin renovations on my house. Pedota's painted lady was a mirror image of mine. They both had massive wrap-around porches, high ceilings, and gingerbread trim. The difference was that his house had been maintained over the years, while mine had been allowed to fall into disrepair.

Bruce scowled at our surroundings.

"What's wrong?" I asked.

"I don't like this guy. Don't feel good about this."

"I get the impression the feeling is mutual," I said. "I'm sure he'd prefer it if both you and I disappeared and he had Hillary to himself."

She gave a Cheshire cat smile. "I've dealt with his type before. Touchy-feely, overconfident, bold." Running her palm along the side of her hair, she said, "I can handle him. Don't you worry."

When Todd finally opened the door again to allow us in, I noticed that he'd changed. Instead of a dress shirt and slacks, he sported a red polo and tight jeans. His feet were bare and he'd liberally applied a cologne that made me want to cough and wave my hand in front of my face. A move like that probably wouldn't help us get what we wanted—a look into his basement—so I powered through instead.

"I don't know what you expect to find," he said as he shut the door behind us. "I've been in my basement a thousand times and I've never noticed any sort of passageway."

"What about an old coal storage room?" I asked.

"Nope." He led us through his living room, dining room, and back into the kitchen. The floor plan made my head spin.

Bruce was feeling it, too. "This is exactly like our house," he said, "only flipped."

Hillary waved her fingers from side to side, vaguely indicating our surroundings. "Your home was profession-ally decorated, wasn't it, Todd?" she asked.

"Might have been," he said. "Whoever decorated did it before Vicki and I moved in. We didn't have a chance to change much before—before she was gone."

I would have liked to hear more about Pedota's former wife, but Hillary was more intent on drumming up business. "It's lovely but I think it could use a little refreshing, don't you?"

Could she be more obvious?

Pedota opened the door to the basement and I was overcome with the damp cloud of mildew that enveloped us. "Sorry for the smell," he said.

He went first and I managed to squeeze in after him before Hillary did. "I never met Vicki," I said.

Pedota half-turned. "You couldn't have known her. She moved out well before you arrived." At the basement floor, he reached up and pulled on a string to turn on an overhead bulb. "More like I kicked her out."

"Oh?" I asked with a leading lilt. "I take it you had some trouble?"

He gave a half snort, half laugh. "I'm surprised you haven't heard about it. The cops have. After Keay got himself murdered at your Marshfield, the detective came to talk to me. Like I had any reason to kill the old geezer."

"Why did they think you did?" I knew the backstory, but I wanted to hear Pedota's version.

Hillary, probably worried that any further talk in this vein might hurt her chances for a renovation job, stepped forward. "The first thing I'd do if you hired me would be to get this basement dried out. You're on high ground here. That"—she pointed to a stale puddle—"tells me you have leaky pipes." Dried water marks around the puddle made it obvious that it had been much larger at one time. Rust-colored drip marks streaked the stone walls and white mold had formed uneven lacy patterns around every crack in the floor.

"Your basement is set up differently," I said as I turned in place. "Looks like one of the prior owners intended to put a room or two down here."

"Yeah, well. This is how it was when we bought it."

Where my bare basement walls were a mishmash of

stone, uneven concrete, and wood, Pedota's walls had been covered. From the looks of it, a long time ago.

There were a few more pull-chain bulbs that Pedota lit as we made our way to the southwestern edge of his basement. He turned on the last one and gestured with an arrogant smile. "See," he said, "nothing."

I wouldn't say there was nothing. Pedota had dozens of cardboard boxes of varying sizes stacked along the wall. Water-stained and buckling from the weight of boxes above, the bottom row was probably the most likely source for the heavy mildew scent in the air.

I wandered a few steps forward, trying to picture where the passage would hit the basement if it appeared in a mirror spot to my house. "Do you mind if I look a little closer?"

Hillary had latched onto Pedota's arm—oh so professionally—and he seemed to resent me for pulling his attention away from her.

"You go ahead and look," Hillary said, waving at me. She hadn't even consulted him. "Todd won't mind." She batted her eyelashes as she stared up at him. Literally batted her eyelashes. I didn't believe women actually did that. "Do you, Todd?"

"Go ahead," he mumbled as she cooed conversation too quietly for me to hear. "Whatever."

Bruce had been subdued throughout. Now he and I exchanged a look as we eased deeper into the basement.

"When do you think this place was last cleaned?" he asked me.

"Take a peek at what's written on the sides of the boxes." I pointed at Vicki's name, which adorned everything along the bottom row. "You can't tell me he isn't bitter. Five years later, he's still holding on to her stuff."

"And leaving it where it's damp so everything gets ruined," Bruce finished. "What a nice guy."

I stole a quick glance back at Pedota and Hillary. They were about fifteen feet away, and I knew they wouldn't be able to hear our whispers. "Yeah, well," I said, "considering what she did, I suppose I don't blame him."

"I'm not seeing anything like the submarine hatch we have on our side," Bruce said.

I'd come to the same conclusion. There wasn't even an old workbench to tear out that might be concealing it. I made my way to the southeastern corner of his basement and took seven steps north.

"You counted that, too?" Bruce asked.

Rather than answer, I stopped and stared at the wall where I would have expected the door to be. "Is there anything different about this part of the basement?" I asked, desperate now. I couldn't imagine Todd Pedota allowing us back for a second search. "Anything at all?"

Bruce tucked his hands into his sides and surveyed. "The lighting's not too good in here." He waved a hand. "I'd say that the section of wall between that beam"—he indicated a tall structure to his right—"and that one"—he pointed about ten feet to his left—"is a different color than the rest of the basement, but it could be my eyes playing tricks."

Boxes were stacked about shoulder-high and covered the base of the wall completely. "Do you mind if we move a couple of these?" I asked Pedota.

Hillary answered, "Go right ahead."

Bruce gave me an amused look. Pedota didn't seem to care in the least. I picked up my first box and winced at the whoosh of stale air that it threw up into my face. "Let's get as many of these out of the way as we can before our neighbor starts paying attention again. I know I wouldn't want strangers moving my stuff around."

Hillary kept Pedota chatting while Bruce and I moved about a dozen or so boxes. I leaned forward to touch the blank wall we'd uncovered. I scratched my fingernails against it and caught a slight hollow sound. I tapped.

"Did you hear that?" I asked.

Bruce nodded, sizing the wall up and down. "Sounds like

that might be fake." He pressed the fingertips of both hands against the wide panel and pushed. "There's a little give."

As if on cue, Hillary scuttled forward. "Did you find anything?"

I wiped my hands against each other, trying to rid them of excess grime. "Could be."

Todd Pedota had picked up on the wall sound and the "give" as soon as Bruce pointed it out. "No way," he said. "No way."

Using both hands, he mimicked Bruce's movements, using significantly more force. The wall didn't move a lot, but it was enough for us all to see.

"Wait," he said, then tried the experiment again in another part of the basement. No give. He tried another spot. Same result. Finally, he returned to the wall we'd uncovered, and pushed at it, hard.

He stepped back. "How did I never notice that?"

I pointed to the boxes we'd moved. "Have these been here for five years?"

He nodded. "We bought the house about two years before that, and Vicki started talking about redecorating. But we never got past the top floor. Got the master bedroom done." He shook his head. "I hate the color so much I sleep in one of the spares. Never made it to changing things in the basement." He stepped back and tucked his fingers into his back pockets. "We had plans when we first moved in. Then she started working for Dr. Keay and that was the end of that."

"She *worked* for Dr. Keay?" I asked. Frances hadn't mentioned that.

"One of his receptionists." Pedota snorted, then added, "More like one of his harem."

"I'm sorry that happened to you."

He shrugged, hands still tight inside his jeans. "Worse was how. You'd think she'd have the decency to tell me she wants out of the marriage. Instead she gets herself involved with a drunken idiot who wraps his fat SUV around a tree and nearly kills them both." Under his breath, he muttered, "Would have made my life easier."

I couldn't stop myself. "Made what easier?"

"Nothing. Forget it." Pedota's mouth went flat as he regarded me for a half second. He waggled his shoulders, as though shaking the moment away. "You're the expert on solving problems. How do you propose we proceed with this? Tear down the wall?"

I didn't have an answer, but because he seemed willing to continue the expedition, I worked my fingers around the edge of the fake wall. Abutted on either side by floor-to-ceiling beams whose paint had begun to flake off over the years, the wall didn't look the least bit suspicious to the casual observer. I could completely understand why no one had bothered with it before now.

Unless Todd and Vicki had gone looking for it when they first moved in—and why would they?—or if they'd begun any remodeling down here, there was no way this simulated concrete would have been noticed.

"Do you have a screwdriver?" I asked.

"Flathead, I assume?" Pedota trotted off to the far end of the basement and returned with one in hand.

"You don't mind if I scratch your wall up a little, do you?" I asked. "I can't imagine this will come off without some damage."

He almost laughed. "Look at this place," he said. "It's a mess and it smells bad. Do whatever you like. I'm curious now, too."

I wedged the flat edge of the screwdriver between the wall and the left-hand beam. There couldn't have been more than a sixteenth of an inch to work with, but I pushed hard and angled until I managed a little leverage.

"I should be doing that," Pedota said, but he didn't make a move to take the instrument from me. Reacting, perhaps, to my reluctance to hand it over, he added, "Go ahead. You've got more experience than I do."

I didn't really, but rather than correct him, I pressed on. "Got it, I think," I said through gritted teeth. The metal edge of the screwdriver had found a sweet spot. I used both hands to push the plastic handle closer to the wall, forcing the fake wall forward.

"It's working," Bruce said. He leaned in and tried to fit the tips of his fingers around the edge as it became free.

Hillary didn't say anything. She watched, hands clasped and eyes bright, from behind where Todd Pedota stood.

He took a step forward. "Need help?"

I was so close I could practically taste it. "No," I grunted as I shoved the screwdriver harder with one hand, and worked to pull at the fake wall with the other. "I think we just about have—"

It came free in a flash, causing me and Bruce to stumble backward. I lost my hold on the screwdriver and it clattered to the floor. The fake wall, which now revealed itself as a thin piece of wood, which had been coated with a gray concrete-like surface, wasn't completely removed from the wall behind it, but it had been dislodged enough for us to get a good grip on two sides and pull.

Bruce, Todd, and I did just that. Hillary watched. It took three tries, but when it came down, it did, fast. The fact that none of us fell on our backsides, ripped open our hands, or lost blood made it a win in my book.

"And there it is," Hillary said with triumph as though she'd singlehandedly uncovered the wall. "Exactly like the one at your house, Grace."

She was right. As though someone had physically lifted it from the wall in my basement and installed it here, the door was identical. The same counter-set handle. The same lock. I wished we'd brought Larry the Locksmith with us on our little trek.

"A door?" Todd Pedota's exclamation made me stare at him in disbelief. Hadn't that been what we'd been telling him since we arrived?

He stepped forward to touch the submarine-like door inset in the metal wall, much the way I had at first. "This must be the handle," he said.

I was about to warn him that it was locked, but he pulled before I could get the words out. To my surprise, and—judging from the gasps around me—everyone else's, it swung wide open.

"But it didn't open from the inside," Bruce said to me. His hands went wide in puzzlement. "How come it isn't locked?"

I didn't know. Todd Pedota waved his hand in front of his face. "Smells like wet dirt," he said, "and rot." He stuck his head in and when he spoke, his words bounced around, hollow. "I thought you said this was a tunnel. It looks like a small coal room to me."

We pointed out the fake back wall. I showed him how to squeeze around it and explained how the passage led to my basement. The wood on this side appeared to be in better shape than on my side. Newer, maybe.

"I don't understand why it wouldn't budge for us," Bruce said, examining the swung-out door. "The wall we tore down was strong, but I have to believe we would have felt some give."

I tended to agree with him. "Hang on," I said, climbing in. "Close the door and let me try to open it from the inside."

For some reason, the hinges on this side of the passage didn't squeal the way mine did, either. I started to wonder if the two ends had been closed up at different times. When Bruce closed the metal door with a bang, I was thrown into absolute darkness. I'd expected that, but it was still unsettling.

Pressing against the door and gripping the handle tightly, I pushed. Nothing. I tried again with the same result. Using the tips of my fingers to walk around the edge, I sought a mechanism that would allow me to unlock it from the inside. Nothing, again.

Bruce shouted to me from the other side. "Should we open it?"

"Not yet," I shouted back.

I flattened my hands against the door and moved them, slowly, searching for a lever, a latch, anything that might unlock the door. Came up empty. Although it felt like I'd been in this dark space for ten minutes, it probably had been no more than two. I gave the door a few more pushes and played with the handle again.

"Giving up," I shouted. "Let me out."

A second later, the door swung open and even though the basement was illuminated only by bare bulbs, I blinked at the sudden light.

"No way out once you're in there," I said unnecessarily. "At least, not that I could find. You get in and then you're stuck."

"Is it the same on your side?" Pedota asked.

I shrugged. "Forgot to check. I will, though."

"Now that this is open, we need to be careful that no one gets trapped inside," Bruce said. "That could be disastrous."

Hillary gave a little shudder. "Maybe Larry can come back sometime and fix these doors so that they can be opened from the inside. That is, if you're okay with that, Todd."

Todd Pedota had his arms folded across his chest, studying the door. With a grin that came across as a leer, he said, "I think it's a marvelous idea."

Chapter 19

FRANCES TRUNDLED INTO MY OFFICE THE following morning, chained glasses perched halfway down her nose, a folder shoved under one arm. She leaned across my desk to press one of her thick fingers down on today's date in my calendar. "You have an appointment at one this afternoon."

I finger-combed my hair, buying time. Whatever this appointment was, Frances was clearly proud to have arranged it. Tugging at the hem of her lilac-littered polyester shell, she righted herself and stared down at me, eyes sharp.

I sat back, hands crossed on my lap.

In her eagerness for me to bite, she fairly vibrated with anticipation.

It wasn't that I wanted to annoy her by prolonging the moment. It wasn't even that I wasn't interested to know who I was meeting with, or why. What kept me from asking for more information in that long moment was the unexpected realization that I wasn't on edge with Frances the way I used to be.

The woman hadn't uttered a snide remark about me or my life in a while. Could it be that—gasp!—we were beginning to get along?

"Who am I meeting with?"

She was close to my desk, but took a half step forward nonetheless. "You'll let me in on it, won't you? I set this up, I surely ought to be invited in to the meeting."

"Why don't you tell me who's coming here, first." When her eyes dimmed ever so slightly, I added, "And after you do, I'll share *my* scoop with you."

"If it's about the secret passageway you found in your basement, that's old news," she said.

"How?" My hands slapped the top of my desk. "That happened yesterday. How in the world do you know about it already?"

She tugged the folder out from under her arm, opened it, and placed a newspaper in front of me. "You made the front page."

Below continuing coverage of Dr. Keay's murder investigation was an "in-depth" story about the discovery of the passage in my home. "Oh," I said.

"Nice photo."

I cocked an eyebrow at her, but couldn't tell if she was being sarcastic or sincere. Judging from the photo they'd chosen to feature, I had to guess she was taking the opportunity to slam. The photographer had caught my expression when I'd first seen the crowd in my basement. My mouth was open, and the hyperbright flash made it look as though my nose had doubled in size. I wasn't the most photogenic person on the planet, but the last picture of me that looked this bad had been taken in seventh grade, when I had braces, streaky hair, and mismatched clothing.

I scanned the article, barely resisting the urge to cover the photo with my hand.

"I'll bet you can buy a copy of that shot from the newspaper if you want."

"Ha-ha."

The story was accurate on a few counts—that we'd found a door, opened it, discovered a passage, and believed it might have been built for the Underground Railroad. The story missed the mention of Prohibition and the fact that the passage connected to Todd Pedota's house. The reporter and his girlfriend had been there for the tramp across the yards, but not for our visit to Todd's home, so the fact that they'd left that part out made sense.

I mentioned that to Frances as I skimmed. "The other part that's missing is that we found a few valuable artifacts in the space."

"Like what?"

I told her about the poison bottles and the other items we'd picked up. "I'm stopping by the historical society after work. Wes McIntyre said he'd do a little homework on prior owners for me."

One side of Frances's mouth curled up. "Oh?" she said with the same sort of tone she used whenever speculating on my love life. "A little homework? Is that what they're calling it these days?"

"Quit your imagining, Frances. I'm seeing Adam, remember?"

She made a face. "How could I forget?"

"Why do you have such a problem with him?"

"Me?" She pointed to her chest in a way that practically begged for an acting award. "I don't have an opinion on the matter. Why should I?"

I rolled my eyes.

"Back to the original topic," I said. "Who's coming in to meet me today at one?"

"To meet with you and the Mister," she corrected me.

"Fine. Who?"

The smugness was back. She gave a little wiggle of glee and said, "Joyce Swedburg."

"Why does she want to see me?" I asked.

"She doesn't." Frances gave an exasperated head shake. "You want to see her."

"I do?"

Now it was my assistant's turn to roll her eyes. "How can you solve this murder if you don't interview all the suspects?"

"First of all, Joyce wasn't here when Dr. Keay was murdered, remember?"

"She may have slipped him something before the party. It had to be her."

"When, exactly, did she inject pure alcohol into him? Before or after he picked up Serena?"

"Before, of course." Frances's posture drooped slightly.

"Okay, got it," I said, as though I was taking her seriously. "Didn't Flynn say that Keay had been attacked shortly before he died? And if Joyce got to him before the party—remember, he had defensive wounds from a fight—why didn't he mention the altercation to anyone?"

"He could have been embarrassed." Frances's words were coming out with far less confidence. "Can you imagine having to admit to being overpowered by your ex-wife?"

"That still doesn't work with the timeline," I said. "Dr. Keay was here for at least an hour before he died. Flynn believes the injection happened during that time."

"Maybe she snuck in when no one was looking."

"Frances. We would have seen her."

"Joyce is a wily one. I wouldn't put anything past the woman." Frances stared up at the ceiling for a moment. "She could have hired someone. Did you ever consider that?"

I pressed the bridge of my nose and took a deep breath. "Despite the fact that it's unlikely that Joyce killed Keay, I am glad you set this meeting up."

"You are?" she asked.

"I know Flynn wants me to stay out of it, but because I helped organize the event, I can't help feeling responsible.

I'd like to talk with Joyce, even if it's only to find out who she believes had motive to kill her ex-husband."

"Told you," Frances said. She spun on her heel and made her way to the door.

"Told me what?" I asked.

"That you wanted to talk with her." She turned to give me a triumphant glare. "I was right again. And that means you should invite me to sit in on the meeting."

JOYCE SWOOPED IN AT TWENTY MINUTES after one o'clock. Wearing a floor-length dress in a shade of pink that made my eyes water and a turquoise necklace that must have weighed four pounds, she leaned over Bennett's chair to kiss him on the cheek. "So wonderful to see you, my good friend. How horrible these past few days have been."

No apology. Not even any acknowledgment that she was late.

I'd stood to greet her. I wouldn't say she pointedly ignored me, but she seemed vaguely disappointed that I was there. She came toward my desk, gave my hand one of those dead-fish fingertip shakes, and lowered herself into the chair next to Bennett's. A faint sheen of perspiration gathered over her upper lip, and now that she was sitting, I could see that her dress clung to her in all the wrong places.

"Dear man," she said to Bennett, "I must thank you again for taking it upon yourself to deliver the news of Leland's passing. So much better than having to deal with that persistent detective." She crossed her legs and pulled a collapsible fan from her clutch, unfolding it and waving it in front of her face. Bejeweled and as pink as her dress, the fan was plastic, the kind tourists buy for ten-year-olds at souvenir shops.

Frances took a spot on the nearby sofa.

Time to get this party started. "Thank you for coming in today, Joyce," I said.

"Your assistant told me it was imperative that I do so." Leaning sideways, she placed a hand on Bennett's knee. "I've heard a vicious rumor that the police believe Leland was murdered. That can't be true, can it?"

Frances and I exchanged a look, both of us silently asking, "Rumor?"

I couldn't help myself. "Are you telling me that Detective Flynn hasn't come to question you?"

"Of course he has," Joyce said with no little bit of impatience. "But that doesn't mean the police are right. When are they ever, really? I talked with dozens of my friends who were here and they all say that it appeared Leland suffered a heart attack. That young detective is hardly a doctor."

Arguing with her that the coroner *was* a doctor and that he had determined Leland's death was a homicide felt remarkably pointless. We weren't here to debate the merits of the investigation; we were here to unearth what we could.

Bennett lifted Joyce's hand from his knee and grasped it in both of his. "I'm afraid it is murder," he said, and with that he returned her hand to her chair. "That's exactly what we'd like to discuss with you today: Who would want Leland dead enough to kill him?" Bennett smiled. "We thought you might know best."

"Well, of course, Leland and I remained on excellent terms since the divorce," she began, "but I'd hardly say I knew what he was up to—beyond his work at the chamber, that is." Her mouth downturned, she sniffed deeply.

"No idea at all?" Frances asked.

From Joyce's startled reaction, it was clear she couldn't have been more surprised if a piece of furniture had addressed her.

"Who knows what sort of riffraff he may have chosen to socialize with? I understand he brought some trollop to the benefit." She forced a shudder. "Disgraceful."

I ignored that. "I would have thought that you and Leland might have been in close contact recently. You were in the middle of negotiations, weren't you?"

Joyce's head snapped up. She glared at me.

Undaunted, I continued, "About the house, I mean."

As if her next words were shards of glass, she edged them out carefully. "I know precisely the negotiations you're referring to."

"It stands to reason that you may have been aware of unusual circumstances in his life. Or of anyone who might stand to benefit from his death."

"I was under the impression I'd been invited here as a social call." Directing her considerable anger toward me, she continued, "It's clear your penchant for solving murders has blocked your sense of reason. You're on a witch hunt. I see that now."

Bennett leaned forward. "Joyce, we're only trying to help."

"I should never have come." Ignoring him, she raised her chin, pulling her shoulders back. "I realize, however, that you won't leave me alone unless I play your little game."

Momentarily dumbfounded by her spiteful speech, I hesitated.

She continued her rant. "Yes, I stand to benefit from Leland's demise." Her glittery hands rose in emphasis. "Of course I do. Who else should have? We had no children, and he had no other family."

I exchanged a glance with Frances, who gave me a surreptitious thumbs-up.

"Yes, the house is mine now. We held it in joint tenancy. And yes, I am the sole beneficiary of Leland's will. Does that surprise you?"

Worked up, she reminded me of an owl with her bold eyes and twisting neck, watching us all, waiting for a response.

Not one of us moved.

"Well it doesn't surprise me in the least," she said, answering her own question. "While we were married, he expected me to take care of all the details like writing wills, arranging for lawn care, setting up grocery deliveries. There is no way he would have ever stopped to think about the future—about paperwork—about the minutiae that day-to-day living requires. He was a zombie before zombies became popular. Undead, living off the lives of others."

She stopped to take a breath. Blinking, she turned again to each of us, then continued in a less agitated tone. "Leland cared about two things: his work as a surgeon and his liquor. The rest of his life was run on autopilot. He achieved a high level of fame early and he expected others to do things for him. By and large, they did. He didn't ever have to *think*. I did that."

Her mouth turned down harder. I couldn't tell if she was trying to make herself cry or if the emotion was genuine.

"I find it difficult to summon sorrow at Leland's death," she said. "How can I, when I don't accept that he was ever truly alive?"

I didn't have an answer for that.

"Leland's death is a financial boon to me, yes." Her eyes flashed. "But I couldn't have killed him. Remember, I wasn't there."

Chapter 20

WHEN JOYCE LEFT, I TURNED TO BENNETT. "What do you think?"

He stared at the doorway for a beat or two before answering. "I feel sorry for her."

Frances had seen our guest out and returned to my office, a big smile on her face. "Told you," she said for the second time that day.

"What now?"

"She's guilty as sin."

Bennett sat forward, tilting his head. "Exactly how did you come to that conclusion?"

"Follow the money, and *cherchez la femme*." Frances plopped herself into the chair Joyce had vacated and folded her ample arms. "It's a classic maneuver. State up front why everyone should suspect you because doing so throws them off. Guilty people would want to hide their motivations, right?" She didn't wait for us to answer. "Wrong. Joyce is no fool. She thinks she's playing us. And from the expressions on your faces, it looks as though she succeeded."

Bennett boosted himself to his feet. "The jury is still out, Frances. Joyce may have had motivation, but she didn't have opportunity. As to the means—" He held up both hands. "No idea." Turning to me, he said, "Let me know what you find out about your house's history, Grace. I'm fascinated by the discovery of that tunnel."

I promised I would. "I'm stopping by the historical society on my way home this afternoon."

"To see Wes," Frances added.

Reading my assistant's innuendo correctly, Bennett asked, "What's this? A new beau on the horizon?"

"Not at all." I glared at Frances, who looked very pleased with herself. "He's offered to help me with researching the tunnel. There's a wealth of information at the historical society. Too much for me to sort through on my own."

Appeased, Bennett again started for the door.

"He's single," Frances added, again in her singsong tone. "Widower."

"Have you been gossiping with your cronies again, Frances?" Bennett shook his head. *"Tsk, tsk, tsk."*

Undeterred by his crony comment, she answered him. "What good is gossip if there's no one to share it with?"

"He's not my type," I said, hoping to put an end to this discussion as quickly as possible.

"Oh? And Adam is?" she asked.

Bennett seemed interested in hearing my answer to that, too.

I hated being put on the spot. "We'll see," I said.

Frances crossed her arms. "That's not much of an answer."

"But it's the best we can hope for at the moment," Bennett said, graciously putting me out of my misery. Changing subjects, he asked, "And Hillary? Are the renovations still progressing well?"

Finally, a question I could answer with ease. "So far, so good."

* * *

I STOPPED SHORT BEFORE WALKING INTO THE historical society that evening. Peering through the door's glass pane, I was surprised to see David Cherk there. The skeletal-faced man leaned one bony elbow on the oak countertop, using his free hand to gesticulate as he spoke. Though his expression remained impassive, his dark brows jumped and furrowed as he conversed with Wes. Wes leaned as far from the other man as he could, which made me wonder if Cherk had bad breath.

I opened the door and stepped inside. "David, you're back."

Cherk's dark brows shot downward as his nose turned up. It wasn't a frown, precisely, but he was clearly not thrilled to see me.

"Thank you for nothing," he said.

As the door shut behind me, I looked to Wes for clarification. He seemed as stunned as I was. "Excuse me?" I said.

Straightening, Cherk gave me a swift up and down with his eyes. "Do you really believe I had something to do with Leland Keay's death? How dare you send your little minion out to drag me back here!"

Realization dawned. Ronny Tooney. "David," I began, "I believe there's been a misunderstanding."

"Is that what you call it?" He slammed both palms down on the oak top and threw his head back, faking laughter. "A misunderstanding. I'd barely set myself up in Belmont when he insisted I come back. And when I say insisted—" He held both wrists out toward me, offering me their undersides to examine. I noticed how scrawny he was, and how blue and prominent his veins were against pale skin. Not much else.

"What am I supposed to see?" I asked.

He flipped his arms, showing me their backs, then twisted up and down once more. "Notice anything?"

If he was showing me any indication that Tooney had manhandled him, I was missing it.

"No. I, um, don't."

"Exactly!" he said in triumph.

Wes stroked his beard and shot me a quizzical look.

"I am pale," Cherk said. "I wasn't out at my shooting location long enough to even get a little sun on my fair skin."

My first instinct was to ask, "Seriously?" but I held that exclamation in. "I never intended to pull you back to Emberstowne from your vacation," I said. "All I wanted was to ask you a few more questions. I apologize if Ronny Tooney was overenthusiastic."

He tucked those pale hands into both elbows, crossing his arms in front of his chest. "Apology not accepted," he said with great pomposity. "Just because you've been instrumental in bringing a few murderers to justice does not qualify you to impinge on innocent people's rights."

This was the second time today that someone had thrown my reputation for solving murders into my face. First Joyce, now Cherk.

"I would have expected the police to ask you to stay in town."

His face creased in a terrifically unpleasant way. "That's only for suspects," he said, taking care to enunciate the word carefully. "Innocent people don't have to follow those sorts of orders."

Not one to waste an opportunity, I asked, "Now that you're here, would you be willing to answer a few questions for me?"

"Why? So you can make me your scapegoat? So you can put me under your little microscope? Your magnifying glass? So you can study me like a trapped bug? I should say not."

He pulled a black bag from the floor near his feet. I hadn't noticed it earlier, but from the way he lifted it, I could tell it was weighty. "The only reason I agreed to return with your hired wannabe was because I'd forgotten a few items."

"Then I don't understand. If you were coming back anyway, why are you so upset?"

"If you have to ask, then I can't explain it to you." He lifted the bag's strap over his head so the sack rested on his hip, like a cross-body purse. To Wes, he made a small twisting gesture with his index finger. "Keep me updated on your finds."

When I looked at what he was referring to, I saw the poison bottles we'd found in the secret passage.

A flash of territorial defensiveness shot up. "Those are from my house," I said.

"Yours? Oh, lucky day." Cherk's mouth went flat and he jostled past me. "Wes asked me to photograph them for the files." He glared at the historical society man with contempt. "You said you wanted to have them evaluated. You never said it was for her."

"Grace has done nothing to hurt you," Wes said. "And these bottles are historically significant. There's no reason why you shouldn't be willing to photograph them for the society."

Cherk sniffed. "I'll be in Belmont if you need me." At the door he turned and gave me a withering look even Frances wouldn't be capable of. "Don't bother me this time. I'm busy." He walked out.

Momentarily speechless, I turned to Wes. "What's with him?" I asked.

Hand across his mouth, Wes shook his head. "I have no idea," he said from between his fingers. "He's displayed flashes of rudeness in the past, but never like that."

I blew out a breath, trying to dispel the indignation that had welled up in me. "He's angry, that's for sure."

"Would you like a glass of water or something before we get started? I don't have much else. There may be a can of soda in the fridge in back."

"No, thank you," I said. "That was a bit unsettling, though."

"I'm sorry."

"Not your fault." I tried to shake off the feeling of anger that had clouded my head while Cherk had been taking me to task. "We're here to talk about fun things. So let's try to turn the evening around, shall we?"

He smiled. "Good plan. Let's not let David's negativity spoil the news."

"Good news?"

"Depends on how you look at it, I suppose," he said. "But I think you'll be pleased." He pulled over two books that were off to the side, displacing the poison bottles. Looking sheepish, he said, "When David came in, he was in such a foul mood, I showed him the artifacts we'd found. I thought it might cheer him up." Wes sucked in his cheeks, as though to imitate Cherk's expression. I laughed. "Didn't help at all. I think he was more angry at himself for forgetting his supplies than anything. You provided an easy target for him to lash out at."

"I'm sorry to hear it." I perched both elbows on the countertop and dropped my chin into my hands. "I'm on a roll today, apparently."

"What do you mean?"

I told him about Joyce Swedburg's visit and how annoyed she was to find that we wanted to discuss Leland Keay's murder with her. "Not that I want to point fingers or anything, but she had a lot to gain by him dying."

"She wasn't at the party though, was she?"

I shook my head. "Unless she hired a hit man—one who was able to overpower Dr. Keay without anyone witnessing it in the middle of an event with a hundred people around him—she's clear."

"Could she have met Keay outside? Maybe ahead of time?"

Now he was starting to sound like Frances. "Dr. Keay came in looking perfectly healthy and not complaining about anyone accosting him. Once he was there, he didn't leave. There's only one way in and out—except for the emergency door, and that wasn't touched. If Joyce is responsible, then she's capable of rendering herself invisible."

Wes cocked his head. "Hmm."

"What?" I asked.

He ran a hand down his beard. "This hidden tunnel in your house gets me thinking. You don't suppose there was any other way into the party, do you?"

"I asked Bennett," I said. "There are plenty of secret passages at Marshfield, but he said he doesn't know of any in that part of the basement."

"Okay," he said, but appeared unconvinced. "Tell you what, after I show you what I found here, we'll take a look and see if there are any clues in the Marshfield Manor blueprints."

"You have them?"

"Some," he said. "David had me pull the plans out before the benefit and was using them to help design his presentation."

"What I wouldn't give for a look."

"I can help with that," he said. "Let's talk about your house first, though."

Fifteen minutes later, I'd learned that my house and Todd Pedota's had been originally built by two brothers. The scrapbooks Wes had pulled out contained photos, newspaper clippings, letters, and other snippets of information that helped us determine that the homes had been built about a decade before the Civil War. By piecing the story together, we gathered that the two men had constructed the tunnel as a shortcut between their homes.

"Because they wanted their families to spend time together?" I asked.

"That's what it looks like." He pulled out the blueprints we'd studied before. "These are not originals from when the house was built. Chances are, those are long gone."

I was a little disappointed. "If the originals are missing, how can you be sure the tunnel was built the same time the homes were?"

"I can't," he said with a wry smile. "I'm surmising. Both brothers were bricklayers, so that would account for the quality of construction we found. The two men moved out of their respective homes at the same time. After they sold, there's no mention of the passage. Seems to me that might have made news in tiny Emberstowne."

"I'd been hoping to uncover a more historically significant reason for the passageway. I wanted it to have been a safe haven for the Underground Railroad."

Wes made a so-so motion with his head. "Want to know what I think?"

"Sure."

"My guess is that the brothers did use it for that very purpose."

"More surmising on your part?"

"Think about it. Maybe there's a very good reason why we don't have the homes' original plans. If the passage was used to protect slaves, then the two brothers might have destroyed the original blueprints so that no one would know the passage existed."

"I like that theory," I said. "If I ever get time, I'll do some homework on the brothers. Maybe I'll be able to find what brought them to Emberstowne in the first place. I'd love to believe that my home played an important part in history."

"I'll bet it did," he said. "By the way, I don't mean to pry, but how uncomfortable is it having direct access to your neighbor's home and—more pointedly—him having access to yours?"

"You're not the first person to ask me that," I said. "It's disconcerting, for sure. The good news is that the metal doors are self-locking. I can't get into his house and he can't get into mine. Believe me, that was the first thing I checked after we visited his side."

"That's got to be a relief."

"For the short term, yes. I'll be looking into a more permanent solution once you're finished excavating the area. You're still willing to help with that, right?"

"I deal with papers all day, every day." He sighed. "Mind you, I firmly believe this is all great stuff. There's a wealth of information here. But, the opportunity to find pieces of history where the town's early settlers left them? The opportunity to dig for buried treasure? That's not to be missed."

I turned to look at the door. "I'm surprised David Cherk wasn't more interested. Seeing as how he's the chief photographer for Emberstowne's history, it seems like this sort of project would excite him, too."

"Yeah," Wes said. "I don't get it. He'll come around, though. He gets upset in a flash then settles down pretty quickly. Before you know it, he'll be at your house—all smiles and sweetness—and you won't be able to get rid of him."

"Ooh," I said with a heavy dose of sarcasm. "I can't wait." I checked the time. "I'm sure you have plenty of things you'd rather be doing than hanging out at work after hours," I said, "but if you wouldn't mind me taking a quick peek at Marshfield's floor plans before I go—"

"I keep the historical society open late a couple nights a week. This is one of them, so no worries. And I think we can safely assume that David won't be back tonight."

"By the way, I meant to ask you about that jar we saw here the other day."

Wes carried the scrapbooks across the room and slid them onto a high shelf. Turning to face me, he repeated, "Jar?"

"The one you thought was David Cherk's developing liquid."

I watched understanding dawn. "Oh yeah. I remember. What about it?"

"Did he ever say what it really was?"

"I never thought to ask him about it. Maybe you should, next time you see him."

I gave him a withering look. "Oh sure. That'll go over well."

"The thing is, everybody in town knows about your reputation for finding answers when the police can't. Your tenacity is legendary."

"Give me a break."

"I'm serious. I told you before that David is odd, but I don't think he's a killer. Still, if he's taking pains to avoid you, you may want to tread carefully."

I'd come to the same conclusion myself. "We're changing the subject, right now. Let's look at those Marshfield blueprints."

Wes walked across the entire length of the room again, this time with keys in hand. I followed until he stopped behind a glass case that held an assortment of Marshfield memorabilia.

"Wait," I said. "The plans have been on display all this time? How did I miss them?" I walked around to the front of the case. "Where are they?"

He bent forward from the waist and unlocked the back of the display. "We keep them in a drawer underneath. There's too much chance of sun damage otherwise, and besides, blueprints are meant to be pored over. There's no joy in looking at them through glass."

He pulled out a set of plans that had to be three times as big as my house's were. Bound in cracked blue leather, they were at least two feet long by eighteen inches wide.

Wes's strained voice gave me an idea of how heavy the book must be. "This is one set. Take a look." He gestured with his eyes as he carried the plans over to the countertop, the only place in the office that was big enough to open it on. "There are separate books for each section of the house and grounds."

I walked around to the back of the case and crouched to peer in. There were at least five other leather-bound sets of plans inside. "Wow," I said. "This is like finding hidden treasure."

"You've never seen these?"

I joined him at the counter. "We do have floor plans at Marshfield. Lots of them. But they look nothing like this."

He opened the cover, sending a quick burst of mustiness

up to tickle our noses. "I'm sure your boss, Bennett Marshfield, has a set or two in that mansion of his."

I leaned over to peek at the drawings. "What part of the house is this?"

He pointed to faint lettering at the top of the page. "This says ENTRANCE HALL. We may have to go through a few of these before we find the one for the basement area where the party was held."

I felt a pang of guilt. "Am I keeping you from anything?"

He waved a hand at me. "Not at all. I live for this kind of stuff." Bending down, he pushed his glasses higher on his nose and began turning the enormous pages, very slowly. His head came up. "Am I keeping *you* from anything?"

"My cat, Bootsie, is probably waiting for me, but otherwise I'm clear."

He nodded. "Good. Now, let's see what we have here."

It turned out that the first of the Marshfield blueprint books we'd chosen was the right one. "Here," I said when we were about halfway through it. Little by little, I'd gotten better at deciphering the handwriting on each page, and when we reached the first page of BELOWGROUND, I paid closer attention.

There were schematics of all sorts, and the two of us, heads together over the open book, tried to make sense of it all. The office was silent, save for the buzzing of the overhead fluorescent lights and the gentle turn of pages.

"Hey," he said. "I'm no expert, but take a look."

I shifted my attention from reading margin notes to the spot he indicated. "What is that?"

We were open to a page that held the plans for the room we'd used as an auditorium—the room where Leland Keay had died. Wes pointed to a rectangle set in the narrowest part of the room. From what I could tell, it would have been positioned behind the temporary stage Cherk had set up.

"I don't know," he said very slowly. His finger traced along the plan to the outer margin, where a scissor-like contraption was drawn, twice, from different angles. Reminding me a lot of an oversized, old-fashioned car jack, it was attached to a rectangular platform in both pictures. One showed the scissor mechanism extended, the other showed it condensed.

"It says WOOD ELEVATOR," I said.

"A wood elevator?" Wes repeated. As though we could read each other's minds, we straightened and looked at each other. Wood elevators were sometimes installed in the homes of the very well off so that servants wouldn't be required to lug fireplace timber in from outside. It saved the servants from having to brave the weather whenever replenishment was required, and it saved the wealthy residents from having to witness the task as it was being completed.

Marshfield had several wood elevators that I knew of. There was a large one in the banquet hall, and others scattered in first-floor rooms. Marshfield had far more basement space than we'd used for the party and the wood for these other elevators was loaded from those locations.

Such elevators weren't precisely the same as secret passages or hidden rooms, but this—if it existed in the room itself and not just on paper—would provide access to the auditorium in a way no one had known about. Not only that, but because supplies were to be loaded from below, that suggested there was another level beneath the auditorium. One I was unaware of.

"Oh my gosh," I said as the implications became obvious. "Bennett didn't know this existed?"

"Apparently not. Or he forgot. If it fell out of use when he was young, he may have never even known it was there."

There were additional pages showing the device from every angle. Clearly, this drawing would have been instrumental to the builder, if the mechanism had been built, that is.

Wes kept shaking his head. "You know what this means, right?"

"That there might be another way in, yes," I said. "But

who could have known about it?" I thought about the workers at Marshfield. We'd had a staff meeting the day after the murder and we'd asked them all to come forward with any leads. No one had.

"Maybe no one did," Wes said. "Maybe this is a coincidence."

In my heart, I didn't believe it was. My brain was reeling with possibilities. "I'll have to check with Bennett to see if he knows where Marshfield's plans are kept. Someone may have accessed them right under our noses. Or—" I pulled my hair high atop my head as I thought of another possibility. "You said that David Cherk had been studying these recently."

Wes blinked slowly. Nodded. "Yeah, he has."

"I have to let Flynn know about this."

Wes stared out the door. "Do you really think David is guilty?"

I held up my hands. "Has anyone else been in to study these plans?"

He shook his head. Then said, "Wait."

I waited.

"Someone else *has* been studying these." His eyes were wide, as though he didn't believe it.

"Who?"

"Joyce Swedburg," he said, looking as surprised to say her name as I was to hear it. "She came in several times and requested these. Now that I think about it, the fact that she, or David, had this book out last is probably why it was on top. Why it was the first one we pulled out."

Breathless, I said aloud what I knew we were both thinking. "That means Joyce Swedburg could have stolen into the party, after all. Joyce may have killed Keay."

Chapter 21

BENNETT, FRANCES, AND I GATHERED IN THE party room of Marshfield's basement the next morning. The space, which had been so bright and glittering the night of the fund-raiser, was now bare and quiet. Even though there were only three of us here at the moment, the patter of our steps echoed in the naked space as we made our way into the auditorium.

I'd asked Wes if I could borrow the blueprints and he'd been happy to oblige. The giant books were, in essence, binders. Working carefully last night, we'd managed to extricate the important pages from the heavy leather volumes. We'd replace them later. Pointing at them now, I said, "Take a look here."

Bennett stood over my left shoulder, Frances my right. Having donned her glasses, she held them low on her nose, using the fingers of her right hand. "I don't know what you're talking about. It's a bunch of lines."

Bennett ignored her. "I see," he said, drawing a finger along the rectangle's perimeter. "This looks like it was part of the original plans, but I have no recollection of it being used, and certainly no knowledge of it even being here."

Frances scoffed as she stepped away. "Look at this place. It's solid." She stamped a heel on the ground as though to emphasize her point. The fact that she wore soft-soled shoes lessened the impact.

"Starting without me? Why am I not surprised?"

We all turned at the sound of Flynn's voice.

"Yes, we're investigating this all by ourselves," I answered in kind. "That's exactly why I asked you to come down here this morning. So you could catch us in the act."

"I wouldn't put it past you," he said. With a particularly malevolent glare at Frances, he added, "Any of you."

"Now that we've gotten our day's quota of insults in, can we get started?" I asked.

Flynn gave a bony shrug, as though nothing I could say would ever matter to him. "What, exactly, are we looking at here?"

I explained what Wes and I had found in the blueprints the prior evening. "It's a wood elevator," I said. "A platform designed to be lowered, loaded with wood, and then raised again. The top would blend in with the floor well enough for it not to be noticed. Most of the wood elevators installed in mansions are set up to bring their supplies to living rooms, dining rooms, and studies. Having one in the basement is a bit unusual."

"Skip the history lesson," he said. "Where is it?"

"We haven't found it yet," I said. "We waited for you to show up. Remember?"

I hated the fact that Flynn and I were at each other's throats nonstop. Still, he was eager to solve this murder and he'd brought information to me even when he didn't have to. I wasn't fooled into believing he viewed me as an equal. It served his purposes to keep me in the loop, but I appreciated the inclusion nonetheless.

"Let's see." He held his hand out and I gave him the

blueprints, expecting him to ask for clarification. After a few moments of study, however, he surprised me by looking up and saying, "If this apparatus is still in place and functional, this may be exactly the lead we've been looking for."

"I'm glad you agree," I said, relieved that he hadn't pooh-poohed my contribution the way he normally did.

He pointed downward. "What's under here?"

Bennett's hands opened then spread, as though he were trying to lift the answers from the ground beneath. "When Grace called me to arrange this meeting, I had my butler, Theo, summon the engineering staff in the entrance hall. I asked them, point-blank, if they were aware of any space, or access, beneath this part of the basement."

"And?" Flynn asked.

Bennett held up both index fingers and tilted slightly to address the young detective. "We have other sections of the home with multiple subbasements, some of which are key to proper maintenance, and some of which are never used anymore. This section, however, has no other access that they know of."

Perhaps reacting to the question that he knew Flynn would ask next, Bennett continued, "The engineering team consists of one director, two managers, and a staff of twenty. I spoke to the three in charge. I trust these individuals, and they trust their subordinates. They have, however, assured me that they will question each and every employee to find out what he or she might know."

Flynn took in the information. "Have you asked them to search for the access point?"

Bennett shook his head. "One thing I've learned from you, Detective Flynn, is that crime scenes must be protected so that any evidence they possess can be preserved and processed correctly. My staff is available to assist if you need them, but Grace and I believed that the investigation would be better served with you in charge."

Flynn's brows jumped fractionally. He cleared his throat

and reclaimed his scowling demeanor. "That was good thinking."

"I would suggest," Bennett said, "that we attempt to locate this wood elevator from in here. I am utterly stumped as to where to search for access to an underground area beneath this room."

Flynn must have used up all his positive reinforcement for the day because he turned to Frances and snarled. "What are you here for? To take notes?"

She'd dropped her glasses to her chest when Flynn had arrived. Now they swung side to side from their jeweled chain as she took two lumbering steps toward him. "Do you really want to get into a battle with me, young man?"

Flynn's face changed, yet again. As though calculating how much he could get away with. I wanted to remind him that she was a world-champion gossip, and if there was anything in his life that wasn't perfectly squeaky-clean, she'd find it and use it to her advantage. He wasn't afraid of her, but maybe he should be. Or maybe he was always squeaky-clean.

Note to self: Ask Frances what she knows about him. Not that I'd ever use it, of course. Fingers crossed behind my back, I smiled.

"What's with you?" Flynn asked.

"Ready to start searching is all," I said, then added, "It's funny, isn't it? We stumbled upon a passage in my house that I never knew existed and here we're looking for a specific one that we're not sure was even ever installed."

"Hilarious," Flynn said. Still holding on to the plans, he paced out a rectangle based on where it looked to be on the blueprints. He bounced his heel against the wood floor and grimaced at the solid sound. "That doesn't tell us much."

"If there is a wood elevator in here," Bennett said, "there would be a mechanism to activate it from within the room." He glanced around. "Probably on one of the walls. In the other areas, our controls are at about this height." He indicated a spot on the wall between his shoulder and elbow.

This was the narrowest part of the large room, the section that had been screened by the temporary curtains and that had served as backstage. I thought, again, about how David Cherk had insisted on setting up the presentation area at this end. While it made sense aesthetically to do it that way, the fact that Dr. Keay had disappeared in this spot now added a potentially malicious intent behind the eccentric photographer's choice.

Bennett began searching the stage-right wall, Frances the one at stage left, and Flynn the one between. They were solid brick and, to my untrained eye, looked perfectly set. I couldn't detect an aberration or misplaced block anywhere. I focused on the floor. We hadn't discussed who would do what; we'd all simply started in.

"Who puts a wooden floor in a basement?" Frances mumbled to herself.

"Rich people," Flynn replied without turning. "People who don't have to worry about their basement flooding every time there's a thunderstorm." Still skimming his fingers along the wall, without looking at me, he added. "Nothing suspicious about that, of course."

Bennett made eye contact with me. "I'm relieved to hear you say so."

I remembered thinking about how the floor in this part of the basement reminded me of the top floors of an old-fashioned department store. Creaky and old, they were not so scarred as to make them unsightly. In fact, wear gave them character. I thought about the squeaks the floor made when stepped on in certain areas. Wouldn't noise suggest an air pocket beneath? Wouldn't a wooden floor installed on a solid foundation remain silent?

I didn't know. I wasn't a builder and there was no one in the room with enough expertise to ask. Concentrating on where the top of the platform ought to be if the wood elevator had been installed according to the plans, I got down on my hands and knees to look closer.

Tucking my skirt in behind me, I lowered my face sideways to the floor. I was hoping to spot a perfect rectangle of unevenness, sticking out like a car door that hadn't closed all the way. No luck. The wooden slats of the floor weren't precisely aligned, or even, but I couldn't detect an out-of-place pattern. To me it looked like a well-worn floor, spied sideways.

I scooched around to try from another angle. Still nothing.

Bennett and Flynn were very quiet as they worked. Frances, however, let loose with regular, exasperated sighs. I ignored her.

Maybe I was going about this the wrong way. I got to my knees and stared down. The oak boards that made up the floor were of varying lengths. They had beveled edges, and that made finding a pattern where boards might split among them all the more difficult.

For some reason this wood elevator—if it existed—was different from the rest of those in Marshfield Manor. The rest of them blended into their floors, but were fairly easily spotted, even if you didn't know what to look for. Why not this one? Was it because Bennett's grandfather *wanted* it to be hard to find?

Flynn interrupted my thoughts. "I've been over this wall twice and there's nothing. This is a waste of time."

I opened my mouth to chastise him about giving up too easily, but Bennett spoke first. He walked over to the detective. "Tell you what, young man. My eyes are older. I may have missed something on my wall. Why don't you go over it and double-check me?"

Flynn didn't argue. "Fine. You can check that other wall while I'm at it, but I'm telling you there's nothing there."

"I believe you," Bennett said. "Frances, how is it going over there?"

She made a noise, but didn't turn around. Bennett gave me a "What did I expect?" look and began scrutinizing the wall Flynn had just left.

They went silent again as I returned to my ruminations. What if this elevator was not meant to be used for wood? What if it had been identified as such in the plans, but its purpose was something more guarded? That would help explain why it was proving difficult to find and why Bennett didn't know about it.

I got to my feet and slapped my hands together to clear off the dust.

Flynn turned. "Giving up?"

"No."

"Then what?"

"Give me a minute," I said. We'd left the plans on the floor nearby. I picked them up and paid closer attention to the distance between the wall and where this wood elevator was supposed to be. I might be a few feet off, I realized. I moved closer to the back wall and decided to try again.

A thought occurred to me. What if the rectangular platform wasn't a true rectangle? What if the designer and the crew who'd installed it had followed the shapes and edges of the wood slats that made up the floor in order to make it blend in better? If they'd done that, there would be virtually no way to detect it if you didn't know where it was.

I felt a rush of excitement. "Does anyone have anything solid, like a pen or a heavy keychain, with them?" I asked.

Flynn turned, his face impassive. "What have you found?"

"Nothing yet," I said.

Bennett pulled a Swiss Army knife from his pants pocket. "Will this help?" He handed it over.

"I didn't know you carried this," I said.

"Old habits die hard."

Flynn had stopped to watch. Keeping the knife closed, I resumed my spot on the floor and began tapping the edge of it against the boards.

"Try this instead." He pulled out a black, cylindrical piece of plastic, about eight inches long and an inch or so wide with several raised ridges. He brought it over to me.

"What is it?"

He yanked the tip, extending it. "You've never seen a police baton?"

I took it from him. "It's heavy."

"It's supposed to be."

I returned the knife to Bennett and resumed my floor-tapping. I looked up to find the three of them watching me. "It's an experiment," I said. "You can keep working on the walls if you like; I want to try this for a while."

Using the blueprint as my guide, I returned to tapping the floor with the edge of the baton, slowly moving in a straight line perpendicular to the back wall, listening for changes in sound.

"I thought you said you had no idea how a floor would sound if there was nothing under it," Frances said.

I stopped long enough to send her a look of disdain. "I've never done anything like this before," I said. "How do I know what I don't know? Maybe I'll figure it out. The only certainty is that I'll never know if I don't try."

She scowled.

Tap, tap, tap.

My mind floated with random thoughts. Flynn and Frances were such crankypants. Maybe that's why they got under my skin so often. And then I thought about Adam. Quite the opposite personality.

Tap, tap, tap.

Allowing my mind to wander helped the tapping become background noise. Every tap sounded the same. Every single one.

Tap, tap. Tup.

Tup?

"Did you hear that?" I asked.

Silly question. They'd all heard it. "Do it again," Bennett said.

I tapped again, recreating the sound. "There it is."

Inching forward a bit I hit the baton against the floor. No

hollow sound this time. "But look," I pointed out when their expressions fell, "the board ended right there. Maybe if I try over here—"

I smacked the end of the baton along the edge of the first board to the right. Solid, solid, hollow.

Ecstatic, I said, "There's a pattern!"

"You call that a pattern?" Flynn's tone was dismissive, but his eyes sparked with interest.

I had an idea. "Frances, would you mind going upstairs and grabbing a roll of tape?"

She made her way over. Now that things were getting interesting, she looked miffed to have to leave. "What for?"

I shot her an impatient glare. "Just, please."

She held her pudgy hands high. "Fine. I'll be right back."

While she was gone, I continued my search for the faint echo-y sounds as I painstakingly made my way, one board at a time, parallel to the back wall.

"Help me remember which boards sounded different, okay?" I asked Bennett and Flynn. They got down on their knees next to me, placing their fingers along the crevices. Frances returned quickly.

"They had this at the front desk," she said, handing me a roll of duct tape. She must have read my expression because her tone became defensive. "What's wrong with it?"

"Nothing," I said, embarrassed to have to explain. "I'm not a fan of duct tape, is all." I thought about how many times my dad had used it to fix things—in the most unsightly way possible—when I was a kid. "I don't like the way it looks."

"Oh, and appearances are so important right now?" She lifted her hands high. "A thousand apologies. I'll go find *prettier* tape."

"That's not what I meant. Forget I said anything. Thank you, Frances."

Taking it from her, I ripped off a six-inch piece and placed it along the edge where I'd first encountered a *tup* where I'd expected a *tap*. We continued marking the hollow lines with tape as I progressed. Now that I knew what I was looking for, we moved pretty quickly. In a little more than fifteen minutes, we had a rough—and ugly—outline of duct tape on the floor.

The four of us stood to examine what we'd identified.

"Looks like a homicide chalk drawing," Flynn said. "For a giant murdered puzzle piece."

I laughed. "It does."

The puzzle piece, about three feet long and about four feet wide, was far smaller than I'd expected.

Bennett strolled around the shape. "If this is a wood elevator, it's not a very efficient one."

"My thoughts exactly," I said. "Whoever designed this took pains to keep it hidden. Otherwise, why so much effort to have it blend in?"

"We don't know it's an elevator," Flynn reminded us. "We could have done all this for nothing."

Frances huffed. "Well, aren't you the Negative Nellie."

This from Frances?

"You know," I said to reclaim their attention, "if this is supposed to be hidden, maybe the switch to operate it is hidden as well." To Bennett, I said, "The activating mechanisms are set at a convenient height on the main level. What if we checked the walls again, this time looking for something located at an *inconvenient* height?"

"Low or high?" Flynn asked.

Bennett and I answered in unison, "Low."

Frances sniffed. "I would have said that, too."

We started in again, this time all four of us working the walls. I was about to join Frances on the stage-left wall, but she gave me a look that told me she resented the implication that she couldn't find the thing on her own.

"Mind if I join you here?" I asked Bennett.

"You and your young eyes are most welcome, Gracie."

We all studied in silence for a few minutes until Frances

gave a whoop. I was startled by the triumphant sound, especially coming from her.

"I think this is it," she said. "Look, look."

She fairly danced as we hurried over. Using a chubby finger to point at a spot about eighteen inches off the ground, she said, "It's a fake brick. I could tell. It felt different, so I tried moving it and—See what I found!"

The woman was as happy as I'd ever seen her. I got to my knees to view the fake brick at eye level. Flynn crouched next to me. Bennett stood behind.

"Don't crowd me out now. Not after I was the one who found it," Frances said. On her knees, she muscled her way between me and Flynn.

I ran my fingers along the outside of the fake brick. It jiggled.

"What are you waiting for?" Flynn said. "Open it."

The fake brick was a small door with hinges along its upper edge. I lifted the door to find two round buttons—one black, one white, identical to the switches that controlled the wood elevators upstairs. The white one was depressed. The black one stuck out.

"I'm going to press it," I said.

"Amazing," Bennett said.

Frances chimed in. "And I found it, remember."

I could feel the tingle of fear and excitement rushing up my back as I knelt there, finger poised. "Is everybody ready?"

"For crying out loud, woman," Flynn said. He jammed his thumb, hard, onto the black button.

I'd expected a *thunk*, a *whirr*, the hum of a motor. Expectantly, we all turned around, disappointed by the utter quiet.

Nothing.

I started to say, "I was so sure."

But the floor shifted. Silently, it began to lower.

Frances's mouth hung open. I could hear her breathing. "Will you look at that," she said.

Flynn's right hand went for his holster and he thrust an

arm out to urge us all back. Only Bennett seemed unsurprised. "Well done, Grace."

"What do you mean?" Frances asked, having regained her composure. "I'm the one who found the fake brick."

"Yes, of course, Frances. We couldn't have done it without you."

She gave a self-satisfied nod.

The perimeter we'd drawn out with duct tape—the puzzle-piece shape in the floor—dropped out of sight faster than I would have expected. Much faster than the home's other wood elevators.

We disregarded Flynn's orders to stay back and approached the edge of the opening as the platform slipped downward, then stopped.

"Wow," Frances said.

Bennett nodded. "Indeed."

I flashed back to the moment immediately before I'd entered the secret passage in my basement. What was it with hidden tunnels lately?

"I'm going in," Flynn said. "You all stay here."

"I'm going with you," I said.

He glared at me. "We don't know what we'll find. You'd better not."

"I doubt the killer is hiding down there. It's been almost a week."

Bennett cleared his throat. "I would feel better if we waited for one of our security team to accompany the detective. Frances, please give them a call, would you?"

"Frances, wait," I said. I placed my hand on Bennett's arm. "I'll be fine, honest. I need to know where this goes. I need to be part of this."

"Gracie, you get too involved with these things. You put yourself in danger."

"But I'm not going alone this time. Detective Flynn is with me." Bennett's jaw was set, but I sensed he was about to relent. It wasn't as though he could forbid me from going down there, of course, but I was always reluctant to risk angering him.

Flynn had dropped into the abyss.

"We'll be right back," I said, "I promise."

Bennett worked his jaw. "Don't be long."

Frances made a clucking noise. "That girl never listens, does she?"

Chapter 22

THE ODD-SHAPED OPENING IN THE FLOOR meant that there were only a couple of places wide enough for me to sit at the edge. Seeing as how I was in a skirt, I couldn't simply jump in the way Flynn had. Not if I wanted to maintain my dignity. I found one decent-sized spot, sat, and tucked my skirt's fabric around my legs as they dangled into the darkness. I thought again about the secret passage we'd discovered at my house, and how dark it had been inside.

"We should get a flashlight," I said.

Flynn's voice was a couple of feet away. "Have one. Come on."

There was enough ambient light from the auditorium to let me see down to the bottom. I eased myself forward and braced my hands on the side of the opening, elbows bent. "Here goes," I said, and dropped in.

I stumbled, but didn't fall. Good thing I was wearing flats.

The space was a little deeper than I'd imagined at first, about six feet down. When Flynn had gone in, he'd landed in a crouch and stayed that way before moving out of sight. I could see that there was a tunnel ahead of us, lit only by the skinny beam of Flynn's flashlight.

He turned around. "You okay?" he asked.

"Yes, fine. What's down there?"

"Gracie, be careful," Bennett said from above.

"First rule," Flynn said. "Don't touch a thing. Here." He dug out two pair of latex gloves and two sets of paper booties. He handed one set of each to me. "Put these on."

"How much stuff do you carry?" I asked. "You had the baton, the flashlight, now all this."

He didn't answer. Instead, he hollered up to Frances to call the department and request an evidence team.

"Now?" she asked. I could tell she'd done that to irk him. It worked.

"Yes, now. Grace and I will do our best not to disturb anything. This still may not have anything to do with the murder, but I don't want to take chances."

I stepped off the platform, surprised to find that the floor down here wasn't dirt, like in my home's hidden passage. This floor was solid. The walls were concrete and rounded, as though we were standing in an oversized storm drain. One tall enough to allow us both to walk upright.

It was dark in front of Flynn. I could only see about ten feet ahead. "Where do you think this leads?" he asked. He raised the light to the top of the circular space and traced it forward. "What's above us in the mansion in this direction?"

I had to stop to think. Getting my bearings, I pointed over my right shoulder. "That way is the front of the house, which means we're not far from the indoor swimming pool." I reached out to skim the concrete side with my fingers. "The deep end of the pool is probably on the other side of this wall."

"Maybe this is an access point for repairs?"

"Could be," I said, but I was doubtful and my tone conveyed as much. We continued to creep forward as the tunnel made a sharp left. "I'm pretty sure that up ahead and to the right above us would be the Birdcage Room. There's not much between here and there except—" I stopped myself.

"Except what?"

"There's another passage that leads from the underground parking into the basement of the mansion. The employee entrance."

He didn't comment. The circular walkway we were in wasn't wide enough for us to continue side by side, so I kept behind him. Now that it had become clear that the ceiling wasn't about to collapse in on us, we'd even picked up the pace. So far I guessed we'd traveled about fifty feet, which meant we were still underneath the house.

"It smells like something. What do you think it is?" he asked.

I lifted my head a little and took in a deep whiff. "Whiskey?"

Flynn half turned. I could see the pleased look on his face. "Same thing I thought." He stopped and glanced around. "When the evidence team gets here, I'll have them look for the source."

We found ourselves at a dead end—a flat iron wall with no discernible door—less than a minute later.

Flynn groaned. "Another puzzle to solve?"

"There has to be a way out," I said. "And I'll bet this one isn't so hard to find. I mean, whoever built this didn't want people to know about it, so they took precautions to keep the mechanism from being easily detected. But once a person was down here, I'm betting they wanted to keep things simple."

I stepped into the flashlight's beam and placed my hands on the circular iron wall, about where a doorknob would be. All I felt was cool, coarse metal. I moved my fingers a little higher up, then higher again. I was at about the mid-space between elbows and shoulders when I found it.

"Here we go," I said.

Flynn came around me, directing his light straight on.

There was a latch like the kind you might see inside a walk-in freezer, the kind where you lift the handle in order to open the door, only much smaller. Rather than have him push past me again, I decided to let him do the honors. "Go ahead. You know you want to."

"Stand back."

Yeah, like I was really going to do that.

He lifted the latch and pushed the door open. I blinked.

We weren't in sunshine, but were definitely outdoors. A gust carrying the scent of fresh-cut grass rolled past us. We heard mowers in the distance. There was an underlying smell of hot, wet greenery, with a sweet twist of honeysuckle. The passageway opened into what felt like a mossy, underground cave with trailing vines covering its sunny mouth. From what I could tell, we were southeast of where we'd started.

I wondered how a spot like this could have gone unnoticed by our caretakers for so long. I'd have to ask them about it. But for now I needed to see where the light was coming from.

Flynn had remained silent but now swung his arm out, stopping me from pushing through the branches and shrubs that had blocked the opening.

"We've established that this leads to the outside. That's good enough for me for now. Let's go back."

"Don't you want to see where we are?"

He gestured for me to return to the dark passageway. "Our evidence techs will be able to tell if anyone has been through those weeds recently. If you and I go traipsing through there, we'll muck it all up for them."

"Good point," I said.

"I know what I'm doing. Even though you and your assistant don't think I do."

"That's not fair."

He turned, briefly. "Isn't it?"

There was a look in his eyes at that moment that I hadn't expected. For that half second it was as though I could see how Frances and I must appear to him. Amateurs poking their noses in. Solving murders and putting themselves in danger. More to the point, in his mind, we undermined his authority. Regularly.

"We never intend to get involved," I said to his back.

I saw him shrug. He flicked the flashlight back on, and we used it until the sharp turn. At that point there was enough light streaming in from above where we'd left Bennett and Frances. He shut it off again.

"Seriously. I realize I've probably been a pain in your side—"

He made an indescribable noise that conveyed "That's an understatement."

"You have to admit that we've helped. Whether we intended to be part of your investigation or not, the fact is that a lot of recent murders were solved because we got involved."

He spun and spoke in a low voice. "I would have been able to solve every single case without your help."

His brows were tight, and even in the dim light I could see the shimmer of fury burning in his eyes.

I chose to say nothing.

"But because you and your wicked witch assistant jump in, no one gives our department any credit. It's all you. All because of you. And the media eats that right up."

I hadn't realized how much antipathy Flynn held smoldering in there. I probably should have, but I'd always reasoned that the end justified the means. "I've never looked to take credit. What difference does it make as long as the killer is brought to justice?"

Still talking softly, he said, "It matters to me."

"That's why you're including us this time, isn't it?" The light was beginning to dawn. If he included us, then he would be able to control the message. If this murder was solved successfully, he could bask in the glow of a job well done.

"It's all about the attention," I said as we neared the opening. Borrowing from Frances, I said, *"Tsk,"* then added, "I expected better from you."

"What do you mean by that?"

Rather than answer, I brushed past him and stood on the platform, looking up. Bennett and Frances seemed relieved to see us. "When Flynn joins me aboard the platform top, how about you hit that button?" I said to Frances. "I'm sure this will hold us both, and I'd much prefer riding than having to climb up there in a skirt."

Chapter 23

BENNETT DROPPED BY MY OFFICE SHORTLY before the end of the day. I was on the phone with Ronny Tooney at the time and I gestured to Bennett to sit, letting him know I wouldn't be long.

Even though I knew that Flynn was looking into where the moonshine had come from that had killed Keay, I didn't think it would hurt for our would-be private eye to lend a hand as well. Given our recent conversation, I'd been surprised when I'd broached the idea to Flynn and he'd agreed. "Go ahead," he'd said. "We have limited resources. And those moonshiners can spot a cop a mile away. Tooney might actually have better luck."

Now, talking with the man on the phone, I reminded him to stay out of trouble. "All we're looking for is who might have bought the alcohol," I said. "I'm not interested in shutting the moonshiners down."

"I'll bet Flynn would be, though," Tooney said.

"Be careful, okay?"

He promised he would.

When we hung up, Bennett asked, "So? Big plans this weekend?"

Frances had followed him in and watched me closely as I answered. "Except for figuring out what to do with the secret passage in my house, no, nothing special."

He smiled. "A young woman like you should be out enjoying herself on her days off."

"With my house in the state it's in—half-finished, with people running in and out constantly—I'm better off staying put."

As he settled himself into one of the wing chairs and indicated for Frances to join us, he asked, "Are the evidence technicians still here?"

"They left about twenty minutes ago," I told him. Frances nodded. "They took a load of samples from the passageway and, at least according to what Flynn told us, found two unlabeled jars that may have held alcohol."

"The killer left evidence behind? That seems sloppy."

"Not if he or she didn't expect us to find the trapdoor."

"True enough," Bennett agreed. "Have you seen where the tunnel ends? You said it opened to the outside. I can't imagine where."

I'd been surprised. "You know where the employee entrance is? Not where we pull in, but the underground walkway that leads into the basement?"

He nodded. Frances had gone with me to look, so she already knew all this.

"The drain tile, or whatever it was we walked through, crisscrosses directly above that. They occupy the same underground space at different levels."

"How did we never hear of this before?"

Earlier, I'd pulled out the floor plans we regularly consulted whenever a structural question came up. They were still on my desk, rolled up on my right. I opened them and indicated the spot where the employee walkway had been constructed.

"I checked back in the records. When this construction was going on, the crew found what they described as an extra-large drain tile—exactly what Flynn and I walked through today. Because they were reluctant to mess with drainage, the decision was made to not attempt to relocate it. They simply dug the walkway a little deeper. Other than that mention, I can find no record of it."

"My grandfather had to have been aware."

I nodded. "That would be my assumption."

"I have a few records of my own. Diaries from my father and grandfather. I'll have a look and let you know if I come up with anything."

"I'd appreciate that. It's a mystery."

"And we know you can't let any of those go unsolved, don't we?" he asked.

"Don't distract her," Frances said to Bennett. "You know she can't resist anything to do with Marshfield history." She crossed her arms. "But none of that will help us find the murderer. The jars, now maybe that's a clue."

"You're right, Frances," I said. "But it's interesting and I'd like to know why the passage is there. What's key here is knowing who else knew about it."

"Joyce Swedburg, for one." Frances beamed. "What did I tell you? I knew she did it. I knew it. Convenient for her to get sick that night, wasn't it?"

"Flynn did say the attack was personal," I said.

Bennett chimed in. "And whoever killed Keay clearly planned this well in advance."

"Serena told us that Dr. Keay told her he was going to meet someone. I wish I knew who that was."

Frances gave a condescending snort. "If we knew that, we'd have the murder solved by now, wouldn't we?" She gave Bennett a look that seemed to ask how oblivious I could be sometimes, and went on. "According to Flynn, who questioned Serena a couple more times, the young lady has nothing more to offer. She said that Keay never told her who he was meeting. A dead end. Now, Joyce, on the other hand—she knew about this secret way in. I think she's worth another look."

"We know that Joyce studied the plans. We don't know if she knew about the trapdoor elevator," I corrected her. "That makes David Cherk a likely suspect as well because he studied the plans before the party, too."

"He did that because he was presenting here." She sniffed. "Perfectly acceptable reason."

"Having a reason to examine the plans doesn't exonerate Cherk, Frances. In fact, it's an ideal cover for a crime like this."

Bennett stood. "Time for me to head back upstairs, but one of the things we need to think about is what David Cherk might have had against Dr. Keay."

"I don't know of anything," Frances said.

Neither did I.

"See?" she said, reading my expression. "It was Joyce. I've been right from the very start."

AT HOME, AFTER THE WORKERS LEFT FOR THE day, I changed into yoga pants and a stretched-out T-shirt before heading into the kitchen to make dinner. As I donned an apron and assembled my ingredients for one of my go-to recipes, chicken with mushroom sauce, I jotted on a piece of scrap paper notes that had nothing to do with the menu and everything to do with recent revelations.

All possible suspects made the list: Joyce, David, Serena, plus a couple of the doctors who had been in attendance at the fund-raiser. I considered them all for a moment and then added Todd Pedota's name. Even though he seemed to have gotten past his anger at Dr. Keay, you never really knew what someone held deep in his heart. People showed you their best selves, and often the truth lay hidden until they were presented with the right moment to act.

Perhaps this had been the opportunity for revenge he'd been waiting for. He didn't seem like a murderer to me, but then again, who did?

I hadn't intended to think about the murder case tonight—I'd planned to relax my brain and put my feet up. Stepping away from a problem for a while often helped me find answers. But tonight I simply couldn't quiet my mind. I knew why, of course: the discovery of Marshfield's secret passage with the hidden elevator. That had certainly widened the net on possible suspects, which was why Joyce and Todd had made it onto my list. I hated to have to admit it, but Frances's contention that it was Joyce who'd done the deed was beginning to be our best guess.

The chicken I'd braised was warming in the oven and the mushroom sauce had almost thickened completely when the doorbell rang.

Bootsie looked up at me as if to say, "Who can it be?" before trotting off to find out.

"Good luck answering the door without opposable thumbs," I called to her departing figure as I shut off the burners, covered the pan, and wiped my hands on my apron.

At the front door, I peeked out the side window, forgetting that the porch lights were out of commission. The old fixture had been removed in the renovation. A new one had been ordered but hadn't yet been installed. Even though it wasn't true dark yet, dusk had begun to settle, and with the shade of the trees blocking ambient light, I couldn't quite make out who it was on my doorstep. All I could tell was that the person had half turned away.

The heavy wooden door—Hillary hadn't decided whether to replace or repair this yet—squeaked as I opened it and Adam spun to face me, holding a heavy armload of gorgeous blooms.

I laughed as he handed them to me. "Oh my gosh, what are you doing here?"

He took a step backward, and even in the dim light I

could see a hint of doubt flicker in his eyes. "I don't mean to intrude, and if this isn't a good time for you, I can go."

"I'm glad you're here," I said. And I was. "I just wasn't expecting you." I held the door open. "Come in. Please."

"You're sure?"

I turned to give Bootsie a warning glare not to run out, but she'd scampered onto a nearby table to get a better view. "I'm not really dressed for this." I pushed the door open wider. "But I'd love company and I made dinner. Are you hungry?"

"Starved. I'd planned to take you out, if you were willing." He sniffed the air. "But it smells great and if you've already gone to all that trouble—"

Adam was a big guy. Although not so tall as to be required to duck through doorways, he didn't leave a lot of clearance. He had bold features, a full head of dark hair, and creased, pockmarked skin. When I'd first met him, he'd sported a chunky diamond stud in one ear, and had been carrying a long black wig. The leader of the rock band SlickBlade, Adam had turned out to be as far from the rocker, partyer stereotype as I could have imagined. I'd learned that during his downtime, his three favorite pursuits were reading, experimenting in the kitchen, and touring historical landmarks. Lately, he'd added a fourth: visiting me here in Emberstowne. A far cry from getting wasted at high-class New York bars with his younger bandmates.

He bent down to pick Bootsie up. "How's the little sweetheart?" he asked as he stroked under her chin. Her eyes closed and she purred loud enough for me to hear.

"You know," I said, as we made our way into the kitchen, "you don't have to bring me flowers when you come to visit."

He put Bootsie down gently and gave me a shy grin. "They make you smile," he said. "Every time."

"Did you ever think that maybe seeing you is what makes me smile?"

He blinked, as though struck by an electrical jolt. "Does it?"

Hope was raw in Adam's expression. This man had made it clear that he cared for me. I hadn't found it in me to return his feelings. Not yet.

I took a breath. I'd been about to say, "Yeah, it does," but my words skidded to a stop as—without warning—Jack's image popped into my brain. I hesitated.

"It's okay," he said with a look on his face that made me wonder if he could read my mind. The bright anticipation in his eyes faded and he worked up a smile. "No pressure."

"I am very happy to see you," I said, but we both knew my response was lame and two seconds too late.

What was wrong with me? Why had thoughts of Jack suddenly burst into my consciousness at that moment? I knew better than to try to sort my confusion out while we stood there staring at each other. Whatever I needed to work out, I would do on my own time. Not now, not after Adam had flown in for a surprise visit. The last thing I wanted to do was to hurt this man.

He had very expressive, very dark brows. They'd tightened for a moment, but he relaxed. "It's okay," he repeated. "We'll talk, maybe." He shrugged as though it made no difference. I knew better. "Or we won't. Right now let's enjoy the wonderful dinner you prepared."

He'd broken the tension between us, yet again. I'd shared some of my relationship history with him, and he'd shared some of his. I didn't know enough, however, to understand what in his life had given him the patience he consistently demonstrated with me.

Adam peeked under the pan cover and gave the mushroom sauce an appreciative sniff. "Mm-mm," he said.

"It's nearly ready," I said. "I need to warm the green beans." Pointing to the covered saucepan at the back of the stovetop, I asked, "Would you mind?"

"You have a spare apron?" He held fingers splayed in front

of his chest. "I wouldn't want to mess up this one-of-a-kind outfit."

I laughed at that. He was wearing a black T-shirt and black jeans. I'd rarely seen him in anything else. "Hey." I handed him a striped apron, as another thought occurred to me. "Do you have a bag? A suitcase? You are planning to stay, aren't you?"

Adam's eyes were wide open windows to his feelings, and for the second time this evening, I watched anticipation dance behind his outwardly calm expression. He tied his apron behind his back and shrugged again. "I didn't want to presume—"

"I have the spare room all ready for you," I said quickly, in case he'd mistaken my meaning. "You're welcome to it. How long can you stay?"

If the mention of the spare room disappointed him in any way, he didn't let it show. "A couple of days," he said. "If that's all right with you. I figured you'll have to go back to work Monday, and the band is overdue for rehearsal."

"No commitments this weekend?"

"We had a couple of things lined up, but when my aunt died I canceled them. The guys in the band weren't too thrilled with me for doing that, but family's family."

"How are the other guys?" I asked.

He shook his head. "No. You first. I want to hear all about what's been happening here."

As we finished preparing the meal and sat down to eat, I brought him up to speed on everything, providing details I hadn't had time to explain over the phone or via e-mail.

In the middle of the telling, he said, "Wait," around a mouthful of chicken. "Let me get this straight: You found two secret passages?"

"Two," I said. "Within a week."

He finished chewing. "Ever see that old movie *Where Angels Go, Trouble Follows*?"

"You mean the Rosalind Russell film?" I asked.

He speared another forkful and popped it into his mouth, then pointed the empty utensil at me.

"So, I'm an angel?" I worked up the best indignant look I could muster. "You'd better not be suggesting that I'm trouble."

He pursed his lips in mock denial. "Heaven forbid."

We discussed the murder and the shortlist of likely suspects for a while longer before I asked again what was new in his life. Adam had a few updates to share about his bandmates, all of whom I'd met, and he talked about their agent, a man whose name I'd recently helped clear.

"All in all, things are good," Adam said. "Jerry sends his regards."

"I'm glad to hear it."

We tidied the table, put the leftovers away for Bruce and Scott to enjoy when they got home, and as I started doing the dishes, Adam picked up a cloth to dry.

"You know," he said, suddenly shy again, "we've been opening for the Curling Weasels a lot here in the East. We may have the chance to open for them in L.A. If the Weasels' manager agrees, it would be a real game-changer."

"Wow," I said, "SlickBlade could become a household name."

"I'm a little afraid of that."

My hands were immersed up to my wrists in warm, sudsy water. I pulled them up to sponge a plate clean. "Isn't that the whole point? Isn't that what you've been working for all these years?" I rinsed the plate and glanced up at him.

His expression clouded as his dark brows tightened. When Adam frowned, it was a full-face effort. Deep lines formed around his downturned mouth and the crinkles around his eyes seemed to double. "I told you once that the guys are more into that stuff than I am."

"I know," I said, "but you also said that a measure of fame allows you to do what you've always wanted—to create music for others to enjoy."

"Exactly, but I'm torn. You know the guys I'm working with. They're great but their priorities are all screwed up." He finished drying one of the bowls and placed it gently on the cleared kitchen table. With a wry grin, he turned back to face me. "Like I should talk about anyone else's priorities and what's right or wrong. Who am I to judge?"

I gave an encouraging nod. "I know what you're trying to say."

"This is the most talented group of musicians I've ever worked with. We have a lot of potential. More than I'd ever dreamed of. The thing is, the guys look to me to lead. About—everything. I handle the bookings, the business. I keep them herded and as sober as I can when we're on the road. I'm like the band dad."

"There are worse roles in life."

"True." He picked up a plate as I turned on the faucet to rinse another dish. "Here's the thing. Another two years, maybe three, and I think SlickBlade will be at the top of its game. I think we'll have achieved enough to keep the guys happy and I think we will have earned enough to allow me to step into more of a consulting role."

I shut the faucet. "You'd stop performing?"

When he looked at me, he seemed to be trying to push every bit of meaning into his gaze. "I don't want to be on the road for the rest of my life. I want to write music and I want to see it performed, yes, but I don't have to be the one performing. I have life plans."

"You want a family."

He nodded and his lips pushed together as though he was afraid to say more, but then he added, "I want to settle down. Somewhere quiet."

"Like Emberstowne?"

"Yeah."

I'd held Adam at arm's length from the very start. Why he continued to pursue me, why he remained so patient and trusting when I'd given him almost no reason to do so, had me mystified. Yet, I enjoyed his company. Very much.

"After living in New York for so long, I'm afraid you'd find life dull here."

He studied me, as he often did. "I don't think I would."

I finished rinsing the final utensil, shut off the water again, and dried my hands. "Adam, you and I need to talk."

"We do," he said as he dried the last of the pile and untied his apron. "But not right now. Show me the secret passageway first."

Chapter 24

ADAM AND I HEADED OUT THE NEXT MORN-
ing to walk into town. As we exited the back door, I wagged
my finger at Bootsie. "You behave yourself for Aunt Hillary
today, okay?"

"Aunt Hillary?" Adam asked when I'd locked up. "When
did that happen?"

We made our way around to the front of the house,
where I waved hello to the workers who were setting up for
the day on my front porch. We took a left at the end of my
driveway. At breakfast, I'd asked Adam if he minded visiting the historical society offices this morning. He'd told me
that he was at my disposal for the entire weekend.

"I don't know what's come over Hillary," I said. "She's
here every day except Sunday, and has been tolerable for a
change."

Before he could respond, I placed a hand on his arm. "I
take that back. Tolerable makes it sound as though I still
can't stand her. That's not it at all. She's actually been

pleasant to be around. It's as though she's become a completely different person."

"People learn to adapt," Adam said, pulling my hand into the crook of his elbow. "That's been the rule of this world from the beginning of time: Change or die."

"Unfortunately, there's been far too much dying going on around here lately." I mulled that for a moment, then added, "I think it helps that Hillary knows the truth now. She's regarded me differently since she found out."

When that had happened, I'd expected Hillary to freak out. As Bennett's stepdaughter, she'd been vocal and vehement about trying to get Bennett to change his will. She wanted him to leave all of Marshfield to her, rather than bequeath it to the City of Emberstowne, as things were currently set up. If I were, indeed, related to Bennett by blood, that would put me higher on the heir scale than Hillary. Not that I wanted anything to do with an inheritance. If it were up to me, I would choose to have Bennett live forever.

Adam placed his hand over mine as we strolled. "She's probably beginning to realize you make a better ally than enemy."

"Could be," I agreed. "Let's hope her good feelings for me aren't temporary."

"My feelings for you aren't temporary," Adam said quietly. He didn't make eye contact and didn't react when I turned to face him. All he did was press his hand a little tighter against mine.

We walked in silence, and as we did, I tried to examine what it was that was holding me back from immersing myself fully in this relationship. I didn't want to lead Adam on if I wasn't interested, and yet, I didn't want to let go. There was something about the man that drew me in. He was kind, interesting, and insightful. But then why when I considered moving forward with him, did I suddenly think about Jack and freeze? I was confused.

"What are you hoping to find at the historical society office?" Adam asked, breaking into my thoughts.

I took in a deep breath and let it out in a sigh. "I'd planned to do a little research at the library, but I found out that they haven't digitized their files yet. Not fully, that is. At this point, searchable records go back only three years."

"What are you looking for?"

"Any mention of Dr. Keay in local publications from five years ago. Stories about the scandal, his time in jail, Joyce's role in getting him out on bail. Whatever I can find."

"They don't keep copies of newspapers from back then?"

"They do," I said, "but the library started sending old files off-site for scanning. They're working backward chronologically, which is why they have only the most recent three years done. The next set—which happens to be the time frame I'm interested in—is currently out of reach. But," I added, "the librarian assured me that the historical society still has quite a bit available in hard copy. I'm hoping to find what I'm looking for there."

"You don't mind me tagging along?"

"Hardly. I'm more worried you'll be bored out of your skull."

He tugged me a little bit closer. "No chance of that."

When we got to the historical society, Wes practically threw open the front door. "Did you hear the news?" he asked. "I was about to call you."

"What news?"

"Flynn." His face was flushed, his eyes wild. "He arrested Joyce Swedburg."

"What?" I asked, feeling slow. "When? How did you find out?"

"She came in and he arrested her." Wes pointed toward the floor. "Right here. They left like two minutes ago."

My head was spinning. "What did she come in for?"

He gave an exaggerated shrug. "I never got the chance to find out. She walked in, I said hello. I was about to ask how I could help her, but next thing I know, three officers ran in, pointing their guns. Flynn handcuffed her, read her her rights, and dragged her out to his car."

"Joyce?" I found myself staring out the window at the curb, trying to imagine how it had all gone down. "That's crazy," I said. "Last I heard there wasn't enough to warrant an arrest. What other evidence did Flynn come up with?"

Wes's face was a mixture of incredulity and resignation. "He didn't tell me anything."

"I don't get it," I said. Turning to the two men, I repeated myself. "I simply don't get it. What changed since yesterday?"

Wes shook himself, as though to throw off his confusion. "Where are my manners?" he asked rhetorically. He extended his hand. "You must be Adam," he said as they shook. "It's nice to meet you. Grace has told me about you."

Adam shot me a pleased, inquisitive look, before sizing Wes up the way men do when they first meet. "And she's told me a great deal about how you're helping her with both the artifacts at her house and discovering the passage at Marshfield."

Wes's face broke into a grin. "It's been a fascinating week, that's for sure. I can't say I've ever been involved in anything this exciting before."

Adam put his arm around me. "Neither have I."

Uncomfortable with the sudden attention, I asked Wes more about Joyce's arrest.

"How did she handle it?" I asked. "I mean, the idea of bringing in a team with guns and taking her away in handcuffs. I can't imagine."

"For the first time in her life, I think Joyce was shocked speechless," Wes said. "I almost felt sorry for her. She cooperated like she was in a daze."

"I don't get it," I said.

Wes frowned. "I don't see her as a murderer, do you?" He didn't wait for me to answer. "She's too . . . posh for that."

"I agree," I said. "I can't see her overpowering her

ex-husband and injecting him with alcohol, simply because she wants to keep her house. I get the feeling she'd view the whole act of killing another person as menial work. She'd avoid it."

"People have killed for less," Adam said.

"That's for sure," I agreed, "but even though the motive is strong, it's hard to picture her engaging in any sort of physical altercation. She's the type of woman who would worry about breaking a nail."

"Exactly," Wes said.

Adam cleared his throat. "Sort of like Hillary before she began work on your project?"

I looked up to find him giving me a grin. "Point taken. Which is why I suppose we can't rule Joyce out completely."

"People change," he reminded me.

"You should have seen her expression when Flynn twisted her arms behind her back. She was completely thrown. I thought she might even cry." Wes looked at me. "You know that never happens."

"Did she put up a fight?"

Wes gave a one-shoulder shrug. "Like I said, she seemed to be in shock. Like the whole thing was a dream and she was sleepwalking." He stared out the front door. "I'm glad you came in. I feel bad for her. I mean, no one was even considering her until you and I pulled out the floor plans and found that trapdoor."

I understood. "If she's innocent, I'm sure she'll prove it. Remember, she's a savvy attorney. Once she's at the station, her first priority will be to contact a lawyer. I have no doubt she has a colleague looking into her release right now."

"I hope so," he said.

"There's one other thing you're forgetting," I said.

"What's that?" Wes asked.

"She may actually *be* guilty."

"Good point." Rubbing his hands together as though to

wash away the subject for the time being, Wes shifted gears. "How can I help you both this morning?"

I told him what I was looking for, specifying the dates surrounding Dr. Keay's scandal five years earlier. "Do you have any documents, like old newspapers or things like that, that might tell me what else was going on in Emberstowne at that time?" I explained what I'd hoped to find at the library.

"Sure we do," he said. "Follow me." Wes led us across the space to a door at the back of the room marked EMPLOYEES ONLY. He opened it and gestured for us to follow. "What you see up front is what makes for the best display. Anyone looking to do real historical research knows that we keep the good stuff back here."

The area was huge, with high, bare windows that streamed sunlight over the tops of darkly scarred bookshelves. "Wow," I said as the commingled scents of old paper, sun-warmed dust, and fresh coffee assailed my nose. "I didn't know the offices stretched this far back."

"The years you're looking for are right here," Wes said as he rounded a far corner. "My predecessor, whoever he or she was, wasn't as fastidious as I am about protecting documents." He wagged his head. "Many of our old newspapers were exposed to moisture. They eventually molded and had to be discarded. When I took over, I made sure that we stored everything in acid-free storage, far from any contact with water. Unfortunately"—he turned and offered a rueful look—"I'm worried that the dates you're looking for might be among those that were tossed."

"Oh no."

"I'm not positive," he said, "let's check."

Wes pulled out several large boxes from a nearby shelf and I pulled one over and began digging. "I apologize," he said. "One of my projects is to get all these files arranged so that they're more easily accessed. I haven't gotten this far back yet."

Wes dug through a different box. "They should be in there," he muttered to himself.

"It's our lucky day," I said as I found one of the dates I was looking for.

"Let me see," Wes said. He eased a yellowed newspaper out slowly from the tightly packed box. Pointing, he said, "Take a look."

The Emberstowne newspaper's headline read: "Esteemed Surgeon Faces Charges."

"Oh my gosh." I took the paper from his hands. "This is great."

"It looks like we have several copies in here," Wes said. "Would you like to borrow that one?"

"I'd love to, thank you," I said. "Out of curiosity, do you have any newspapers for the next day, maybe into the following week?"

He reached in again to look. "So you can follow the rest of the story?"

"Exactly," I said. "I've been relying on others' memories from five years ago. I think that if I read the actual articles, I'll have a better sense of the timeline and flavor of how things happened. And if you happen to have the newspaper from a day or even two before this one"—I held the issue with the scandal headline aloft—"that would be great, too."

"Why would you want that?" he asked.

"If there's one thing I've learned, it's that you never really know what's important until you find it. I'm wondering if there was anything else going on in Emberstowne at that time."

I dug a little longer, pulling out newspapers from the day before the Keay scandal and from several days after. "Whoever killed Dr. Keay sent a message by injecting him with alcohol," I said. "To me, that says that the murderer was angry. No, more than angry. Whoever did it was livid with rage, and the killer equated Dr. Keay with being a drunkard. Which, according to all accounts, he wasn't anymore."

"What you believe, then, is that whoever killed Dr. Keay did it because of something the doctor did while he was intoxicated?" Adam asked.

"That's the theory I'm holding on to."

"Right now, the only person who lost anything was Joyce Swedburg," Wes said.

"That we know of. There may be others. Plus, you're forgetting Todd Pedota," I said. "His wife was the woman in the car with Keay when he crashed."

"Your neighbor?" Adam asked.

"The same."

Chapter 25

ADAM AND I WALKED TO A COFFEE SHOP IN the slightly busier part of town, about a mile from the historical society. After ordering, we made our way to their outdoor seating area, where a handful of tables circled a verdigris sundial. Surrounded by heavy-headed sunflowers and burnt-orange daylilies, the cobblestoned courtyard was beautifully screened from the street. With classical music piped in around us, it was a perfect, quiet spot to relax.

"Not very accurate, is it?" I asked, absentmindedly running a finger along the sundial's edge.

Adam twisted to read the time. "Two in the afternoon? Yeah, I'd say it's a bit off." He consulted his watch. "It isn't even noon yet."

"I suppose it's here for decoration, but if you make the effort to install a sundial, wouldn't you try to get the time right?"

We sat at a nearby table and he grinned as though I'd said something funny. "Not everyone pays as close attention to details as you do. That's one of the things that makes you so special."

"That doesn't make me special. I think everyone is curious. I just happen to act on that curiosity more often than most people do."

Adam smiled. "I stand—or should I say sit—corrected. You're not special in the least."

I laughed at that. "Thank you. What did you think of Wes?"

"I like him," Adam said. "He's a wealth of knowledge. I'm glad he's helping you on this. I can't say the same about your neighbor, even though I haven't met him. I'm not thrilled about you having an open passage between your house and a possible killer's."

"Todd Pedota may technically be a suspect in my book, but he's certainly not of any interest to Flynn."

"You were shocked to hear that Flynn arrested Joyce Swedburg, right?"

I sipped my tea and nodded.

Adam leaned forward, fixed me with a firm gaze, and lowered his voice. "With Flynn's track record, I'd lay odds that Joyce Swedburg isn't guilty but that Todd Pedota is."

I laughed.

"What's so funny?" he asked.

"You," I said, feeling a quick lightheartedness I hadn't expected. "You haven't met Joyce, you haven't met Todd. I'm sure you barely remember Flynn from last time."

Adam straightened. "Oh, I remember him all right."

"My point is that you haven't gotten to know any of these people, but you're being drawn into the drama of it all."

He wrapped both hands around his tea. "Can't help it. It involves you."

Except for a teenage couple in the far corner of the outdoor space, we were alone. I leaned toward him and spoke quietly. "Why, Adam?"

He knew what I was asking, but I watched guardedness come across his expression. "Why what?"

I placed my hands around his. They were warm. "Why are you here?"

He stiffened. "Isn't it obvious?"

"We need to have that talk."

His hands trembled, barely enough for me to notice, but I did. Not wanting him to feel self-conscious, I pulled back.

"This isn't the time," he said.

"I think it is." I waited for him to argue again, but instead he looked away. He lifted his glass and took a deep drink of tea. Even if he refused to make eye contact, I had to forge ahead. "You've come to visit me a couple of times now. You bring me flowers. You seem genuinely glad to see me."

"I am."

"But . . . why?"

He didn't answer.

"I've given you nothing," I said.

His gaze snapped to meet mine. "You've given me friendship."

"I get the sense you want more."

"I'm a patient man."

"But what if I can't give you what you want? What if—" This was hard to say, but it needed to be asked. "What if you and I never move forward? Your patience will be wasted."

The hurt in his eyes slipped in and out so quickly I almost missed it.

"If you tell me to go away, I will," he said simply. "I hope you won't, because I'm good for you, Grace. You may not see it yet, but I am. And you're good for me."

"And you know this how?"

"I don't know. I just do."

"That's vague."

"You don't see it yet, but it's there."

His pronouncement tweaked me. "You do realize you're coming across like a know-it-all. Like I'm a silly female who doesn't know my own mind, but not to worry: Big, strong-shouldered Adam is here, and he's going to take care of me, whether I like it or not."

His eyes clenched as though pained. When he opened them again, he looked away. His mouth pulled in tight and his gaze went glassy. He shook his head and stared out toward the sunflowers but I wasn't sure he was actually seeing them. I wasn't touching him, but I could see his body vibrate.

He breathed in deeply through his nose, settled himself, and turned back to me.

"I'm not an enigma, like your friend Jack," he said finally. Was there a touch of anger there now? I thought so. "You don't have to work to figure me out. I've been straight with you from the very start and I told you that I would continue to be that way for as long as we remain friends."

"I know that."

"What you don't know," he said so quietly I could barely hear him, "is *why* I believe we're right for each other."

I was almost afraid of what he might say next. Adam was a great guy, I could recognize that on a logical level. He was kind, compassionate, determined, and a hard worker. I liked him, a lot. From time to time I even felt more than friendship for him. But not enough. Never enough to allow this to turn into a full-blown relationship. Not yet. And I couldn't be sure I'd ever feel that way.

"Why, Adam?"

He shook his head. "What I feel for you, Grace, is strong and profound, and utterly different than anything I've felt before in my life. I'm thirty-seven years old and there are parts of my life I've wanted to share with you, things I haven't spoken about to anyone. But you aren't ready. You may never be ready." He squinted into the sun and lowered his voice further. "Every time you smile at me, my heart gives a little lurch. I know that doesn't happen for you and I thought that would be okay for now. I thought I could get you to change your mind."

I wanted to interrupt, but I wasn't sure what I'd say.

"When I hear myself trying to explain why we're right together, I come across exactly as you described: a know-it-all. Or worse, a crazed lunatic who doesn't know when to walk away." Still not looking at me, he wore the saddest smile. "I'm beginning to accept that you may never feel for me what I do for you. Maybe it's time I move along."

"Are you breaking up with me?"

"If we were a couple, yes. But we aren't."

I reached across, to touch his arm with my fingers. He pulled away.

"Adam, I'm sorry."

"For what?" Finally making eye contact, he tried to smile again. "For being honest with me? Don't ever be sorry for that."

My head was swirling. Was this what I really wanted? I knew we were at a turning point. We might stand up and leave right now. We might stay and talk longer. Either way, I knew that when we did leave, it would be after I'd made a decision. A make-or-break decision. Adam was asking me if I wanted to cut ties with him. I cared for the man. I didn't want him out of my life. But was it fair to him to maintain this arm's length when he wanted so much more and I didn't know what I wanted?

A breeze stirred up, causing the heavy sunflower heads to bounce and wave as though mocking me.

"I'm the one who's sorry," he said. He shifted in his seat, his entire body facing mine. "You're so smart, Grace. So inquisitive. Look at all you've done here in Emberstowne since you arrived. You've solved murders, for crying out loud. How many people can say that?"

I didn't understand where he was going with this.

"Maybe my mistake was to show up here, to try to make you care about me before you were ready. You're not used to that. I'm not a mystery to be solved. I'm just big, eager Adam. What you see is what you get."

"That's not true—"

"It is as far as you're concerned. Understand me, Grace. I don't blame you. I blame myself. You deserve to be treated well, you deserve all that's best in the world. Because you *are* the best in the world. But you're not ready for that."

"What do you mean?"

"You're still attracted to Jack. Don't deny it. I hear it in your voice when you say his name. Nothing wrong with that, but you're drawn to him in a way you can't explain. Am I close?"

My breath caught. How did he know? I gave one quick nod.

"He was distant and aloof when you were interested in a relationship and suddenly attentive when you were not."

I bit my lip, almost wishing I hadn't shared so much of this with Adam. At the same time I was perversely curious enough to want to hear the rest of his analysis.

"Jack was broken, and he's in the process of putting himself together again," Adam said. "He's doesn't yet know himself fully, which means you can't know him fully, either. He's a mystery to be solved. And you can't resist."

"That's not true."

"Isn't it?" He tilted his head again. "At the very least, he's unfinished business. You need to find closure before you can move on. That closure might very well mean that you and Jack end up together, I don't know. But you need to find out what the right answer is. For you. Got that? Not for Jack. Not for me. Until that happens, you're denying yourself happiness. And you deserve to be happy."

My throat went hot.

"I don't do the jealous thing," he said. "I'm not angry that Jack is still in your life. What's right for you is right for you. I happen to believe that what's right for you is me. But until you believe that, it really doesn't matter what I think, does it?"

He stood, picked up his tea glass, and shook his head

when I started to rise. "Tell you what. How about you wait here for a little bit? Give me a half hour's head start. The workers are in and out of your house all day today, right?"

Numb, I nodded.

"Then the doors are probably open. I'll go in, pack up my stuff, and get out of your hair."

"Adam—"

"Do what you need to do," he said. "But remember one thing above all: You deserve happiness." Swallowing hard, he hit me again with that sorrowful smile. "Do I want you to find that with me? You know I do. But I can't make it happen and I'm starting to understand that my coming here didn't do either of us any good. I need to leave."

My heart was heavier than it had been since my mother died. I knew Adam was right about my feelings for Jack, but the realization of the hurt I'd caused took my breath away. I could barely form the words. I couldn't look at him. "You're leaving? For good?"

"That will be up to you."

My gaze flicked up to meet his.

"I'm going to pretend that you and I never met. Heaven help me, it will be one of the hardest things I've ever done. But I'm taking the pressure off, Grace. You do what you need to do," he said again. "Whatever that is. Maybe you'll realize that you can never care for me the way a man and woman should if they want to spend time together. Then again, maybe you can. My hanging around here isn't going to make it easier for you. So, I'm going."

"I'm so sorry, Adam."

He waved off my apology. "You can't make another person love you," he said. "It's time I realized that. Give me a half hour," he said again, then turned away.

I gave him his half hour. I gave him more than that. I sat staring at the sundial until clouds gathered overhead and time disappeared.

Chapter 26

FRANCES STORMED INTO MY OFFICE MONDAY morning. Nose in the air, she kept her arms folded across her chest. "You have been summoned."

Her body language screamed "annoyed," so she couldn't be talking about Bennett. "Flynn?" I asked.

"No, this time it was your little lap dog," she said. "Ronny Tooney."

"Has he found something?" I stood. "Is he here?"

She wagged her head, and her ample chins shimmied in response. Her feet were planted shoulder-width apart and if it hadn't been for the crossed arms, I would have thought she was about to tackle me. I knew Tooney aggravated the heck out of her, but this level of anger was out of proportion.

"He's drunk," she said. The words came out hard and sharp, like a bite. "Drunk as Dr. Keay was when he keeled over in front of us."

"Are you sure?" Tired of having to guess what was going on, I brushed past Frances to hurry into her office. "Where is he?"

"Home, of course. The man is an idiot, but he's no fool."

I pressed my fingers to my temples. "Explain what's going on, Frances. Without the commentary, please."

She rolled her mouth as though fighting to keep the snarky comments from escaping. "He called a minute ago. Wants you to come out to see him. At his house." She raised an eyebrow at that. "He claims he has information for you that's important but he's too drunk to drive. Want me to tell him to come in when he sobers up?"

"No, this is great."

"What are you talking about?" she asked.

"This could be the break I was hoping for."

I raced back to my desk, grabbed my purse, and started for the door. Frances stared at me, openmouthed.

"Well," I asked, "are you coming along or not?"

WE WERE BARELY OUT MARSHFIELD MANOR'S front gates when Frances shifted in her seat to face me. "What happened with the boyfriend?" she asked. "You know, the bandleader hippie guy."

I signaled to turn right at the intersection, and took my eyes off the road long enough to gauge her face. Her tadpole brows sat suspended high on her forehead, and she blinked at me. Her look said she was all innocence. I wasn't buying it.

"He's not a hippie." I returned my attention to my driving. "Far from it."

If she hadn't been confined by her seatbelt, she probably would have jammed her fists in her hips. "Everybody knows he dumped you at the coffee shop," she said.

"He didn't dump me."

"You dumped him?" Her tone suggested she found this scenario unlikely. "I thought this was Mr. Right for you. You keep insisting you're over Jack and that this new boyfriend was the one." She studied me, her beady eyes bright.

"I want to make sure you're okay. Not depressed or anything."

I'd never said that Adam was "the one," but I couldn't fight more than one battle at a time. "You want to make sure you get the rest of the story straight so you have something to share with your grapevine gremlins around town. Is that it?"

"We're interested in your well-being."

I shot her a look of contempt. "For your information, the breakup was mutual."

"Oh?" She stared pointedly out her side window. "That's not what I heard."

She wanted more, clearly. She wanted details. I wasn't about to oblige. It had been hard enough explaining Adam's departure to Scott and Bruce. They'd been supportive in that if-you-really-think-this-is-the-right-move-for-you-then-we're-behind-you sort of way. But I could tell that they'd both been disappointed. Who was I kidding? I was disappointed. Much as I wanted to, I couldn't shake the feeling that I'd made a terrible mistake. More than once over the weekend, I'd been tempted to call Adam. I'd wanted to apologize; I'd wanted to ask him if we could remain friends.

But I knew that in this case, it was all or nothing. Anything less than "all" would be cruel and unfair. I knew that my wanting to call him was more about assuaging my own sadness than anything else. Calling him would be selfish. I had to steel myself to fight the urge to try to make things better. While doing so might temporarily ease my conscience, I knew in my heart that it would only make things worse for him. I couldn't do that. He deserved better.

I'd done a great deal of thinking all day Sunday and I'd come to the conclusion that Adam was right. I needed to find closure with Jack. Until I did, I was in limbo, unable to move or make decisions. I didn't like it one bit.

"Want some advice?" Frances asked.

"No."

"You have to get Jack out of your system, one way or another."

I pulled my lips in so tight they hurt.

"Oh, figured that out for yourself, did you?" She gave a self-satisfied nod. "He knows about your breakup, by the way."

I gripped the steering wheel tighter.

In my peripheral vision I watched her study me again, give a shrug like nothing mattered, and then turn her attention back out the window. "My 'gremlins,' as you so affectionately call them, made sure he got the update. I thought you ought to know."

TOONEY LIVED IN A COTTAGE ABOUT FIVE miles away from Emberstowne's busiest area, across the railroad tracks that, as in many towns, separated the haves from the have-nots. I was fortunate to live in an area that featured painted-lady mansions and manicured lawns—not because I was wealthy, but because my mother had left the house to me.

Here, down a rural road, among ramshackle houses that barely seemed storm-worthy, Tooney's home sat deep on a lightly wooded lot. His house was about the size of a large two-car garage, with a cement block foundation and faded siding. We pulled up onto the adjacent gravel driveway and got out of the car.

"This looks like him," Frances said. "Old, rumpled, and ready for the bulldozer."

"Frances," I snapped. "Cut it out."

We stepped onto his porch, an eight-by-sixteen-foot platform made up of warped plywood boards nailed onto uneven two-by-fours. It didn't creak so much as moan as we made our way to his front door.

"What? You want me to say something nice about the place?" She looked at the cottage, gave it a quick once-over, taking in the battered screen door, the windowless front façade, the folded lawn chairs leaning against the wall next to the door, and the black bags of garbage around the near corner. Smooshing her lips to the side, she said, "Sorry. Can't."

There was no doorbell, so I opened the shaky screen and knocked at the heavier door inside. It swung open.

"Izzat you?" Tooney's voice bellowed. "C'mon in."

I clapped a hand to my mouth as we entered. The hot stench of sick, sweet liquor mingled with sweat was overwhelming. It propelled me back, with sharp stinging memory, to Dr. Keay's last moments before he died.

There was one piece of furniture in the room, a low red couch, shoved up against the far wall, which was also painted red. Tooney sprawled sideways across the sofa, one arm draped to the floor, the other raised in the air, waving hello. His shirt was open to the middle of his chest, his pants were rolled up to his knees, and his hairy feet were bare.

Frances pulled a handkerchief from her purse and held it to her nose. She stormed up to Tooney, demanding, "When did you last bathe?"

He looked up at her with drooping basset hound eyes, shook his head, and burped.

"Heavens," Frances said, and turned away.

"Hiya, Grace," he said, slurring the end of my name. "Iss so good to see you." He pointed at Frances with effort. "But why'd'ja have to bring that one along?"

Frances pulled the hanky away from her mouth. "Oh, were you hoping to be alone with her? Is that it, Mr. Tooney?"

His face smashed in on itself, like he wanted to frown as hard as he possibly could. Slapping the air with his hand, he said, "Nah, nothing like that." Again, with effort, he sat up. "Whaddya take me for? Grace is like a daughter to me. Aren'tcha?"

I chose not to answer. A window air conditioner had

been built into the wall near the ceiling, though it didn't seem to be running at the moment. I crossed the room in two strides, reaching up to turn it on.

He rolled his head back to stare up at me. "Good idea, Gracie. Iz gettin' warm in here."

"Only the Mister calls her Gracie," Frances said.

Tooney slapped the air again. His tongue made its way around his lips.

"Thirsty?" I asked.

Both hands came up fast and he reacted as if I'd asked him to strip naked and dance the Hokey Pokey. "I've had enough, thank you very much," he said. "Can't handle any more."

"I meant water. I'm sure you're dehydrated."

I didn't wait for him to answer. I made my way to the kitchen, passing Tooney's bedroom and bathroom along the way. Both doors were open, so I wasn't snooping, not exactly. I simply took an extra moment to glance in at them. They were as small and dreary as his living room. The entire home was floored in adhesive tiles, some of which were missing. Tooney's bedroom consisted of a bumpy double bed, a pitted dresser, and orange walls with broken drywall near the floor where a baseboard should be. At least there was a window in this room. Shabby but tidy. I had to give him that.

The bathroom was cramped, painted hot pink, and featured an aluminum shower stall that would be narrow even for me. I had no idea how a man Tooney's size managed to get clean in there. A matching metal medicine cabinet hung on the wall over the toilet. There were prescription bottles on one shelf, but I thought it would be too much of an invasion of privacy to peek at what was in them.

The kitchen was painted a vivid green and fluorescent yellow. What was it with all the bright colors? The sink was clear, the countertop—what little there was—clean. He had a toaster and a coffeemaker in addition to the refrigerator that hummed in the corner, but otherwise the room was empty.

I opened the cabinet closest to the sink and found three drinking glasses. Two were juice size, one was a tumbler. I checked the fridge for ice water, found nothing but an opened package of hot dogs, a container of strawberries, and four cans of beer. That wasn't going to cut it.

A lonely bag of creamed corn sat in the freezer. No ice. "Tap water it is," I said. I waited for it to run cold, filled the tumbler, and brought it to Tooney.

In the short time I'd been gone, Frances had dragged in the two lawn chairs from outside and had set them up across from Tooney's couch.

"He expected us to sit next to him on that," she said, pointing to the sofa. "The nerve."

I handed Tooney the water, and he gulped it down, barely breathing until it was done. "Thanks," he said, handing the empty glass back.

"What, you think she's your maid now? Expect her to hurry off and get you a refill?"

"Frances," I said.

She grabbed the glass out of my hand, huffed, and stormed out of the room. "We drove all the way out here to talk to the man. What are you waiting for?"

The lawn chair's aluminum frame scraped against the tile floor as I pulled the seat closer and sat in it. "What happened, Tooney?"

"I think I found them." He smacked his lips a few times. "I'm really sorry I am in this condishh—condition."

"How much did you have to drink?"

"Not mush."

I arched an eyebrow at him.

Frances returned at that moment, handed him the refilled glass, and stepped back. "That's a lie," she said.

He adopted an exaggerated sincere expression. "No, really. I don't drink a lot. Maybe a beer, y'know, once in a while. I had two shots of the stuff. These guys make it in their barn."

Frances and I exchanged a skeptical look. "Two shots?" I asked.

"Maybe three?" He held up four fingers, then five. Shrugged. "Can't remember. Here." Half-draped over the couch's arm, he reached down and pulled up a clear, unlabeled jar. "This is it," he said. "Totally illegal."

I took it from him. "I've seen something like this before."

"The evidence technicians said they found two empty jars in the hidden passage," Frances reminded me.

"Yeah, but I never saw those. The techs bagged and removed the evidence before I got back down there." I held the jar and turned it from side to side.

Frances watched me. "Where did you see it?"

"It looks a lot like one that belongs to David Cherk."

"Oh?" she asked. She sat in the other lawn chair and leaned forward. "What was he doing with moonshine?"

"First of all, I don't know what was in David Cherk's jar. He's a photographer. It could have been developer."

"But you don't think it was, do you?" Frances's eyes glittered. "Do you think Cherk was in cahoots with Joyce?"

I took a deep breath. "Let's not get ahead of ourselves here." I turned to Tooney, who appeared to be having a tough time tracking our conversation. "What did you find out?"

"I found 'em," he said, nodding. "Took me a coupla days but I found the guys who make this stuff."

I needed to exercise patience. "That's wonderful. Now, why don't you tell me who they sold it to."

He shook his big head. "They're afraid of the cops, y'know. Took me a lot of effort to infla- infila—"

"Infiltrate?"

"Yeah. That." He wiped the back of his hand across his nose. "I can't tell you who the people are who made the moonshine. They made me promise."

"That's fine. All I want to know is who else bought from them recently. They told you that, didn't they?"

He stuck a pinky finger in his ear and wiggled it around.

Frances was giving me the evil eye. "He's useless," she said under her breath.

Tooney brought his arm up and pointed a shaky finger at her. "You—need—to—shut—up."

Frances's mouth dropped open and she sat straight. "How dare—"

"Frances, let it go," I said. "Talk to me, Tooney. Who else did they sell moonshine to?"

"A guy. Male."

"Who?" I asked.

"I couldn't ask too many questions, y'unnerstand," he said. "I had to be sneaky about it. I told them that a coupla friends might be innerested in buying from them, too. Asked them if maybe my friends were already customers."

"And?" I asked, wishing he would get to it.

"No names. Never names." He held up an index finger and wagged it back and forth. "Wouldn't even let me say my name. So—" He held both hands out to the side. "No help there."

"How old was the guy?"

"No idea." Tooney gave an exaggerated shrug. "Y'see, these guys who make the stuff are old. They been doin' this since before even I was born. Everybody looks young to them."

"What did you do?"

"I said that one of my friends had dark hair and kinda looked like a skeleton."

"You described David Cherk?"

He nodded, his top lip heavy over his bottom one. "They said nope, no skeletons came in."

My shoulders slumped. "So you got nothing."

"Didn't say that." He worked up a smile. "I like it when you're proud of me, Gracie. Makes me feel good."

Frances loosened her pout long enough to interject, "Her name isn't Gracie."

"I asked if anybody seemed, like, suspicious, when they bought the moonshine," Tooney said.

"More suspicious than you, you mean?" Frances asked.

He was so intent on imparting information that he seemed to not hear her. He leaned very far forward and I could smell the booze on his hot breath. His eyes were yellow and rimmed in red, and he looked as though he might crash any moment.

"They told me about a guy who comes in and buys four bottles at once. I got the impression he was a regular customer."

"What are you trying to tell me, Tooney?"

"The guy said that his wife left him. Said he wanted the stuff to drown his sorrows." Tooney lowered his chin and stared at me from beneath wiry brows. "Who does that sound like?"

Chapter 27

WHEN I GOT HOME LATE THAT AFTERNOON, I didn't walk straight in. Even though my brain was chock-full of clues about the murder and my heart was heavy because of Adam's departure, I stopped for a moment on my driveway. I wanted to take some time to appreciate the positive changes Hillary had brought to my home.

All her hard work, coupled with her surprisingly adept management, had paid off. The exterior was in the process of being painted—Hillary's choice, pastel blue—and all the new windows were in. The porch, which had once been as shabby as Tooney's, was now on the way to becoming breathtakingly beautiful. All that was left—outside at least—was to finish up with bright green, purple, and pink trim. As Hillary had promised, the house was beginning to look like something out of a high-class fairy tale.

I took a deep breath. Tooney's investigation hadn't provided as much help as I'd hoped for, but Flynn had been happy to see us. More accurately, he'd been happy to see the jar of moonshine when we'd dropped it off with him.

He planned to give it to the coroner for comparison with the alcohol that killed Keay. If they proved to be a match, I knew Flynn would go after the distillers in a flying tackle. Heck, he might go after them anyway, for fun.

I stood outside staring, letting myself slowly relax. Until a voice behind me said, "Looks wonderful."

I turned and my heart gave a little skip. Like Adam said his did when he looked at me. But the voice behind me belonged to Jack.

A thousand thoughts raced through my head at once: *Did my stomach flip-flop because of attraction? Was it merely surprise? What the heck is going on? Why is Jack here right now?*

And then I remembered.

"So you heard," I said.

He massaged the stubble on his chin. "Yeah."

I fought a rising tide of anger. I couldn't quite put my finger on what was driving it, but I couldn't tamp it down either.

"Is this how it works?" I asked. "The minute I break up with Adam, the entire town conspires to get the two of us together?"

He had the decency to look embarrassed.

"How's Becke?"

He kicked a stone and watched it skitter away. "Why is that important?"

"Because it is." I knew that wasn't much of an argument, but a light was beginning to flicker alive in my brain.

"She's fine."

He wasn't wearing the khaki shorts and sweaty T-shirt I'd been used to seeing him in, back when he was in charge of landscaping at Marshfield. Today he sported dark jeans, a collared shirt, and shiny loafers.

I took a step closer to him. He smelled good, really good, and my heart raced a little bit when that whiff of aftershave caught me unawares.

And yet, his being here was wrong.

"What do you want, Jack?"

"Isn't it obvious?"

"You and I don't even know we'd be good together," I said, realizing as I spoke the words that they were true. "Yet we've been trying to forge a path together. What you and I should probably really be trying to do is make ourselves work, first."

He scratched the side of his eye, still looking away. "What more do I need to do?" he asked. "I quit Marshfield to go back to school. I'm following up on what I've wanted to do from the start. I'm serious about putting my past behind me and making a new life for myself."

"You've done a marvelous job of that," I said. "I admire all you've done."

When he met my gaze, I could see anger burning there. And something more. Exasperation. He hadn't expected a discussion; he'd expected me to welcome him back with open arms.

"But?" he asked.

I could do no more than tell him the truth. "I don't know you. Not really. I have this ideal in my mind, this image that formed when we first met. But that's not who you are."

"Are you telling me that you don't like who I've become?"

I shook my head. "Months ago, you told me you had no interest in Becke. That you were simply helping out an old friend. I told you that if you were serious about a relationship with me then you had to settle things with her first."

He hunched his shoulders and spread his hands, his face tightening. "You were dating Adam," he said. "What was I supposed to do?"

"You don't get it, do you, Jack?"

"What I get is that you're single again. Why shouldn't we give a relationship a try?"

"What about Becke?"

"What about her? She'll understand. She knows that we're not serious."

"No, Jack, she doesn't know that."

He gave me one of those "You don't know what you're talking about" looks. "I've told her I'm not looking for an instant family. We're just friends."

"Friend with benefits?"

He shrugged. "It doesn't mean anything."

All of a sudden the flickering light morphed into a high beam, illuminating in ways I'd never imagined.

"Sure, you may have told her you weren't serious, but what do your actions say?"

"My actions brought me here."

Frustrated, I thrust my hands out. "Jack, listen to me. You're not being fair to her."

"Are you kidding? Do you know how much I've done for her?"

"Yes, and that's exactly my point. You took her in, gave her a place to live."

"And that's so bad?"

"Of course not. But look at it from her perspective. You're her knight in shining armor. You're taking care of her, taking care of her kids. You hang out together. You brought her as your date to the benefit. You gave her your grandmother's dress to wear."

His voice was low but strained. "Is it so wrong to be a nice guy?"

"Whether you're intending to or not, you're leading her down a path. Is it being a nice guy to pull her hopes out from under her the minute someone else is back on the market?"

He ran a hand through his hair, his upper teeth tight on his bottom lip.

"She wants the happily-ever-after with you, Jack," I said. "You've let her believe that it's possible."

"I'll break it off with her today," he said. "I promise. Then can we talk?"

I dropped my hands at my sides and struggled to not

raise my voice. "You don't understand." A little whisper in my head reminded me that I hadn't understood, either. Not until this minute.

"What I understand," he said, "is that you and I have been attracted to each other from the very start. We've hit a lot of roadblocks and yet here we are, still attracted to one another. And now both of us are single."

"You're not."

"I will be. I told you that."

"No," I said.

"What do you mean, 'no'?"

"Months ago, when I told you that we could talk after you settled things with Becke, I meant it. Now I'm going to tell you something else that I mean: It doesn't matter if you break up with Becke. It doesn't matter if she moves across the country and you never see her again." I thought about Adam. Thought about what he'd said. "I deserve better."

"Better than what?"

It hurt to say the words, but I'd finally found the truth. And the sooner it was out there, the sooner we could heal. "I deserve better than this."

He stared at me like I was a creature that had just crawled up from the lawn and was clapping tambourines while dancing a jig. Inside, maybe I was.

Right before my eyes, Jack lost that edge of excitement, that rugged handsomeness that had always drawn me in. In a swift, astonishing *Poof*, he morphed from the man of my dreams to a scoundrel. A guy who didn't consider another's feelings before taking a step that would undoubtedly hurt her. If he was the kind of person who could so casually wound Becke, then what would stop him from doing the same to others? To me?

All of a sudden, I saw him for who he really was, and not who I hoped he might be. His family troubles and his struggle to get back on his feet had been enough to keep me close, encourage me to help, and garner my sympathy. Jack

had been distant from the start and all this time I'd rationalized his selfishness away.

"I can't believe you said that." He opened his hands,
closed them, and then opened them again.

For the first time since I'd fallen for Jack, I felt free.
Surprisingly strong. Happy.

I could have softened the moment with a wish for us to
stay friends, but it probably wouldn't have helped.

"Good-bye, Jack," I said.

He didn't move. When I got to my front door, I turned
and he was still there, still staring.

"Good luck," I whispered. "You're going to need it."

"YOU'RE HOME," HILLARY SQUEALED WHEN I
walked into the kitchen. "I was about to call." She lifted her
skinny wrist and spun her dangling bracelet watch around
so she could check the time. "You're usually home a little
sooner than this. Why are you late? We've been waiting for
you. You missed seeing your neighbor Todd Pedota by
moments. He stopped by to ask about the passage and if
we'd learned anything more."

I barely paid attention to what she was saying because
she wasn't alone. David Cherk was leaning his backside
against the countertop near the sink, sipping from one of
my mugs. Wes sat at the table, a pile of drawings spread in
front of him. Even from upside-down, I could tell that he'd
sketched the passage between my house and Pedota's. A
gentleman I'd never seen before had pulled one of the four
chairs around and sat next to Wes, a magnifying glass in
hand.

They all looked up at once.

"What's going on?" I asked.

David Cherk regarded me with a bored air as he lowered
the mug from his lips to hold it in both hands. "Lucky me,
I get to photograph your historical find."

"I thought the newspaper people already took care of that," I said.

Hillary scurried around on her tiny high heels to pat me on the arm. "That was for local flavor, this is for posterity. David has agreed to use his considerable skills to document the passageway." She held her hands up in the air, making a frame with her fingers, like a director convincing a starlet that he sees her name in lights. "Your house will be immortalized at the historical society office. Isn't that exciting?"

"I don't know, Hillary."

David dropped the cup next to the sink with a clunk. "This guy," he said, pointing to the man I didn't recognize sitting at my kitchen table, "wouldn't let us take even a single shot without your approval."

I turned to the man. "I'm afraid we haven't met," I said, extending my hand.

He stood to shake it and was about to speak when Hillary interrupted. "Oh, silly me. That's right, you haven't met Frederick. You remember me telling you about him, right? My business partner?"

Frederick was a lump of a guy. Balding and short, he wore a gray suit and a silky red bow tie. He squinted hello at me from behind rimless, round glasses. He had pasty white skin and blond brows. I guessed him to be around fifty-five.

"Nice to meet you, Frederick," I said. "Hillary speaks very highly of you."

"And of you," he said. He had a nice face and a friendly smile. Of course, he might be lying through his teeth.

David waved a hand between us. "Hello-o—? The pictures? I've been waiting for you. Patiently, I might add. Can we get started here?"

Frederick let the rude intrusion roll right off his back. He sat down and returned to working side by side with Wes. They had two of the poison bottles on the table in front of them, and Wes was indicating where in the passage we'd found them.

I wasn't keen on the idea of photographing the passage. Not yet. Maybe I was still feeling the effects of my interaction with Jack, but I wasn't in the mood to be particularly agreeable.

"I don't think this is such a good plan," I said.

Cherk threw his hands in the air. "Oh, brilliant. I come out all this way and she changes her mind."

"I haven't changed my mind," I said with more than a little oomph. "I never agreed to it in the first place."

"Oh, um," Hillary interjected, tapping my arm. "I thought it would be helpful."

"You agreed to it?"

She nodded. "When he got here, though, Frederick told me that we really needed to wait for you to approve, first. I thought it would be a mere formality. Why *wouldn't* you want to do this?"

"Thank you for letting me have a voice in the matter, Frederick," I said.

He smiled up at me then returned his attention to the drawings.

"Are we too much in the way?" Hillary showed teeth when she smiled. "We should have done all this before you got home. We could have had the shoot finished and have been out of your hair before you even got here."

"Her house, her decision," Frederick said without looking up.

Hillary bounced her head from side to side. She turned to me. "What can I say to convince you this is a good idea?"

"I don't know that you can, Hillary," I said, but I could feel my resolve waning. There really wasn't any reason the passage shouldn't be photographed for the historical society's archives. Maybe someday a future owner of the house would look for the records. These pictures could help them like the Marshfield blueprints had helped me.

"Please, Grace? I know that David is eager to get started."

"Her house, her decision," Frederick said again, this time a little more forcefully.

"You're right, Frederick," Hillary said. "I'm sorry. I shouldn't push."

I don't know if I was more taken aback by Hillary's acquiescence or by David Cherk's unkind glare.

"So I made the trip for nothing," he said.

"Wait a minute," I said. "This came out of the blue. I need a minute to think about it."

"It's an easy yes or no," David said.

"What, exactly, do you plan to photograph?" I asked.

David rolled his eyes dramatically. "The entrance, the pathway. A couple of locations where artifacts were found. From what I understand, the walls are solid brick. I'd get a few shots of those. This is good for the town's history, for helping to bring the past alive for our citizens." He pushed himself off from leaning against the countertop. "Or maybe you don't care about stuff like that."

Wes looked up at me, silently apologizing with his eyes.

"Fine," I said. "But be careful. The doors lock automatically, and if they close behind you, you're stuck."

Hillary squeaked her delight.

I was frustrated, tired, and annoyed. By all of them.

"It looks like you'll be here awhile," I said to David. Glancing at the rest of the people gathered in my kitchen, I said, "I'm going upstairs to say hello to Bootsie. Then I'm grabbing dinner out." To Hillary, I added, "Please be sure to lock up when you leave."

She gave me a chipper smile. "I always do."

Chapter 28

"FRANCES," I CALLED FROM MY OFFICE LATE the next morning, "did you take any papers from in here?"

My assistant came into view at the doorway. "What are you looking for?"

I'd gotten up from my desk and was now searching around the rest of my sizeable office. Enormous mullioned windows spanned one wall, above built-in filing cabinets. I sorted through papers that I'd left atop the cabinets, my back to the fireplace. Tilting my head upward to stare at the coffered teak ceiling, I tried to mentally retrace my steps.

"I borrowed old newspapers from the historical society the other day," I said. "I started to go through them at home, but I didn't have time, so I brought them in today. I thought I might have a chance to read here at work."

Her brows came together. "What kind of old newspapers?"

Except for these papers on the filing cabinets, I kept a relatively clutter-free office and knew I hadn't put anything away in the past couple of hours. Walking over to my desk,

I picked up the newspaper with the headline "Esteemed Surgeon Faces Charges." "I picked this one up the other day, along with a couple others from that time—a day before and a few after the scandal hit. I had five different full editions in all. Now I have only four."

"And you brought them in today?"

I massaged the bridge of my nose. "I was in a hurry this morning and didn't notice that anything was missing. I couldn't have left it at home." Talking aloud now, I brought up a mental image of my kitchen. "They were on top of the microwave when I grabbed them. I would've noticed if I'd left one behind."

"Maybe one of your roommates took it?"

I doubted it. "I'll check, but they knew why I'd brought these home. I can't imagine they would have removed one from the pile without telling me."

"Has anyone else been in your house since you brought them home?"

I nearly barked a laugh. "Only half the town," I said, then sobered. "You don't think someone would have stolen an old newspaper, do you? What could they possibly want with it?"

Frances held up three fingers. "One, you may be dealing with a kleptomaniac. Who knows why any of them steal? Two, whoever took it didn't know it was important and they needed an old newspaper to line a birdcage, or maybe clean windows. Or, three, you're on the right track and the killer doesn't want you to read what's in that missing paper. Of course that would mean that the killer—or *her hit man*—was in your house recently."

"I need to call Hillary," I said, pulling up my cell phone and dialing her number. The call went to voicemail, so I hung up.

"Why didn't you leave a message?" Frances asked.

"She'll see a missed call and call me back."

"But she won't know why you were calling."

"I'll tell her when she gets in touch."

"I don't understand. If her voicemail comes on, why not leave a message?"

I was about to explain how accessing recordings on cell phones was far more trouble than returning a call, when Flynn walked in. He usually wore pale button-down shirts, dress pants, and a jacket. Today, however, he'd donned blue jeans, a gray Henley with the first few buttons undone, and a leather shoulder holster. The biggest change to his appearance, however, was his hair. Or, I should say, the lack thereof. He'd shaved himself bald.

I struggled to find something to say.

Frances had no reservations. "You've been watching too many *Die Hard* movies. Looks like you're channeling Bruce Willis."

He scowled at her. "I have a lead on that moonshine," he said. "Your hired detective did some good this time."

Still shocked by the change in Flynn's appearance, I couldn't even manage a reply.

"Turns out your guy, Tooney, may not have been the only local who knows where to get moonshine."

"You found out who bought the alcohol from them?" I asked.

When Flynn nodded, his newly shiny head caught the light. This was going to take some getting used to.

"Well, who?"

"Dr. Keay."

Frances sat. "He injected himself?"

"I didn't say that," Flynn said. "My department is investigating the moonshiners so I can't tell you the specifics of how we found out, but Dr. Keay was one of their regular customers."

"But," I said, "he was sober. For years."

Flynn shrugged. "People lie. I see it every day. Seems he was one of their best customers."

I was still digesting that when Flynn continued, "The

theory we're going with right now is that whoever killed Keay knew that he was still on the sauce and threatened to blackmail him."

"Then why kill him?" I asked. "You said the attack was personal."

"Blackmail is personal."

"Injecting him and poisoning him doesn't make any sense if the killer was looking for money," I said.

"You got a better theory?"

It wasn't much, but I held up the newspapers and explained what I'd been looking for. "I think that whoever killed Dr. Keay did it because of something that happened around the time the scandal hit. Because of something Dr. Keay did back when he was a raging alcoholic."

Flynn shook his smooth head. "Doesn't fit. If Keay was buying moonshine, he never *stopped* being a raging alcoholic. He just got better at hiding it, is all. Whoever killed him knew how to do it, and they knew because they knew his habits."

"What if it wasn't blackmail? What if it was a personal vendetta?"

He waved both hands at me in an attempt to shut me up. "I didn't come here to discuss theories with you. I came here to tell you that Joyce has been released. We didn't have enough to hold her."

"You let her go?" Frances asked. "How could you? She did it. I know she did."

"There's this thing called the law," he said with heavy sarcasm. "I'm charged with upholding it. We had to let her go due to lack of evidence."

Frances turned her cheek to him. "I don't know what's wrong with you people. The answer is staring you right in the face and you unlock the jail cell and set it free."

Flynn's mouth pulled to the side. "We did get another tip that we're checking out right now. Can't say more than that without jeopardizing the investigation. I'll tell you this

much, though: We're working on a warrant. Don't be surprised if we announce an arrest before the week is out."

"Another arrest? For the same crime?" Frances bright-
ened. "You think Joyce had help? Like a hit man?"

Flynn gave her a weary look. "Didn't I say that I can't
tell you more without compromising our work?"

I wanted to ask him why he'd bothered offering that
much information if he didn't expect questions, but I already
had my answer. The man desperately needed to prove that
he was ahead of us this time. He was here to show off.

"Good luck, Detective," I said, even as Frances scowled.
"Thanks for the update."

MY CELL PHONE RANG LATER THAT AFTER-
noon, while Frances was in my office. Hillary's name blinked
on the device's display.

"You see," I said, right before I answered. "Better than
leaving a message."

Frances didn't say anything.

"Grace, I have the best news," Hillary said when I
answered. "Have you heard? You must have, otherwise why
would you have tried to call me earlier?"

"The reason I called—"

"Your renovation is going to be featured in a national
magazine," she said with dolphin-pitched merriment. "*Painted
Lady Monthly*. It's a glossy. Can you believe it?"

"No, I—"

"Frederick reminded me that you'll need to approve this,
but Grace, of course you will, right? Can you imagine how
much of a boost this would give my business?" She didn't
wait for me to respond. "My *fledgling* business? Not so
fledgling after this. I know how private you are and how
much having people in and out of your house all the time
grates on your nerves, but if you could do this one eensy-
weensy favor, I'd be so grateful. Frederick would, too."

"That's not why I called," I said. "We'll talk about the magazine later. For now I need you to answer a question for me about all those people who are in and out of my house every day."

"The *Painted Lady* will want an answer soon."

"Concentrate for a minute on what I'm saying, Hillary." I waited a beat, ignored her tiny sigh of annoyance, and continued, "I need you to answer some questions for me first. Only then will I consider it." I knew I'd regret the implied promise later, but once Hillary got an idea in her mind she was a steamroller until she achieved her goal. To get her to focus I needed to dangle the prize and not give in until she complied.

Another annoyed sigh, but this time she said, "Go ahead."

"I had some newspapers in my kitchen the other day." I spoke slowly. "I brought them in on Saturday but I didn't have much of a chance to look at them until today, when I took them with me to work."

"Are you talking about the old newspapers that were on top of your microwave?"

My mouth fell open. Frances, reading my expression, asked, "She saw them?"

"Those are exactly the ones I'm talking about, Hillary," I said. "Can you tell me if you saw anyone, anyone at all, handling them?"

"What's going on?" she asked. "Will I be getting someone in trouble by telling you?"

"Bear with me," I said. "Who touched them?"

"Almost everyone." My heart sank, and I gripped the phone tightly, waiting for more information, hoping that she would offer some clue as to who took the missing paper.

"Are you alone?" I asked.

"I am at the moment."

"Good, now think for a minute. Tell me everything you can about the newspapers and who looked at them."

"Okay." Although I couldn't see her consternation, I

could feel it. "Let's see, the first person to notice the newspapers was Frederick."

"Why would he be interested in them?"

"Are you sure I'm not getting him into trouble?"

"What did he do with the newspapers?" I asked.

"Frederick is a good man," she said. "I'm sure he wouldn't do anything to mess your house up on purpose."

"Focus, Hillary. Tell me what happened."

"The only reason any of us noticed the papers was because Frederick pointed them out. He asked me why you had a pile of five-year-old newspapers on top of your microwave. I said that I didn't know."

"Who else was there?"

She thought for a minute. "Everyone you saw the other night," she said. "David Cherk, Wes McIntyre, me, Frederick. Oh, and at that point there were a couple of other people, too."

"Who?"

"One of David's student friends was there to help him with the shoot, and your neighbor Todd. I think he really believes I'm interested in him." She gave a very teenage-like giggle. "Oh, and the reporter who did the story on the secret passage. I think that's it, but I may be forgetting someone."

All these people in my kitchen when I hadn't even been home. "What was the reporter doing there?"

"Follow up, he said. Anyway, the best I can recall is that Frederick started paging through the papers and—" She stopped.

"And what Hillary?"

"You're not going to like this."

"Spit it out."

She gave a quick sigh. "Frederick said something about the papers being a fire hazard in the kitchen and he thought they should be tossed out. He wouldn't do that, of course, without your permission, but he asked again what you could possibly want with newspapers that old. He offered to put them somewhere other than the kitchen, so it would be safer."

"Safer? Than on top of the microwave?"

"Frederick is a little paranoid about such things. He's very clean."

"What happened? He obviously didn't move them. They were still there when I grabbed them this morning."

"Wes explained to the group that you were looking for information about what else might have been happening in Emberstowne when Dr. Keay's scandal broke. He suggested that we leave the papers exactly where they were because it was important to you. That got everyone talking about you and how you've become the town's amateur sleuth. David Cherk said that he thought fame had gone to your head."

I didn't care what people thought about my amateur sleuthing, but I tucked that remark away, nonetheless.

"So the only person to handle the papers was Frederick?" I asked.

"David got bored while we were waiting for you, and he started reading through them. I think the reporter guy did, too. Yes, he did. He mentioned something about how news coverage is so much better today than it was back then."

"Anyone else?"

"I can't say for sure. I was in and out of the kitchen a few times, checking on Bootsie and making sure the workers were doing what they were supposed to be doing."

"Thank you, Hillary."

"What about the magazine? Can we schedule a shoot? They're really eager to get out here."

"Wouldn't you want to finish the interiors first?" I asked, in an effort to buy time.

I could almost hear disappointment register like a coin in a vending machine. "That's probably a good idea. I hate to push them off, though." A beat later, her cheer returned. "You know I can't wait to get my hands on your home's interiors. Wait until I tell Papa Bennett about the magazine feature. He'll be so proud."

"One thing at a time, Hillary."

"We should probably have them come out to shoot the exteriors while the weather is good, don't you think? When can we give them the okay? The sooner the better, and the house project should be done by the week after next."

Hillary had done a good job. I couldn't take that away from her. And if allowing a magazine to feature my house helped her drum up business, who was I to complain? "One favor, Hillary."

"Name it," she said.

"Let's wait until Dr. Keay's murder case is closed. Okay?"

Chapter 29

THE REST OF THE DAY LEFT ME LITTLE TIME to work on my murder investigation efforts. I did check on Rodriguez, who had been released from the hospital and to whom we had—finally—sent flowers. I also called Wes at the historical society and told him that one of the newspapers he'd lent me was missing. Even as I apologized profusely, he assured me that it was okay and that he probably had another copy, so not to worry.

"I have to believe someone took it," I said. When I mentioned the fact that the issue had gone missing from atop my microwave and that Hillary had told me that David Cherk paged through the editions, he was silent for a half moment longer than I'd expected.

"Something wrong?" I asked.

"Probably not, but . . ."

I waited.

"I remember the conversation, and I'm pretty sure your neighbor Todd Pedota took a look at them, too."

"That's right. I'd forgotten that Hillary mentioned he'd been there."

"Let me check the files. I don't want to waste your time if we don't have another copy."

"I appreciate that."

He must have cupped the phone between his ear and shoulder because I could hear his exertion as he moved boxes to conduct the search. "What's the date of the one you're looking for?"

I told him.

"Hmm," he said, which didn't sound promising. "I have September thirteenth, fourteenth, and sixteenth of that year. I'm missing the fifteenth. The one you're looking for."

"I am so sorry, Wes," I said. "I should have been more careful."

"Don't sweat it. I'm sure I'll be able to dig up another copy. I'll get on it right away."

"It's not your fault it's missing," I said. "You entrusted these to me. I'm the one who ought to find a new copy to replace this one. All I need to know is where to look." I apologized again.

"Grace." Wes's voice was a balm in the midst of my self-flagellation. "Don't worry about it. I have a few connections at the newspaper. I'm sure they'll be able to help. I'll get another copy, and as soon as I do, I'll let you know. Fair enough?"

"Thanks so much," I said. "I wonder who took it. Even more, I wonder what's in it."

"We'll find out," he said.

The only other thing I found time to do during the day was check on Tooney. Even though he seemed to have fully recovered from his inebriation the day before, I couldn't help thinking about his tiny, threadbare home. Everything about the man led me to believe he was lonely. I wondered if there was more I could do for him.

Otherwise, I kept busy with my managerial and curatorial

duties. We'd received three very large, separate shipments of treasures from three different auction houses and I inventoried and recorded each piece from each shipment before anything left my office to be shuttled to storage. From there we would determine which pieces went on display, which would be transferred to Bennett's personal rooms, and which were relegated to storage, indefinitely.

On top of that, I had timesheets and accounts payable to approve, checks to sign, and a monthly inspection to run. I barely kept my head above water, and even though I wanted to do more to find out where that missing newspaper went, and I wondered who Flynn had targeted for arrest, I couldn't find time for either.

Now, on my way home, I gave one other topic some thought. My busy schedule of late had kept me from overanalyzing the state of my love life, but quiet drives in the car were perfect for such musings. Timing, they say, is everything. From the beginning I'd believed that the only reason Jack and I hadn't managed to kindle a romance was because our timing was off. I'd been wrong.

Timing had played a part, but now—maybe because I'd met Adam—I'd begun to view Jack differently. I'd known him from afar. Handsome, mysterious, distant; Adam had been right about that. The more Jack hid from me, the more I wanted to know. Now that I knew him better, however, I didn't care for what I saw. Becke might not be the kind of girl men bring home to meet their mothers—heck, I didn't think she'd be the type to bring home to meet your parole officer—but that didn't justify his casual dismissal of her feelings. Jack had turned out to be one of those guys who said one thing but did another.

Adam, on the other hand . . .

I pulled up to my house in time to see Frederick leaving. He drove off, Hillary standing at the edge of the driveway waving, holding Bootsie's leash while the cat scampered. Bootsie had snagged a bright orange leaf between her paws.

As I got out of the car, she looked up at me as if to ask, "Now that I captured it, what do I do with it?"

Hillary greeted me by saying, "Wait until you see the paint chips I picked up today. I have amazing plans for your kitch—"

She was cut short by two cars racing up and screeching to a halt right next to us. Both vehicles were black four-door sedans with large spotlights mounted next to their driver's side-view mirrors. The cars held two occupants each, men who jumped out as soon as their vehicles shifted into Park. The men ran up the driveway of the house next door.

If there had been any question as to the nature of this onslaught, those doubts were stricken seconds later by the arrival of two squad cars. They didn't blare their sirens or flash their lights, but the sudden appearance of such a strong police presence made my jaw drop.

"What's going on?" Hillary asked.

One of the first people out of the unmarked black cars had been Flynn. He directed the other officers. Two in plainclothes went to Todd Pedota's front door, accompanied by a cop in uniform. Two uniformed officers, along with the last plainclothes detective, ran around to the back. We lost sight of them as they turned the far corner.

Hillary and I moved closer to find an unobstructed view of Pedota's front door. About fifty feet away, Flynn glanced over at us. He raised his hand in greeting then held up a finger, telling us to wait. He then pointed two fingers at his own eyes and then aimed them toward the house. The message was clear: "Wait. Watch."

Hillary seemed more shaken by Flynn's appearance than the police activity. "What happened to his hair?" she asked.

I didn't answer.

The officers in front banged on the door, announcing their presence loud enough for the whole neighborhood to hear. Even Bootsie seemed interested. She'd given up her leaf, content to sit and cock her head one way, then another, as though trying to figure out what all these strange humans were doing at the house next door.

Todd Pedota was either not home or not answering.

The uniformed cops out front donned heavy body armor and helmets. They now dragged up what looked like a three-foot-long metal column with handles. Two officers, working together, grasped the handles and rammed the solid column against Pedota's front door. It shuddered, but held.

Hillary thrust Bootsie's leash into my hand. "That's an antique door," she said, and started off to stop them, arms raised over her head.

I scooped up Bootsie and ran after her. "Hillary, you can't get involved."

She'd made it almost to the bottom step of Pedota's house when the antique door cracked, splintering open. I caught up to her, watching her shoulders slump. "Couldn't they have broken the glass in the front window and gone in that way instead?"

I didn't know what to do, so I patted her shoulder.

The uniformed officers dropped the battering ram and opened the front door fully to allow the detectives, including Flynn, to race into the house, guns drawn. The uniforms followed. We heard shouting, lots of it. Fascinated and not feeling particularly threatened, we stood on Pedota's front lawn, waiting to see what might happen next.

Because we were so close to the action, we weren't aware of another car pulling up. Didn't hear Todd Pedota running. Didn't notice him whatsoever until he sprinted past us. "What happened?" he asked, half-turning. "Did someone break in?"

We didn't have a chance to answer. He had made it up about two of his front stairs when Flynn emerged. The young detective yanked handcuffs from the back of his belt. "Todd Pedota, you are under arrest."

Pedota backed up, shaking his head, shouting, "What? Me? What for?"

Flynn took a step toward him. "Things will go easier if you cooperate."

"What's going on?" He turned to me. "What did you tell them?"

Still holding Bootsie, I did my best to raise my hands. I was as confused as he was. "I have no idea what's going on."

Flynn kept his gaze lasered on Pedota. The man's face had gone red and he'd begun to tremble. "Turn around, and put your hands behind you."

One of the uniformed offers trotted over to stand behind Pedota, in a clear show of force. There was nowhere to run.

Another officer emerged from the front door and said, "I've called the evidence techs," he said, "but we're taking pictures, too."

Pedota's voice was nearing shriek level. "Pictures of what?"

Flynn sauntered forward, giving me a quick, smug smile that claimed victory. "You are under arrest for the murder of Dr. Leland Keay," he said. "Now turn around."

Chapter 30

FLYNN WATCHED AS THE SQUAD CAR CARRY-
ing Todd Pedota pulled away.

"Did you have to knock down that beautiful door?" Hillary asked him. "There's no replacing it now."

"There's no replacing Dr. Keay, either," he said, shooting me an "I can't believe her" look. "Would you rather we
allow a killer to live down the street from you?"

"Of course not," Hillary said. She wrinkled her nose.
"But it was all so brutal."

Flynn reached over to scratch under Bootsie's chin. She
purred contentedly, and I wondered if she remembered that
the detective had once saved her from getting lost.

"I don't understand," I said. "Why would Pedota kill
Keay? And why now? His wife has been gone for five years.
And he doesn't seem to be terribly broken up about the
divorce. What's his motive?"

"It's gotta be the wife leaving." Flynn stopped petting
Bootsie and took a step away, the familiar scowl replacing

the soft expression he'd worn moments earlier. "If there's anything else, we'll find out. Believe me."

"I don't understand," I said again.

He smirked. "That's the beauty of all this. You don't need to."

Frustrated, I looked away.

"I *can* tell you a little more, though," he said. "We'll be releasing information to the media soon, so it's no big deal if you find out early."

My interest piqued, I nodded. "Go on."

Flynn half-turned, and pointed, gun-like, at Pedota's house. "Know what we found in there?"

I waited. Hillary's eyes were huge. "What?"

"Two jars of the same kind of moonshine that was used to poison Dr. Keay." He waited for that to sink in. "He left those jars right out in the open. Middle of his kitchen table. Must have figured we'd never put it together, but we did. Know what else we found?"

We both shook our heads. Bootsie squirmed.

"Syringes. A box of them." Flynn gave a self-satisfied lip smack. "You know, like for injections? Yep, I think this case is about to be closed." With a superior look on his face, he added, "No thanks to you."

"A box of syringes. On his kitchen table," I repeated. "Why would he still hold on to all that if the deed was done?"

"Maybe he had plans for a second victim. We'll find out." Flynn shook his head. "Stupid move on his part to keep the stuff in his house. Without it, we probably wouldn't have had enough to convict. Now we do."

"That's great," I said, without feeling.

Eyes narrowed, Hillary watched me closely. "You don't think Pedota is guilty, do you?"

I told the truth. "I don't know what to think." To Flynn, I said, "Maybe if I knew where your tip came from?"

"Leave the police work to the professionals this time, okay?" He smirked again. "I could just see you and that old-lady assistant of yours if you were searching the guy's house." Raising his voice falsetto, he held his hands up, fingers pointed down as though miming being afraid to touch something. "Oh, should we look in here? Do you think we'll mess his poor house up?" Bringing his voice back to normal, he added, "You would have been too polite to find the syringes. Your assistant, on the other hand—"

"What do you mean polite? You said they were on his kitchen table."

"Yeah." He laughed. "But they were in a box that was taped shut. And marked PERSONAL AND CONFIDENTIAL. You probably would have been too afraid to open it."

A *zing* shot through my brain. "David Cherk," I said.

Flynn started to walk away. I grabbed his arm, something Bootsie didn't like one bit. She tried to wriggle free. I held fast.

Flynn yanked away as though I'd stabbed him. "What?"

"That's David Cherk's box."

"You're nuts."

"No, listen to me," I said. "He had a jar, very similar to the one Ronny Tooney got us from the moonshine people."

"So?"

"And there was a box that belonged to him, marked PERSONAL AND CONFIDENTIAL, too."

"Do you have any idea how many things the post office handles that have those words marked on them?"

I did, but I pressed on. "What if you're wrong? What if Pedota is innocent and David Cherk is guilty?" I asked.

Flynn grinned. "He's not." He tapped the side of his head with two fingers. "I've got a sense about these things."

He walked away, sauntering as usual.

"You believe he's wrong about all this, don't you?" Hillary asked when he was out of earshot.

"What do I know?" I said. "He might be way ahead of me this time."

She tipped her head and wrinkled her nose again. It was

her trademark move to express annoyance, but it also
served to broadcast when she didn't agree. "I wouldn't bet
on that."

THE NEXT MORNING, AFTER CATCHING THE
news about Pedota's arrest and hearing hints about the evidence that had been found at the scene, I thought about Hillary's comment. In her own way, she'd expressed support, and
I figured I owed it to myself to continue investigating.

I'd alerted Frances to my plan and so she sat in my office
as I dialed Tooney.

"Another well-being check?" he asked when I said hello.
"If you keep calling me every day, Grace, people will begin
to talk."

Frances leaned forward, having heard every word he'd
said. "You should be so lucky," she shouted.

"That last call was simply to make sure you were fully
recovered," I said. "Today it's all business."

His lighthearted tone disappeared immediately. "What's
up?"

"Three things," I said, ignoring Frances's quizzical
glance and the fact that she held only two fingers up. "And
if you wouldn't mind keeping this on the down-low, I'd be
very appreciative."

"You know I will," he said.

"I do know that. You are always very discreet. Okay,
here's what I need: You saw that Todd Pedota was arrested
last night."

"How could I miss it? It's been all over the news."

"I'd like to know the source of the tip that Flynn received
that allowed him to get a warrant to search Pedota's premises."

Tooney grunted acknowledgment and I could hear the
scratchy sounds of him writing notes. "What else?"

"I'd like you to find me a copy of a local newspaper from

five years ago." I gave him the date of the stolen copy. "Would you be able to find a replacement for me?" I asked. "Let me forewarn you that the library has its collection out for computerizing and the historical office lent me their only copy. I'd like to replace it, which means that I need the actual physical paper, not a digitized version."

"What happened to the one you borrowed?" he asked.

I told him.

"No idea who stole it?"

"There's a pool of suspects, including Todd Pedota. Maybe I've got blinders on but I don't see the motive there."

"You got it, Grace. I'll do my best."

"I know you will."

"That's two things. You mentioned three."

I took a breath. Frances was going to love this. "It's about your rates, Tooney."

He made a sound of disappointment. "I knew I shouldn't have tacked on the bill for repairing my ripped suit after those guys roughed me up in New York last time. I figured it fell under expenses."

I thought about all he'd had to endure during that experience a few months ago, and how his help had been invaluable in making connections we hadn't known existed.

"You asked me about that, remember?" I said. "Before you added it to the bill. By all means, you should have charged us for that."

"Then, what?" he asked. "What did I do wrong?"

"Tooney, you've been an enormous help to us. Much more than I could have ever anticipated. I'd like to put you on retainer." I named the monthly fee I'd decided to offer him.

He drew in breath. "That's a lot of money."

"You're worth every penny." When he started to speak again, I interrupted. "I really hope we don't need your assistance in the future. But if we do, it'll be nice to know you're there for us."

I could practically hear his happiness brimming over the

phone. "Always," he said. "I'll always be there for you. And Mr. Marshfield, too."

When I hung up, Frances stood. She glared at me. "You happy?"

I knew she wasn't asking sincerely, but decided to play along. "As a matter of fact, I am."

"That's what he's wanted from the very beginning. Don't you remember when you first started working here and Tooney snuck in, pretending to be the police when Abe was killed?"

"Of course I remember."

"This very minute you handed him what he's always wanted, and you delivered it on a silver platter. What were you thinking?"

"Frances, he's helped us. A lot. That effort deserves to be recognized."

"You put him on retainer."

I scratched the side of my head for effect. "That pretty much sums it up."

"You feel sorry for him because he lives in a shabby house. For all you know, he has a million dollars squir-relled away in a bank account somewhere and he's laughing at you behind your back."

Not for the first time, I wondered what had happened in Frances's life to create such a vortex of negativity in one person.

She barreled on. "There are a thousand private investi-gators in the world more experienced and more savvy than Tooney is. And they probably don't charge as much as you're paying that loser."

I remained seated and gave her a smile. I knew that my composure was driving her nuts and that made me even calmer. "I'm sure you're right about that, Frances, but there's not one other PI in the world who cares about Marshfield, and all of us, the way Tooney does."

"You're a bleeding heart," she said and stormed out.

"Is that supposed to be an insult?"

She shouted from the other office, "You're darned right, and I'd appreciate if you'd take it that way."

BRUCE, SCOTT, AND I SAT IN OUR LIVING ROOM that evening, watching the rain sluice against our new windows. With a bottle of wine, and soft music playing, I was in a perfect place to relax. I tried.

"Have you noticed that the house isn't so drafty anymore?" Scott asked. He glanced over to the bare panes. It would be a while before we had draperies and curtains in place again. And if Hillary had anything to do with it, none of our original furnishings would return. "Things are really shaping up."

"We're very lucky," Bruce said. "Are you happy you agreed to this upgrade?" he asked me.

"I am," I said. "Believe it or not."

My roommates had brought home a new vintage today, a Meritage they'd decided to sample before offering it in the shop, and we sat in what were becoming our regular spots— me in the wing chair, Scott sprawled on the sofa, and Bruce cross-legged on the floor, playing with Bootsie and one of her favorite toys.

I took another sip. "It's good."

"You've said that four times," Bruce said. He lifted the plastic wand high in the air, causing Bootsie to jump for the stuffed mouse dangling from the end of it. "Are you fibbing, or is your mind elsewhere?"

I leaned sideways to rest my glass on the table next to me. "Busted," I said. "I can't seem to quiet my thoughts."

"Care to share what's bothering you?" Scott asked.

I dropped my head back and stared up at the ceiling. The peeling paint there only served to remind me that phase two of Hillary's renovation would be starting up soon, keeping the house in turmoil that much longer.

"It might be easier to tell you what *isn't* bothering me."

One of them said, "Go ahead."

Righting myself, I held up fingers as I listed things one by one. "The house is really looking great."

"I concur," Bruce said. Scott nodded.

I held up a second finger. "Hillary hasn't been half as difficult to work with as I'd expected."

"I think that deserves two points," Scott said. "I really expected that having her around would be a nightmare. It's been an adjustment, for sure, but not nearly as much as we thought."

"The final thing I'm not bothered by"—I waited until they both made eye contact—"is cutting ties with Jack."

Both sets of brows jumped at that.

"Really, really?" Bruce asked. "Or are you saying that to convince yourself?"

"Really, really."

As though she understood, Bootsie took that moment to forsake the fake mouse. She bounded onto my lap and propped two paws on my collarbone and stared at me as though attempting to divine my true thoughts on the matter. "I'm not kidding," I said to her. Addressing all of them, I continued, "I don't understand it fully, but I think I saw Jack as unattainable. And that was his allure."

"Now that he's pursuing you, that makes him less interesting?" Scott asked. "I'm not buying it, Grace. That makes you sound shallow, and you're not."

I caught myself wrinkling my nose à la Hillary and forced myself to relax. "I appreciate the vote of confidence, but I think what happened was that I wasn't fully healed from the breakup with Eric when Jack came into the picture. The fact that Jack was emotionally unavailable made things easy for both of us. We were able to play the attraction game. Made us both feel good while it lasted. Most of the time, at least."

"And now?"

"Now I realize that there isn't the substance that I expected to see, that I believed I did see."

My roommates went silent. "You remember we vowed not to give you any more advice, right?" Bruce asked.

Bootsie circled my lap, pawing at the tops of my legs before settling down into a warm cat curl.

"I remember."

The two men exchanged a glance.

"What about Adam?" Scott asked. "Simply asking a question," he added quickly, even though I hadn't pushed back. "We're wondering how much time you need before making a decision where he's concerned."

"I don't know," I said, stroking Bootsie's fur. "All I can tell you is that it's good to be me, by myself, for a while. I think he knew that, and I believe that's why he's giving me room to breathe."

"Smart man," Bruce said.

The doorbell rang, preventing us from discussing my love life any further. Because I had Bootsie on my lap, Scott answered the door. Bruce and I heard him talking with a man, and a moment later, the two walked in.

Ronny Tooney stood in the doorway in a trench coat, soaking wet. He held a dripping fedora at his waist and wore a shy expression. "I hope I'm not interrupting."

I got to my feet. Not a problem, because at Tooney's entrance, Bootsie had leaped down. Now she circled his pant legs.

"Is everything all right?" I asked. "Come on in."

Tooney shook his big head. "I don't want to bother you all. I came to give you this." From inside his trench coat, he pulled an opaque plastic bag. "Here's that copy of the newspaper you wanted."

"Tooney," I said with amazement. "How did you ever get your hands on this so fast?"

His cheeks went pink. "I know a gal who works at the paper. They keep a few copies of each edition. They don't like to sell them unless it's for a good reason. I told her it was important so she pulled a few strings for me."

"Thank you so much. Did you page through it at all?"

He gave an eager nod. "Didn't find much. 'Course, I'm not sure what you're looking for."

I clasped the newspaper to my chest. "You are the best, Tooney."

Bruce had gotten to his feet. "Would you like to join us?" he asked. "I'll pull out another wineglass."

Tooney seemed embarrassed by the invitation. "No, I'd best be getting home. I may have an answer for you about Flynn's tip soon."

"That would be great," I said.

He gave a little nod, said good night, and headed back out into the rain.

Delighted by the replacement paper Tooney had delivered, I scooped Bootsie up from the floor and hugged her close, the newspaper tucked tight under my arm. "You know who that was, don't you, sweetie? That's the man who helped me when we rescued you."

Bruce shut the front door and returned to the parlor. "You ask me, Grace, I think you rescued *him*."

Chapter 31

"THIS IS THE MISSING NEWSPAPER, THEN?" Frances asked the next morning. She toddled around to my side of my desk and perched her glasses on her nose to read over my shoulder. "Finding any clues?"

"Not yet," I answered, paging through more slowly this time. "I'm beginning to wonder if the first copy wasn't stolen. Maybe it was simply misplaced and this is a wild-goose chase."

"Gotta chase geese once in a while if you want to keep your legs strong."

I gave her a skeptical look.

"Old sayings have to start somewhere," she said. "And I think that one's pretty catchy. Just wait. Pretty soon you'll be hearing it around town, and you'll be able to tell folks where it originated." She pointed to her bosom. "Right here."

"I'll keep that in mind." Having read all of pages one and two, I concentrated on page three, again.

Still hanging over my shoulder, Frances asked, "How many issues have you gone through?"

"Five in total. I read through the others, but because this was the edition that went missing, I thought I'd give it extra attention."

"And what have you found out?"

"Not much. To be honest, the words are beginning to blur."

I'd already been through this entire newspaper three times this morning. I was currently on my fourth go. This was our local publication, which focused on scintillating stories about town hall meetings that established dates for festivals and awarded property variances. There was a front-page blast that covered an ongoing trouble with borer-infected trees. I could recount the score from the Little League team's win, and knew the details of the high school's career fair that year.

Because Emberstowne catered to tourists, there was the requisite piece on Marshfield history, which I skipped. There were also several articles that suggested other sights to see in the area. These, accompanied by photographs, didn't hold much interest, either. I assumed most were stock photos of the nearby national park and the nightlife along Main Street.

I studied the police blotter, but nothing of note jumped out at me: a couple of reports of disorderly conduct and a shoplifting mention or two. No familiar names. We even had a society page where three couples had announced their engagement. All good, but nothing that helped me.

"And I wondered why they thought my secret passage was a big deal. Compared to the news from this date, that's headline material," I said.

"Not much happens around here," she agreed. "Which is why Dr. Keay's scandal kept the newspapers flying for days. They really milked that story for every cent it was worth."

Turning my attention back to the newspaper, I tuned her out. The advice columns and restaurant reviews were probably not worth my time, and I glossed over the pictures. There were three of the town hall meeting and one of the

Little League team. In the touristy section there was a shot of a happy group posed outside of Marshfield's front gates, under the mini-headline "Mansion Welcomes German Visitors." There was a night shot of a couple posed beneath the Promise Clock with the headline: "All the Time in the World." And another Emberstowne moment captured forever: "Preparing for Fall Festival," which featured a group of shopkeepers displaying autumn-themed wares. I had to imagine the season's oranges, golds, and purples, because the paper had been printed in only black-and-white.

I continued to turn pages.

Frances made a sound like *hmph*. "Could be that the stolen newspaper was a red herring."

I turned in my chair to look up at her. "Come again?"

"You don't know what a red herring is?"

"Of course I do, but I want to hear your thoughts on this."

"What if whoever stole the newspaper did that because he wanted you to think the newspaper was important? What if it was to tie you up in knots and keep you confused?"

I sat back. "You could be right."

She struck at her chest with her fist. "Be still my heart. You admit that?"

I didn't bother giving her the withering glare she deserved. "You know you're right most of the time, Frances. I've told you that. No need to get dramatic."

Sitting forward, I turned back to the page before.

Frances inched closer, crowding my elbow. "What is it?"

"Take a look," I said, "David Cherk is credited with taking these touristy photographs."

"Is that important?"

Cherk was credited for having taken most of the pictures that had been published in the local newspaper five years ago. That wasn't my understanding of the man's career path, but things change, and I thought that maybe that was the sort of job that paid the bills before he'd become so well known for his historical photography.

"I can't imagine why it would be," I said.

"Then why bring it up?"

I shut the paper and shoved it to the side. "Because I'm an idiot. We have a suspect in custody who was caught red-handed with evidence, and for some inexplicable reason I can't let it go."

Finally stepping out of my personal space, she dropped her glasses back down to hang from their chain. "You need to take a break," she said, and left the room.

After returning to the newspapers and studying Cherk's shots until I could practically see them in my brain when I shut my eyes, I decided to take Frances's advice. I called Wes to ask him if I could drop the newspapers off tonight. He told me the historical office would be open until nine, but there was no rush.

Frances returned a little later, just as my phone rang.

"It's Tooney," I said.

She made the equivalent of jazz hands and said, "Oh, don't keep the poor man waiting. He's such a valuable employee now. He's on *retainer.*"

I ignored that and answered the phone. "What's up?"

"Hey, Grace," he said. "Glad to catch you. Remember you asked me to find out about the tip that sent Flynn to Pedota's house?"

"I remember," I said. "Did you find out anything?"

"You may not know this, but I tried to join the Ember-stowne Police Department at one time."

"I may have heard something about that."

"Oh." He sounded disappointed. "Listen, I may have washed out, but it wasn't because I didn't try."

"What did you find, Tooney?"

"I was trying to provide context."

"Of course. Now, though—"

"Right, right. Okay, here's what I can tell you. I made a few friends when I was working to get on the force. They got through the exam, I didn't. But I guess they thought I wasn't so bad. We go out and have a beer once in a while."

"You talked to them?"

"I did. That's important because I'm sharing a confidence here. They told me because of professional courtesy. They didn't know I was asking on your behalf."

"So I need to keep my source quiet. Is that it?"

"You need to not know what I'm about to tell you. You can't mention anything about it to Flynn. Otherwise, he'll know exactly how it got out."

"Go ahead, Tooney. You have my word that I won't spill."

"According to the officers, that reporter who was at your house visited Flynn. He brought an envelope filled with photos of the inside of Pedota's house. He said that his source told him that Pedota killed Keay."

"Who was his source?"

"He wouldn't say. Claimed First Amendment rights and protection via the state's Shield Law."

"An anonymous tip?" It took me a second to process that. "What if it was the killer who took those pictures? He could have set it all up to frame Pedota."

"Yeah, but how did the tipster get into the house to take the pictures? Pedota must have let him in. Either that or that house got broken into. But would the killer risk that just to set up a photo shoot? And Pedota never reported any kind of break-in."

"I can't believe that was enough for Flynn to get a warrant."

I could almost hear Tooney shrug. "This is a small town and Dr. Keay was a big shot. Even the judges want to see this case closed in a hurry. Flynn said it was like working with Deep Throat."

"It's *nothing* like working with Deep Throat."

"I'm sorry, Grace. I'm telling you what I know."

"No, Tooney, I'm sorry. I'm taking my frustration out on

you." I inhaled and then let the breath out slowly. "Thanks for the update."

When I hung up, Frances hovered. "Photographs? Are you thinking what I'm thinking?"

"David Cherk?" I asked.

She nodded.

I rubbed my knuckles against my bottom lip. "We've never come up with a motive for Cherk, have we?"

"None."

"This is crazy." I stood and stretched. "I'm giving it a rest for a while."

"There's something else you ought to give a rest."

"What's that, Frances?"

"You're listening to that music too much."

My stomach did a little nosedive. "What are you talking about?"

She pointed toward the iPod on my desk. "You think I can't hear when you have that SlickBlade album playing?"

I felt my cheeks warming. With no defense to that, I said, "I'll try to keep the volume down in the future."

AFTER WORK, I WENT HOME AND CHANGED into jeans and a T-shirt. The workers had called it quits for the day, and Hillary had left a note that she'd see me bright and early the next morning.

Home alone, I picked Bootsie up, snuggled her close, and said, "It's just you and me tonight, sweetie."

She struggled to get out of my arms and jumped to the floor, quickly disappearing around the corner and out of my room. I slipped on a pair of flats, went downstairs, and had leftovers for dinner.

I sat at the kitchen table and fired up my laptop. Bootsie crawled around the corner to see what I was up to and sat on the chair next to mine as though she understood and approved of me looking up SlickBlade's schedule. They were playing tonight, warming up again for the Curling Weasels.

Not that it mattered. I wasn't expecting to hear from Adam. He'd made it clear that any move had to come from me. I missed his friendship and our easy banter, but I wasn't sure I was ready to invite him back into my life.

I clicked through an exhaustive array of band promo shots, listened to a few of their songs, and checked out their Wikipedia listing, among other things.

"Why do I always seem to make the wrong choices?" I asked Bootsie. "And better yet, how do I start making the right ones?"

I shut the laptop and blinked in surprise, discovering that my kitchen was almost dark. I flicked on the overhead light and remembered, belatedly, that I'd planned to drop the newspapers back at the historical society tonight. I glanced at the clock. Almost eight. Wes had said there was no rush, but I suddenly craved human conversation. I chucked Bootsie under the chin. "No offense," I said.

Gathering up the newspapers, I considered giving them one final perusal, but I didn't have it in me. I packed them into a bag, tucked it under my arm, and took off out the back door.

My kitchen had been dark, but outside it was merely dusk. The air was crisp and clear. It was a perfect late-summer evening with the spicy promise of fall.

I decided to walk. Lights had come on in the houses down my block, and trees cast long shadows on the spacious front lawns. Kids, back at school for a week or so now, were probably sitting at kitchen tables doing homework, while parents stood close by ready to help, hoping not to have to step in.

Even though it had been a number of years since I'd been in school, I remembered those days well. I closed my eyes for a moment to appreciate the smoky scent of wood burning nearby. A bonfire, maybe. As much as I loved my roommates, their business kept them busy most nights and I found that lately I craved more. That was part of the reason why I'd decided to make the trip tonight and why I'd enjoyed my time with Adam as much as I had. Companionship.

I shook myself to stop that train of thought. I needed time to consider everything Adam had told me. He was right in so many ways.

When I arrived at the historical society's offices, it was fifteen minutes before closing time. "Too late?" I asked as I walked in.

"Never," Wes said from behind the counter. "How's it going?"

I placed the package on the countertop between us. "I've been better," I said. "But I'm not here to complain. I'm here to return these."

"This might help your mood: I have some information on those poison bottles for you. One of them looks like it might be worth more than we expected. A lot more."

"That's great news."

"You don't sound very happy about it."

I allowed a sigh of self-pity to escape. "I'm sorry. I am happy about that. Other things on my mind."

When he opened his mouth to say something, I held up a hand.

"Got it," he said. "I won't ask."

"Thanks. I appreciate it."

He opened the bag and began removing the newspapers. "Did you find anything in these that might help you?"

"Not a darned thing," I said. "Total waste of time."

He began sorting them in date order. "Hey," he said. "You found it. The missing issue."

"Got a replacement, actually," I said. "Marshfield Manor's P.I., Ronny Tooney, managed to procure it for me. So we're all straight again."

"You're amazing." He gave me a smile. "It's a good thing you got here when you did," he said. "I'm closing up right on time tonight. Joyce Swedburg called a little bit ago. Wants me to stop by."

"Joyce? What's up with her?"

"It's about the Promise Clock again. She said that the workers who are refurbishing it found some cache of documents hidden in a secret compartment beneath the actual mechanism. She wants me to come to her office to take a look at them."

"Why doesn't she bring them to you?"

"That was my suggestion, but she swears I have to come to her."

I didn't like that. "Don't you think that's odd?"

"Joyce is odd."

"What time are you meeting her?" I asked.

"Ten."

"That's late." All of a sudden I was getting a very strange feeling about this meeting. "Do you want me to come with you?"

"I think I can handle her," he said. "Although I'll admit that Joyce can be a spitfire sometimes."

"That's not what I meant."

"I can read exactly what you're thinking on your face," he said. "But remember, it's Joyce we're talking about. She believes the sun rises and sets based on her schedule."

"What exactly does she want you to look at?"

"I wish I knew. She's being coy."

"Maybe you should alert Flynn."

He burst out laughing at that. "And tell him what? That I'm going to visit one of the wealthiest socialites in Emberstowne? He'd probably accuse her of being a cougar and wish me the best of luck."

"That's not funny."

"Trust me, everything will be fine. Flynn arrested the guy who killed Dr. Keay. And you probably heard that charges against Joyce have been dropped. You and I both agreed that she's hardly the murderous type. I'm safe."

I started to interrupt.

"Beside, I'm not going alone," he added quickly. "David Cherk's going with me. What could possibly go wrong?"

"Wait. What? Why?"

"She wants him to photograph the box of documents as we open it. It's not quite as dramatic as the door in your basement, but as the head of the historical society, I ought to be part of it. More important, I *want* to be a part of it."

"I don't disagree with that, but every bit of this is crazy. Who calls meetings at ten o'clock at night?"

His voice rumbled. "Rich people who don't care about other people's schedules or needs. We know that's an accurate description for Joyce."

He was right about that and I could tell I wasn't going to sway him. "Cherk won't be much help if you get into trouble. I'd bet he'd run. Or try using you as a shield."

"Would it make you happier if I rescheduled my meeting with Joyce for another day? I'll do it if you want me to."

"It would," I said, massaging the bridge of my nose. I'd never seen Joyce as the killer and I still didn't. The Cherk twist was what had me most concerned. "I'm probably being foolish."

"Then I'll reschedule for a saner time of day." He glanced up at the clock. "I'll call her in a minute. Let me go in the back and get the storage box for these first. I won't be long."

He disappeared through the same door Adam and I had gone through when we were here looking for the newspapers in the first place. I'd been so sure that they would hold a clue. And when the one edition had been stolen—or more likely misplaced, as it appeared to have been now—I'd been doubly convinced.

I wandered behind the counter to take a closer look at the wall of drawers, imagining all the secrets they held. As I edged past the desk that had been tucked into the nook, I caught another look at the photograph Wes kept there. His wife, he'd said. I picked up the picture. He clearly missed her. I remembered the day he talked about how she'd—

I felt the *zing* up my back first. I'd seen this photo. Recently. I pulled the framed picture closer to my face. The shot had been cropped. Studying it closely, I could see that another person had been cut out and only a shoulder was visible. The top of the photo had been cut out as well. Very little of the background had made it into the frame, but what remained was distinctly recognizable.

Above Wes's wife's smiling face was the edge of the arch on the outskirts of Emberstowne. The arch that housed the Promise Clock.

I raced back to the newspapers, pulling out the one I'd studied over and over, the one that had been misplaced. I turned to page four.

There she was. Wes's wife and another man standing together, their arms around each other, smiling big. "All the Time in the World," the mini-headline read. I took a closer look at the caption. "Lynn Reed and her husband, William, pose beneath the Promise Clock. 'We're so happy to be here,' Lynn said. 'After my surgery Tuesday, Dr. Keay says I'll have all the time in the world.'"

No.

No, it couldn't be.

I needed time to think this through. But Wes would be back any second.

He'd told me that his wife had died of an aneurysm. He'd never mentioned Dr. Keay. The picture of Wes's wife was in color. So, who was this man in the black-and-white version in the newspaper? I pulled it closer. Thin, lanky, clean-shaven. It took a long few seconds, but I recognized Wes. Five years younger, forty pounds lighter, no beard.

Had Wes killed Dr. Keay? Could this simply be some weird coincidence? Why was his name different in the caption?

My heart thudded so loud that my ears hurt. I struggled

to steady my breath. I could hear him moving about in the other room. In a moment he'd be back through the door and—

The photo burned in my fingers. I spun and raced over to the desk, dropping it back onto the surface in such a hurry that my shaking hands knocked it over, making it clatter. Biting my bottom lip to keep from whimpering, I righted the frame, straightened it as best I could, and made for the open space between the counters.

The newspapers. I'd left them open. I spun back, reaching over to slam the paper shut. I didn't want him to know I'd put it together. Maybe there was a perfectly good explanation. Maybe I was overreacting.

I could worry about that later. All I knew was that I had to get out. Now.

The EMPLOYEES ONLY door opened and Wes emerged. He dropped the box onto a nearby table and hurried to my side. "What's wrong?" he asked.

My face was flushed, sweat burst forth from every pore, and my breath came in short bursts. I opened my mouth to answer, but no words came out.

In a heartbeat, I watched his gaze dart from the messy pile of newspapers to the photo on his desk. Comprehension washed over his features. "Oh, Grace," he said. "You couldn't have waited one more day?"

"One more day?" My words came out high and limp. "Sure." Reaching to gather the newspapers, I mustered a cheery tone. "I can bring these back tomorrow. No problem."

"Grace." He took a step closer. "That's not what I mean and you know it. I can see it in your eyes."

I was still between the countertops. Holding up a finger, I said, "Don't make it worse. Don't compound the crime."

"I was afraid this might happen," he said. "Don't move, Grace. Please."

He didn't break eye contact and I couldn't get around the counter without pushing past him. "You told me your wife died of an aneurysm."

"She did," he said. "Now back up. Please. I don't want to hurt you. But I will."

I backed up, banging my behind on the desk. He pointed to the drawers that held my house plans, far along the wall. "Take a couple steps that way."

As I inched sideways I toyed with leaping over the counter. It was too high to make it in a smooth vault and there wasn't enough room for a running start. I couldn't fight him in hand-to-hand combat. Wes had the advantage of height and weight. He'd take me down in a second.

Never shifting his attention from me, he slowly reached into the nearest desk drawer, dug beneath a sheaf of papers, and pulled out a gun.

"I had a feeling," he said.

All the blood in my body rushed to my feet. This man, someone I'd considered a friend, had killed Dr. Keay and now was about to kill me. "I'm telling you, Wes, we can talk this out—"

"No talking," he said quietly. "There are things I want you to know, but first I need to take a few precautions."

"I don't understand."

Keeping the gun trained on me, he made his way to the front door, where he flipped the OPEN sign to CLOSED and slammed the dead bolt home. He then dimmed the lights. "One thing at a time. I need you in the back room. Hurry up."

This was a very quiet part of town. Any faint hope of a passerby seeing me in here faded as I made my way through the EMPLOYEES ONLY door. The windows were high and I didn't remember an exit door from the last time I'd been in. I wished I'd paid better attention.

I walked slowly, constantly checking over my shoulder, hoping to buy time. I needed to think of a way out of this. Nothing came to mind. "Stop," he said when we reached a study table.

I stopped.

He pulled out one of the table's heavy wooden chairs. "Right here."

I turned. "You want me to sit?"

"Yes, please."

"What if I don't?"

"Grace, I don't want to hurt you. You're an innocent and you should stay safe. I'll make you sit if I have to, but I'd rather not."

Stay safe? With the gun pointed to my chest, I couldn't come up with any way around it. I sat.

"Here's what will happen," he said. His words were soft, but his voice trembled. "I'm going to tie you up. Tape you up is more like it." He reached over and grabbed a wide roll of duct tape he had sitting on top of a box nearby. "I planned for this contingency. I worried that you might figure everything out before I was done. When you brought that newspaper back tonight, I knew you had."

"But I didn't. That is, not until just now."

"Either way, you're an impediment. I have to keep you securely out of the way until the job is finished."

"Finished? What else do you have left to do?"

"You really haven't figured it all out yet, have you?"

Using his teeth to help rip long stretches of tape from the roll, he maintained a vigilant hold on the gun. Every ounce of my being urged me to bolt. To run. But I knew I wouldn't get four steps away before he'd take me down.

"Hands behind your back, please," he said.

I complied, dropping them onto the seat behind me.

"It would be better if you brought them together around the back of the chair," he said, as casually as anything. "Your reputation for overpowering your captors makes me skittish. I don't want to take any chances tonight."

I placed my hands around the back of the chair. It was wide enough to make the positioning uncomfortable, but narrow enough for my wrists to cross. He wound a long piece of tape around them.

"Sorry," he said. "I've never done this before."

Hoping his ineptitude would work in my favor, I tried to keep my wrists far enough apart to buy me wiggle room later, but he must have sensed that. He snugged them tighter. Once taped, they didn't budge.

"I'm not going to put any of this over your mouth. There's no chance anyone will hear you, even if you scream bloody murder."

That didn't mean I wouldn't try.

He must have read my mind because he said, "No, really. When I first moved here, I originally planned to lure Dr. Keay into this back room. I did sound testing first, to make sure I'd be able to deal with him in private. The stuffed bookshelves work as an effective acoustic barrier."

"Why didn't you kill him here?"

"The more I thought about it, the more I realized that, as delicious as the prospect was, there was no way to accomplish that and still get away with it," he said. "The location would make me suspect number one. But it all worked out for the best. My patience paid off. Killing him during the clock fund-raiser turned out to be poetic justice."

"Would your wife be proud of what you're doing?"

"She's not here to answer that, is she?" he said with a flash of anger. Softening his tone, he continued, "You need to understand: I'm not a murderer at heart. I hope you can appreciate that."

I said nothing.

"I know you're disappointed in me and I suppose I can't blame you. But don't you agree that the world is better without slime like Keay and his pretentious ex-wife in it?"

"You're going to kill Joyce, too?"

"One more day," he said. "Couldn't you have given me one more day?"

He ripped off a strip as long as his arm, and reached for my right ankle with his gun hand. I tried kicking the weapon away, but he simply dropped the gun and grabbed my ankle tight. I couldn't get up because my hands were back behind the chair.

"Grace." This time his voice was a warning.

I stopped fighting, concentrating instead on figuring a way out.

He didn't say much more as he taped one ankle, then the other to the legs of the chair. "There you go," he said when the job was complete. "Comfy?"

I didn't answer.

Standing, he picked up the gun and placed it on the table next to me. Far away, though. I couldn't have reached it without a stretch, even if my hands hadn't been bound.

"Joyce didn't call you to meet her tonight, did she?" I asked.

His shoulders came up. "A lie. One of many."

"Like your wife dying of an aneurysm?"

"That," he said, pointing a shaking finger at my face, "was true. If she'd had the surgery she'd been scheduled for, he would have found it before it stopped her heart. He could have saved her."

Wes's eyes grew red. He worked his lips. "Lynn had had heart problems for years. When we flew out here for our consultation, Dr. Keay told us he could fix her." Blinking, he fought to speak over his choking voice. "He told us—no, he assured us—that Lynn would have a normal life. That she'd be transformed, forever. That we'd have all the time in the world. He lied."

"Aneurysms are tricky things," I said. "I'm no medical expert but—"

"If she had had the surgery, she would have lived," he said through clenched teeth. "But she didn't get her chance because the old lush had to go out and get drunk. Had to get in an accident. Because he was in jail, he couldn't perform the scheduled surgery."

"You wouldn't have wanted him performing surgery in that condition," I said.

"Don't you get it?" he asked. "If he'd gone home and sobered up, he would have been fine two days later. Everybody said that's how it went with him. But no. This time he overdid it. And his stupid wife decided to teach him a lesson so she made him stay in jail for those days." His voice was trembling and he was shaking. "Two days. They canceled Lynn's surgery. They said that we could reschedule. But she died that night."

"I'm so sorry," I said. And I was.

Wes took his time tidying up. While he worked, he made noises that led me to believe he was holding a conversation with himself. He kept a close eye on me, and whenever his attention turned my way, I stopped trying to stretch against the duct tape holding my hands together. The minute he returned to his tasks, I resumed mine.

He reclaimed the newspapers and the storage box from the other room and brought them to the table next to me to work. "Those poison bottles we found in your secret passage really are valuable, by the way. That wasn't a lie. I did quite a bit of research on them."

"You did quite a bit of research on the passage in my house, too, didn't you?" I asked, already knowing the answer.

He met my eyes but didn't reply.

"There is a way to unlock from the inside, isn't there? You planted that evidence at Todd Pedota's. The bottle and syringes didn't belong to David Cherk, did they? You took those photographs that the reporter gave to Flynn."

He shrugged.

"Sneaking into the fund-raiser via that wood elevator was a huge risk," I said. "Someone could have seen you."

"An unavoidable risk, and yes, I was fortunate no one saw me, but I did what I had to do." Raising his voice as he put the newspapers back in the box and covered it, he said, "Your poison bottles are in one of my desk drawers. You'll find them there later, I'm sure. I hope you get a good price for them."

With a grunt, he hoisted the storage box onto its proper shelf.

"My guess is that you'll be found here tomorrow or Saturday," he said. "Someone will notice that the offices aren't open, and I'm sure the police will break in, looking for me. They'll find you instead."

"And where will you be?"

He disappeared into the other room again. When he returned this time, he had my purse with him, his hand deep inside. He stopped pawing through it long enough to answer my question. "Gone," he said. "I've had five years to plan this. As soon as I'm finished with Joyce, it will be like Wes McIntyre never existed."

"Why not leave now? What good will killing Joyce do?"

From deep inside his beard, a chilly smile emerged. "Patience these five years has brought me many rewards. Keay at the clock fund-raiser was only part of it." He pointed to his chest. "Whose idea do you think it really was to have the event in the Marshfield basement? Mine. Joyce is so self-absorbed, however, that she never noticed how I guided her to that decision. Little by little while she was here studying plans, I set up the pieces so that they would fall into place."

"I should have realized," I said. "You had all the answers. You pointed to everyone else. That should have tipped me off."

"It did. Unfortunately for me, a little too soon."

"Wes, please. Consider disappearing. No one needs to know. By the time they find me, you'll be long gone. You don't need to harm Joyce."

He actually laughed at that. "Don't you see? Joyce is basking in the glow of wealth. She's inherited everything from her ex-husband and thinks her life has taken a spectacular turn for the better. Right now, when she believes everything has gotten as good as it can get—I'm ending it for her. The same way she and her disgusting, drunk husband did for us." He closed his eyes for a second, then opened them and grinned more widely. "I'm telling you, it's beautiful. Poetic."

Convinced grief had driven the man insane, I stopped trying to reason with him. I wondered if, once he was gone, I could hop in the chair and move it forward into the front area, where I would have a better chance of being seen and heard. That was assuming, of course, he left the door open between the rooms. That was another big if.

He returned to my purse and pulled out my cell phone. "I'll take this with me to Joyce's office, and toss it in a garbage can there. That will give the police an interesting trail to follow. At least until you're found." His expression grew thoughtful. "I don't envy you the next couple of days. I know they won't be pleasant. You'll be hungry, you'll be thirsty." He frowned. "I would have let you use the facilities before I tied you up, but that would have been too much of a risk."

"Wes, please. You don't want to do this. You really don't."

He leaned on one of the bookcases and regarded me. "I'll tell you what I don't want to do," he said. "I don't want to kill your boss."

"Bennett? What does he have to do with any of this?"

"Didn't he tell you he was meeting Joyce tonight?"

My entire body sagged.

"I guess he didn't," Wes said. "Joyce is sweet on him. Sweet on his money, is more like it. She invited him out to dinner tonight."

"But he—"

"No, I don't think it's going anywhere either." He made a face that was supposed to be comical, but came across eerie and cruel. "Especially after tonight. If it hadn't been for you, they might have had an enjoyable evening and retired to their own beds afterward. But plans changed. My timetable for taking Joyce out was thrown off. That's your fault."

He pointed. "You did that. As soon as you pulled out that newspaper for the day before the scandal, I knew I had to scramble. Just in case you made the connection. Because of you, I had to reconfigure everything and pick a new killing date. Turns out, that's tonight. It's Bennett's bad luck that he'll be there."

"No, no." My voice came from some primal center of my being. "Can't you simply tie him up?"

Wes shook his head. "Won't work this time," he said. "Sorry." He crouched to my level. "I really am. But there's no way around it."

"But," I tried again, "you've avenged your wife's death by killing Keay. There's no reason to do this. You've gotten what you wanted."

He stood up again. "Revenge," he said, almost to himself, "is one of the purest motivations for killing." He gave me a condescending smile. "Tonight, for the first time in five years, Joyce is going to get what she truly deserves. Bennett, if he's still with her, will be unfortunate collateral damage."

He picked up a weighty leather bag and threw it over his shoulder. "Can't be helped. Sorry."

He left me then. In the dark. Alone.

Chapter 32

SCREAMING AND HOPPING DID LITTLE MORE than render me hot, sweaty, and frustrated. Forcing my body upward with as much power as I could muster while balancing on my toes—the only parts of my feet that maintained contact with the floor—I'd managed to move no more than two inches forward from where I'd begun. All the while, I'd worked my wrists against their duct tape bindings. The tape was made of fabric, wasn't it? It ought to rip, shouldn't it?

I wiggled my hands and twisted my legs, doing my best to loosen the duct tape's grip. No luck. I expelled a long breath of despair.

Clenching my eyes, I visualized making headway, and tried hopping and scooching again.

And again.

Another two inches. Maybe.

I'd seen this maneuver in movies: the heroine, taped to a chair, hops across the room to safety. Or at least to a place where she can call for help.

There's a reason they call it fiction.

My chair still firmly attached to my backside, I leaned as far forward as I could, doing my best to peer around the five-foot-tall shelf next to me.

There were obstacles in the path to the door. Lots of them. Large boxes, piles of books, and other pieces of furniture lined the aisle. Clearly, Wes had anticipated my attempt to bounce my way to the front room. Forget the obstacles: There was no way I'd make it to the door. Not to mention the fact that he'd been sure to close it completely. Even if I could make it that far, I'd have a devil of a time trying to get it open.

"You gave me way too much credit," I said aloud.

Jerking my wrists up and down, then twisting them as far as they'd go, one way and then the other, I fought the duct tape's clutches. Wasn't this stuff designed to be flexible?

I shut my eyes and gritted my teeth. Summoning every bit of concentration I could marshal, I tensed my wrists and twisted. Tensed and twisted back.

My eyes popped open when I felt a little bit of give. Not a lot. But some. Enough, I hoped.

"Come on," I urged the tape as I struggled against it. "Give it up. You can do it."

Sweat beaded up at my hairline, above my lip, and under my arms. Strings of perspiration wended their way down my sides.

More give, a little looser. The tape fought back, but slowly began to stretch. "Come on," I said again. "I swear if you let me free, I'll never make another disparaging comment against you."

Talking to duct tape. What was wrong with me?

I was getting more give with each and every twist of my wrists.

Twist, tense. Pull. Twist, tense . . .

One shocking instant later, I was free.

Bringing my hands up, I quickly wrenched the last

remaining pieces of tape from them, wincing as the pale blond hair on the back of my wrists was yanked out, leaving welts on my skin.

I bent over and fought the tape around my ankles. He'd had more time to get these tight and solid and it took far longer to unwind when the tape kept catching on itself, sticking whenever an end came free.

My brain began a countdown. Wes had been gone about ten minutes, maybe a little longer. I raced to the front office, gauging where the closest telephone might be. I picked up the landline phone. It was dead. He'd thought of everything.

At the front door, I threw open the dead bolt and ran out. On this cool evening, with most of the businesses on the street closed for the night, there were zero tourists strolling. I had exactly one second to decide: Should I run up the street who-knows-how-far to find a phone at the first open establishment? Or should I run down the street, three blocks to Joyce's place of business?

With Bennett's life in the balance, I took off for Joyce's law office.

My lungs were burning and my legs crying out by the time I made it there. A small storefront establishment with a plate glass window, the place was dark and appeared deserted. I yanked at the front door, but it was locked. Banging against the glass, I shouted for someone to open.

Nothing.

I cupped my eyes and peered in through the door. There was a lamp burning at the very back of the place, but I could detect no movement whatsoever. I knew that the historical society probably looked exactly like this when I'd been tied up in back, so the quiet didn't fool me. They had to be here.

I backed up, looking at the building from every angle, searching for another way in. I was about to run around the block to the alley to find the back entrance when the front door jangled open.

"What do you want?"

The fifty-something man at the door wore a rumpled shirt with its sleeves rolled up, and a furious look on his face. His collar was open, his tie askew.

"I'm calling the police. Get out of here." He shoved at the air, in emphasis. "Are you drunk?"

"Please, call the police. Where's Joyce?"

"What are you talking about?"

"Joyce Swedburg? Where is she?"

"She left. About five minutes ago."

"She's in trouble. Where did she go?"

"I don't know," he said.

"Was she alone?"

But he'd slammed the door.

I banged on the glass again, shouting, "Call the police. Call them."

Inside the office the man stared out at me, his index finger swirling near his temple, as he mouthed, "You're crazy."

I stepped away from the building. I ran my hands up the sides of my head, into my hair. Wes had lied again when he'd said he was meeting her here. Where could they be?

And then the answer hit me so hard I staggered. Wes had pronounced Keay's killing being poetic justice. Why? Because it had happened at the clock fund-raiser. Because Wes and his wife had been promised all the time in the world. Because they'd taken that photo of themselves under the Promise Clock.

My gut had comprehended even as my brain caught up, and I realized I was already running.

There was only one place Wes would take them.

Chapter 33

IF I HAD CHOSEN TO RUN AND CALL FOR HELP when I'd first burst from the historical society, the police would be on their way to Joyce's office, rather than the clock, right now. By the time we would have discovered that Wes wasn't there, it would have been too late for Bennett. I'd followed my gut, rather than standard logic, and it had been the right choice. I was depending on my gut again as I raced through town, knowing clearly that if there was any chance of saving him, it was up to me.

It might still be too late now, but I fought to banish that thought. Had something happened to Bennett, I was sure I would have felt a shift in the universe. I would *know*.

I believed he was still alive. He had to be.

By now, at least twenty minutes had elapsed since I'd broken free of my restraints. With nothing in my mind beyond reaching them before Wes had the chance to carry out his plans, I ran, arms pumping, lungs screaming for air.

I bellowed as I ran, "Call the police. Send them to the clock!"

The streets down this part of town weren't touristy. Weren't busy at night. No one saw me. No one heard me.

I ran down the middle of the street, hearing the blood pump in my ears with a reassuring *thud, thud, thud* that matched my steps as my feet hit the pavement, faster than I'd ever run in my life before.

After what couldn't have been more than two miles, but felt like ten, I made the turn that brought me face-to-face with the deserted stretch of town. The Promise Clock sat in lonely gloom, high above the barren street. Tonight's clear sky had grown overcast, and what little moon there was played hide-and-seek behind high clouds.

I scanned the area. Scaffolding supported the crumbling arch; traffic cones warned against potholes in the middle of the road. I skirted around piles of fresh-cut lumber and navigated past bags of concrete mix. A stack of construction horses, blinking their incessant orange warnings, leaned against a nearby wall. Supplies were piled about, giving me ample room to hide and time to consider my next move.

My breaths came out ragged and ridiculously loud. I sounded like a person who'd been held underwater and who'd finally come up, gasping desperately for air. I tried closing my mouth in order to hear better. I struggled to listen for noises, to figure out where they might be, but my body fought me, dragging in breath after heaving breath.

I held a hand against the cool brick of a nearby wall, bending at the waist, laboring to quiet myself. A sudden sinking feeling made me weak at the knees. What if I was wrong? Tragically wrong?

But he'd said it was poetic justice. For his wife.

They had to be here.

I stayed close to the walls of the silent buildings. Still about a block down from the archway, I couldn't see them, couldn't hear them. It was too dark.

Keeping to the shadows, I crept forward, trying to hear conversation over my irregular, heavy breathing, trying to see movement that was out of place. I had no doubt that Wes would take the time to let Joyce know precisely why he'd brought her here. He was a methodical man, a patient man. He wouldn't squander this opportunity to tell Joyce exactly what sins she was about to pay for.

That could buy me time. Or so I hoped.

Keeping my back to the sturdy walls, I walked my fingertips along the bricks and ducked into a deserted doorway to stop and watch.

My breathing began to even out; my lungs took pity on me and didn't force me to suck great pulls of air every second. I worked to steady myself further.

Please, I begged silently. *Not Bennett*. I didn't want Joyce to die, but if Bennett were hurt, it would kill me.

I spotted another open doorway ahead. Holing up there would bring me within about a hundred feet of the archway. Keeping low, I made my way over, ducking in and crouching, scanning the street, the arch, the scaffolding beneath the clock, the street—

My gaze shot back to the scaffolding. My heart jumped into my throat.

I hadn't seen them at first because Joyce and Bennett were seated on the street itself, bound tightly to the metal pipes of the two story scaffolding, shaded from the pale moonlight by the clock's arch. Their hands were duct-taped, their mouths covered. They didn't struggle against their bonds because Wes stood before them, talking, gun in hand.

He had his back to me as he paced back and forth, addressing his captives. I couldn't make out what he was saying, but I noticed how he kept looking up at the clock, as though checking, double-checking, then triple-checking, the time.

The clock's hour hand pointed between the ten and eleven, the minute hand directly to the nine: 10:45. Was he waiting for the clock to chime eleven before shooting them? To muffle the sound of gunshots?

And in one panicked heartbeat I got it. I knew why Wes had said he was sorry. Why killing Bennett couldn't be helped. I knew what had been in the leather bag that Wes had carried away—the bag he no longer carried. I knew exactly what he planned to do.

Wes had had a third victim in mind all along.

He wouldn't be satisfied until the Promise Clock had been destroyed, too.

My hands flew to my mouth to keep myself from yelping. I closed my eyes and tried to conjure up in my mind the photo of Wes and his wife. What time had been on the clock that day? What time was it in that picture?

Wes's head tilted again. Another glance at the time. While I still couldn't hear what he was saying, I could make out his cadence. His pace had picked up.

Wes outweighed me and I had no doubt he was stronger. Tackling him unarmed, even with the element of surprise on my side, would be suicide. Worse, it would accomplish nothing.

I took a quick assessment of my surroundings. A construction zone meant that there had to be heavy objects around me. Kneeling on the ground, keeping my attention on Wes, I crawled forward toward a pile of detritus, desperate for anything I could use as a weapon.

My fingers gripped a brick. Not the kind with holes, used to build homes in subdivisions, more like a landscaping brick used to erect retaining walls. Wider at one end than the other, it was thick and solid, too big for my small hand. But, I hoped, heavy enough to do the job.

With the clock ticking—literally—I hoisted the brick to one side, tight atop my shoulder. Holding on to it with both hands, I ran at Wes as swiftly and silently as I could.

Joyce or Bennett must have reacted to my presence, or maybe Wes heard my approach. He spun at the last second, turning the gun on me.

He wasn't fast enough. I rammed the brick at him the

very same second the gun discharged. I didn't hear the brick *thunk* into his head, but I felt the solid connection. Hot fluid—blood—poured out around me. Whether it was from the gash on his head or the hot burn along the side of mine, I didn't know.

He and I toppled to the ground and his head suffered another blow, cracking against the cobblestone street. He lost his grip on the gun—I watched it somersault away. Wes's eyes clenched in manic pain. His arms went limp. His mouth went slack. His eyes opened, then grew wide and wet. Tears flowed from their far corners, tracing down his upturned face.

"How long?" I shouted, as I scrambled to my feet.

He closed his teeth, grimacing as he tried to get up. By the time he answered, "You're too late," I had kicked the gun out of his reach and was running to Bennett's side. "Duct tape stretches," I screamed.

My brain mocked me: *Those are lame last words. You'd better hurry.*

Joyce had managed to work her mouth around the duct tape and was now screaming for help. I struggled to loosen Bennett's restraints. He'd worked his lips around the sticky tape, too. "Get Joyce first."

"Not a chance," I said.

Above the din of Joyce screaming, the moans coming from Wes five feet away, and the searing, heavy thrum of my racing heart, I heard the clock above us step forward another minute.

"Go, Grace. Get out of here," Bennett said. "There's no time."

I'd released one of his hands and he reached over to help me undo the other.

"Less than a minute left," he said. "Go, Gracie. Please."

"Not without you." My fingers were wet—sweat, blood—who could tell? I lost the tape's free end. It doubled back on itself, sticking tight. I didn't have time to play with it, to work the end free again. I bent down and used my teeth to gash the tape. Too thick, but it budged. Blinking blood out of my eyes, I grabbed hold with my teeth again and ripped at the tape, rewarded for my efforts as the fabric split apart.

The moment Bennett was free, we both attacked the tape holding Joyce. In total freak-out mode, she shouted, screaming about crazies, and bombs, and how she couldn't die. All the while I maintained a silent countdown in my brain. We had thirty seconds left. Maybe. She thrust and bucked and fought as we tried to get her loose.

"You're not helping," I shouted at her.

"Stand back, Gracie."

Bennett had pulled out his pocketknife. He reached in and sliced it across the tape, slashing the binding in two. I pulled one end, he the other, and as Joyce was freed, she tumbled sideways to her knees then wobbled to her feet and began an ungainly run down the way I'd come. Bennett and I got to our feet and rushed to follow.

She glanced back, which caused her to stumble and fall, the way lithe young women in horror movies always do. Bennett and I grabbed her. Joyce was neither lithe nor young, but we hauled her as far from the clock's vicinity as we could, dropping her unceremoniously near the bags of concrete mix. Ten seconds left, I guessed. Maybe.

Bennett grabbed Joyce's arm and half pulled, half dragged her over the mound of concrete mix bags, as I turned to go back.

"Gracie," Bennett called to stop me, but I'd already started away.

Wes had gotten to his knees. Crawling, he made his way toward the scaffolding beneath the clock. I knew we had mere seconds left. "Wes," I called. "Turn around."

He looked over his shoulder and shook his head.

I drew on every ounce of energy I possessed, running toward him, convinced I could drag him from the clock.

I hadn't gotten far when I was lifted, bodily, and carried

away by two strong arms, one around my waist, the other snugged under my knees. "No," I screamed, fighting. "No!" It was no use. Whoever had me, held my head tight against his chest. I heard his breaths coming hard as he ran, shifting my weight as he zigzagged, navigating a path to get away.

My savior had run about ten steps when the blast hit. An explosion of sound, sensation, and heat shook the ground, knocking him to his knees, spilling me from his arms. He leaped forward, shielding me. I instinctively covered my head as the explosion shot pieces of scaffolding, plaster, bricks, and wood to rain down over us.

I made myself small until the last of the debris skittered by. When it was quiet, I lifted my head, turning to see who it was who had protected me.

"Tooney," I said, grasping his arm. "Are you okay?"

He struggled to his knees. "Yeah. You?"

As he bent to help me up, I waved him away. "I'm all right," I said. "Find Bennett."

Chapter 34

POLICE SPOTLIGHTS RENDERED THE STREET-
scape bright as day, making the area look like the final
scene from a blockbuster disaster movie. The authorities had
arrived en masse, quickly taking over, quietly assuring us
that they had the matter under control.

I glanced up at where the clock had been, where two
jagged, empty arms now reached for each other across a
giant, gaping hole.

Time had stopped, at least for the Promise Clock. Along
with killing Keay, Wes had managed to carry out that part
of his quest for vengeance.

Bennett was fine. Except for having lost a shoe in the
wreckage, and having the back of his suit singed from the
heat of the blast, he'd managed to escape with a pair of sore
wrists and bruised knees.

The blood that had soaked my shirt and hair was beginning to dry. Parts were getting crusty. Some of that blood,
we'd discovered, was mine. The single shot Wes had discharged had skimmed me, directly above the left ear. Had

I been positioned one centimeter to my right, the bullet would have missed completely. One centimeter to my left? I preferred not to think about that.

Bennett and I sat next to one another sideways on a low gurney, blankets wrapped around our shoulders, even though we weren't cold. Someone had handed us each a water bottle, and it took a while before I remembered that I wasn't supposed to grip it until my knuckles turned white— I was supposed to drink from it.

Joyce had suffered scrapes, which had left her knees bloody. She screeched a lot and insisted on being taken into the hospital for observation. We were happy to see her go.

I watched as she was carted away, her shrill complaints cleaving the night air, drowning out the hum of conversation. When the ambulance shut the back doors, silencing her nonstop wails, I turned to Bennett. "You went on a *date* with her?"

His cheeks reddened ever so slightly. "I have no romantic interest in her, you know that, Gracie."

"Then why did you agree to it?"

"Joyce and I have been colleagues for many years." He took a long drink from his water bottle. "I surmised her intent, but a gentleman doesn't act on romantic presumptions." He eyed the bandages on the side of my head. "How are you feeling?"

"You can't change the subject." I nudged him with an elbow. "What happened?"

"Always curious, aren't you?" He took another drink. "I decided that if she made an advance, I would be kind but clear in letting her know that I had no interest in changing the nature of our professional relationship."

"And did she?" I asked. "Make an advance?"

"My goodness, Gracie." He took a deep breath. "She did."

I twisted so I faced him fully. "And?"

"When I told her we had no future together, she waved a hand in the air, quite dismissively. She told me it had been worth a try, and then invited me to join her to see what amazing artifacts Wes McIntyre had discovered at the Promise Clock."

"You didn't think it was odd to be meeting him there so late?"

He shrugged. "I did, but after having dispelled any romantic notions she may have harbored, I believed it would have been ungentlemanly to allow her to venture out on her own."

"Being a gentleman almost got you killed."

A corner of his mouth quirked up. "One of the hazards of the job."

A second later I jumped to my feet. "Tooney!" I said when he came into view from around the front of the ambulance.

After having assessed that none of his injuries were life-threatening, the paramedics had taken our favorite private eye away for closer examination of the cuts and bruises he'd sustained. His regular shirt was gone and he stood before us in sagging slacks and white undershirt. There were blood spatters all over him and a bloody handprint across his T-shirt's chest. A wad of white bandaging encircled his neck like a clerical collar.

"Oh my gosh, Tooney," I said. "Are you all right?"

"Perfectly fine. They want me to go in for a few stitches." He pointed a thick finger. "Back of my neck got sliced up pretty good." He turned and I saw that the paramedics had piled on the gauze. "That'll hold for a while, but I'm taking their advice and going in. They insist on driving me. Said I might have lost too much blood to go on my own."

I reached out and touched his arm. "Thank you," I said. "You saved me."

As if to punctuate my statement, the coroner's van pulled up at that moment. They waited for authorization from the police before moving to collect Wes's body—what was left of it, anyway.

"I thought I could get him out of there," I said quietly.

Bennett had gotten to his feet. He stood next to me and put his arm around my shoulders. "There was nothing you could have done."

I swallowed, thinking differently, but it wouldn't do to argue.

A paramedic called to Tooney. "Let's get you in," he said.

My hand was still resting on the private eye's arm. "Gotta go," he said with a sad smile as he pulled away.

"We'll go with you," I said.

"Nah, I'll be fine."

Bennett adopted his most authoritative voice. "Mr. Tooney, are you telling us what we can or cannot do?"

Tooney's eyes went wide. "No, sir."

"Then we shall accompany you. We Marshfields don't allow our friends to sit in the emergency room by themselves."

Tooney's mouth tightened. He gave a brief nod.

As we walked over to the ambulance's wide open back doors, I pointed to the center of his shirt. "That's an awful lot of blood."

He smiled a little. "That's your handprint," he said.

"From when you picked me up?"

Another quick nod.

My heart twisted. This man had risked everything to save me. Gratitude welled up from a place so deep inside, I couldn't speak.

Tooney added, "I was really glad when it turned out that most of it wasn't your blood."

I brushed hair out of my eyes with the back of my hand as the whole horrible sequence of events replayed itself in my mind. "Why were you here?" I asked. "How did you know?"

He climbed into the back of the ambulance and offered me, and then Bennett, a hand up to join him. "I'll tell you on the way."

Chapter 35

I DIDN'T KNOW WHAT AGGRAVATED FLYNN more: the fact that he'd arrested the wrong person—twice—or that he'd missed all the action under the Promise Clock.

He met us as Bennett, Tooney, and I were leaving the hospital. He wanted to talk right then and there, but I told him we'd meet him later and suggested he come by the following morning. "It is morning," he said, banging an index finger against his watch. "It's three in the morning."

"Tomorrow afternoon, then," I said.

"But I need to know what went down."

"And you will," I said. "Tomorrow afternoon."

Bennett had called for a car to pick us up, and I'd arranged for Tooney to stay at Marshfield's Hotel tonight. We'd also engaged a nurse to stay with him there. She'd keep an eye on him, just in case. Tooney had suffered a concussion in the blast and we didn't want him going home alone in case he needed medical assistance overnight.

We pulled away from the hospital with Flynn pacing angrily outside its front doors.

Tomorrow the detective would have a thousand questions, and as I settled into the soft backseat of Bennett's gorgeous Packard Phaeton, I studied my companions. Bennett, hands clasped in his lap, had shut his eyes and lowered his chin to his chest. Tooney stared out the window opposite mine, his thumbs twiddling. He worked his bottom lip.

The doctors had removed three pieces of shrapnel from his back. I reached over and touched his knee. "Are you in pain?"

"Nah. My hide is tough. Plus, they numbed me up pretty good."

"You sure you're okay?"

He nodded. "You're not mad at me?"

"For saving my life?" I laughed softly, so as not to wake Bennett. "How could I be mad at you for that?"

"You used to accuse me of stalking you. I kind of did tonight. You have to know it wasn't like that."

"I do know," I said.

On our way to the hospital, as promised, Tooney had told us how he'd come to be in the right place at the right time. He'd thought long and hard about something I'd said—that the killer might have gotten into Todd Pedota's house in order to frame the man for murder—and believed my idea had merit. It dawned on him that someone might have used the secret passage between our homes to accomplish that, and he came to my house to share his suspicions with me.

I hadn't been there. He started asking people where I might have gone and was about to give up when he tried the historical society. Even though it was closed for the night and the lights were dark, the front door was unlocked. With a sneaking suspicion that something was not right, he went inside and found the ripped-up duct-tape bindings and my abandoned purse.

The problem was that no one had any idea where I'd gone. No one, except the man at Joyce's place of business, who'd called the police to report a crazy woman banging at his office door. When the cops heard the man's story, they knew I was that crazy person.

Tooney talked to the guy and discovered which way I'd run off. Thank heavens for easily irritated, nosy people.

I'd asked Tooney how he'd known to come to the clock. He'd shrugged his big shoulders and told me that it was a hunch. "Remember I told you that I paged through that missing newspaper when I got that replacement copy?" he'd said. "The only mention of Dr. Keay in that whole edition was in the caption under the clock. I don't know. It clicked, I guess."

Now, in the back of the quiet car, I said, "You're a treasure, Tooney. I don't know that I'll ever be able to thank you enough."

Tooney offered a lopsided grin. "You put me on retainer, remember? That's like having my dream come true. Told you I'd always be there for you, Grace." He flicked a glance at my boss, who—I suddenly realized—may not have been slumbering after all. "You and Mr. Marshfield."

As we sped through the quiet streets of Emberstowne, I thought, not for the first time tonight, about calling Adam.

As much as I wanted to, however, I knew I wouldn't. Not yet. When that day came—if it did—I wanted to do so without hesitation. Without holding back. I wasn't there yet. Adam had been right again. I needed time. And after all that had happened this evening, I needed sleep, too.

THE FOLLOWING AFTERNOON, BENNETT, Tooney, and I shared our overnight adventures with Frances, who listened without interrupting, her lips pursed, her eyebrows jumping up as the story unfolded. We sat in my office, overlooking the south gardens, where the tree leaves were beginning their slide from green to gold, orange, and red.

Instead of taking my seat behind my desk, I'd arranged a circle of chairs. Frances had taken the one I'd have chosen, with its back to the window and face to the door, but that didn't matter. My purple-clad assistant was in a wholly cheerful mood. After we'd brought her up to speed, she chortled, "That'll show Flynn, won't it?"

When Flynn showed up, he seemed far more eager to share what he'd learned than to hear the details of our story. After demanding an update on Rodriguez, who, he assured us, was recovering extraordinarily well, we let him talk.

"McIntyre was Wes's wife's maiden name. He adopted it when he moved here to exact his revenge on Keay. Wes's real name, as Grace discovered in the newspaper caption, is William Reed. He changed that and his appearance so no one would recognize him from his original visits here with his wife. They came twice. Once for consultation, and several months later for the surgery." Flynn shook his head. "That whole disguise and name-change thing was overkill. Nobody remembers random visitors."

"Maybe you should start paying closer attention," Frances said.

I shushed her.

Flynn seemed not to hear. "Wes, or William, apparently shadowed Dr. Keay for some time. He discovered that the man had returned to his old drinking habits."

"I can only imagine how much that infuriated Wes," I said.

Flynn nodded. "The doctor, of course, didn't want anyone to know that he was still getting drunk, so he began buying his supplies from a local distillery." He held up a finger. "An illegal one. We believe Wes threatened to blackmail Keay, and that's how he arranged to have the doctor meet him in secret at the fund-raiser. He really planned this one down to the smallest detail."

"I'm not surprised. Wes was a methodical guy," I said. "He didn't take any chances."

"He did by letting you live."

I turned to stare out the window. If I hadn't hit him so hard with the brick, Wes might have been able to escape the blast. He might have made it out alive. I worked my fingers in my lap and said nothing.

Tooney reached over and covered my hands with his. He leaned to whisper, "You saved Bennett, you saved Joyce. You did what you had to do."

I could feel heat in the back of my throat. "And you saved me."

Frances piped in, breaking the moment. "Hey, Flynn."

"*Detective* Flynn," I corrected.

Frances lifted her chin, leaning forward. "*Detective* Flynn," she said with exaggerated deference, "did you hear that Joyce called here this morning? Told Grace that if she ever needs legal assistance, it's on her. For the first time in that woman's life, she seems grateful for something."

Having delivered her pronouncement, Frances straightened her shoulders and sat back again.

"That's something at least," Flynn said, not at all impressed. "What does she plan to do with all the money that was raised to refurbish the clock?"

Bennett took that one. "The Chamber of Commerce will discuss it further, of course, but that area is still in need of improvement. They'll come up with a plan. I highly doubt, however, that their vision will include replacing the clock, now that it's been destroyed." He held his hands out, as though open to suggestions. "They're also discussing the idea of using some of the money to help fund additional programs at the hospital, in Leland's name."

"What kind of programs?" Frances asked.

"A couple of ideas being bandied about are to either provide more resources for those battling alcoholism, or to increase funding for heart disease research."

Frances shifted her shoulders. *"Hmph."*

"I'll let you know what the chamber decides," Bennett said.

I had a question to ask that I hoped Flynn knew the answer to. "Todd Pedota has been released, hasn't he?"

"First thing this morning," Flynn said. "He said something about wanting to move out of this lunatic town before he goes crazy himself."

Bennett pointed to Frances. "Keep on top of that. If Mr. Pedota puts his house on the market, I want to buy it."

"What would you do with another house, Bennett?" I asked. "You've already set Hillary up in one of the neighboring homes. I know it's none of my business. But I am curious."

"Consider it another mystery to solve," Bennett said with a twinkle in his eye. "I'm betting you'll have it figured out in no time."

FROM *NEW YORK TIMES* BESTSELLING AUTHOR

JULIE HYZY

GRACE
TAKES OFF

A Manor House Mystery

When curator and manager of Marshfield Manor, Grace
Wheaton, and her boss, Bennett Marshfield, turn up at the
Italian villa of one of his oldest friends, they're troubled to
discover that most of his friend's impressive art collection is
fake. Someone has been selling the real deals and replacing
them with skilled forgeries.

Unfortunately, Grace and Bennett have to fly home the
next day, so there's no time to investigate. But on the plane,
Grace catches a woman trying to poison Bennett. The
woman, of course, isn't talking, but by the end of the flight,
there are two dead bodies. Now Grace will have to wing it to
find a mile-high murderer...

"Readers will
—*Chicago S*

juliehyz
facebook.com/Ju
facebook.com/The(
penguir